Redemption is near at hand. Let our journey begin and follow through.

Avery Blackman – I Was Born A White Slave

A Story Told By
Haywood Hogan II

Clarah

"Alright now, Miss Clarah, get ready to push!" old Doc Feeley encourages as he is poised at my bed's end, his shirt sleeves crumpled without direction on his swollen forearms, his jacket carefully draped over the bartered rocking chair in the corner. Once brightly lit candles now belch blackened smoke from burning low. Darkness refuses to sleep, as pure exhaustion creeps through my eyelids, hungry for its own attention. It must be near dawn by now. Thoughts of your face in my mind are the only relief from the scorching pain. Our child's zest for its first breath becomes undeniable.

Doc shouts for me to push again, and again, harder, and harder. I oblige with all that is within my youthful strength. Pushing with everything I have left, as determined to see our child born as I was steadfast in keeping your identity a secret. Our closet is the only protection I can offer you, my love. Daddy would surely abandon our child and let the life seep out of my body at the comfort of his own hands if he ever were to find out that I was with child and without a husband. He would whip me near senseless. But my love for you will hold fast and so will our child, remaining intact within its natural carriage. Our blessing is coming now, without question. I desperately want to shout out so you can hear me.

Snapping back to the reality of where I am, this isn't how I wanted to have our baby. Out here in the barren cold fields, surrounded by wood piles and mosquitos, it's coming now whether I'm ready or not, the heavens have spoken to send this gift anyway.

Wordless cries carrying across wide fields spread news of your son's birth with no response. I feel something loosen within me, and suddenly, the high, thin wail of a newborn fills the air. I crane my neck, trying to see our baby as Doc Feeley clears his airway, cleans, and wraps him. I reach my arms out for our son as the sweat begins to cool on my brow, but Doc isn't looking at me. He turns and shuffles off into the shadows, taking my heart with him.

I beg intensely as he disappears down the path, but he is gone quicker than my voice can carry. Struggling to my bare, cold feet, intent on hurrying after him, weakness suddenly takes me over, and I nearly faint before finding my center. Determined, I wrap my shawl around my shoulders and follow. If I don't reach them soon, I may never get to see our baby. Closed mouths did everything within the powers given by God to silence my secret, but even deathly cries of conviction are not enough to persuade Doc to let me keep our child.

My trembling, moisture-drenched body sways side to side down the beaten path with the afterbirth still dangling without release, as sharpened branches reach out, scratching against my naked arms and weary legs. Trying to focus my eyes to peer through the darkness of the unseen trail, I am unable to see Doc Feeley or the baby. A dim light glimmering through the branches above allows me to see a small opening where the tree's part ways at the roots' end.

Fear spurs me on, faster now. I shiver as I step deeper into the pitch-black, cool morning air and pull my shawl tighter around me. My eyes search frantically until I catch a glimpse of Doc's white shirt in the dim light as he slips further into the trees. He's heading for the blue creek. Panic grips me, and I begin to give chase. The dew on the grass is slippery with

2

every emotionally charged, fast-paced step. Reaching the creek, my weakened body can no longer stretch another agonizing step. Doc is already kneeling by the water's edge, but I can still hear that beautiful, high, thin wail. Faith pushes me onward, knowing that my baby still breathes.

Doc doesn't hear me approach over the gurgling of water. Grabbing a rock in the shape of our future with both hands, I slowly lift it high above my head and bring it crashing down upon the back of his skull with a thunderous roaring growl of more than human strength. He lets out a faint grunt as he collapses into the water's edge, surrounded by peeking grass blades. The baby slips from his grasp into the creek; and I throw myself in the creek's bed after him.

As soon as he is safe in my arms, I know that I can't go back... there is no returning home.

Splashing through the water to the other side of the creek, my legs push as fast as they can carry me. The bare branches grasp at my shawl on one side, the muddy creek sucks at my bare toes on the other. I stumble and fall for the last time. My body unable to recover from the beating pressed on me; there is no getting back up.

Darkness plays musical chairs with my mind, but no matter, I have no strength left within me to move on. I give in to what has become of me. A small chuckle cherishes my face as I share a pleasant smile with our son. He has your eyes.

As the sun rises, I place my slumbering child safely aside and begin to gather ripened berries in a cornered piece of my ragged edged skirt. I feel almost normal for a moment as I lick the juice from my finger's tips.

I smile once again. I am a mother now.

Avery

If this rocker that holds my rickety and frail body could tell the long-held story of my past, it would finally bring me the unspeakable happiness that has always seemed to elude me.

The day that I was born was the day that I should have been robbed of living. If this too shall pass, then I should have passed along with it.

It is said that I am pure in blood, of the purest white people that ever walked the fields of the South. Yet I have been treated like the filthiest of animals... neglected and mistreated by society for simply existing... not worth breathing the air that others suck in freely, not belonging to any significant clan, not allowed to share my feelings with anyone except myself, by myself, with myself, alone. I am purebred, a pedigree of pureblooded whites. Yet I was born into slavery; I am a slave.

Years have long passed from the day that Momma Ruby first laid hands on my milky skin, frozen in fear and trembling of starvation. The plantation that I grew up on was one of slave traders, masters of lynching, reverends of lies and deceit. A place of mass suffering in which stories were told of niggas past and present, the harsh teachings of how to be a good nigga, a loyal nigga, a well behaved, hardworking, obedient nigga. And that, I was not.

The lights are dimming quickly for me. There are no loved ones to pass the time with, no heirs for hand-me-downs. All loved ones known over time have long been sold, killed, died, or simply succumbed to the vastness of this treacherous land, never to be seen or heard from again. The only company I have is that of a nine-year-old, bothersome, dirty boy from the backwoods who comes and goes as he pleases. We sit for hours on end, staring out into trees that dance in the wind, as the sun repeats its rise and fall of days coming and going. My story is told to a child who will never remember a word that is spoken to his deaf ears. Just stupid.

My hands are tattered rags of repetition, never recalling a day of warmth in petrified winters nor rest of comfort in warm springs. The only joy my soul ever knew was from the love and care of Momma Ruby... allowing for a quick nightly rest upon her breast, ever so closely standing guard all night for my protection from discontented vultures seeking my death daily. Not being like others around me, death continuously sought to devour me.

The Master

This child is an abomination, an evil trick placed upon me by the devil himself. How dare this child wear the fair skin of my ancestors to mask being a true nigga child, born out of deception and unruly heathenism. If ever I lay eyes on the two who created this child, or any who bore witness to the hidden truth, they will have only God to blame for the pain I inflict on their naked skin, backs raw as the flesh of animals hunted for their hides. Just the sight of this child makes pure hatred leak from my pours.

It is completely and utterly inconceivable that any self-respecting white Christian of pureblood would abandon their child, leaving it to perish at the hands of Mother Nature's vigorous elements. This could only be a mulatto child. There is no other answer. It shall wallow like a pig in the hands of the filthy slaves from which it was conceived. Maybe the child should be drowned out back in the watering hole or hung from a limb by its feet to starve and slowly rot at the hands of fly maggots. That will deter all slaves from anything but masturbation.

My decision is swift, justice is done. The child will serve his master, day in and day out, sun-up till sundown, forever as my property... my albino nigga slave boy. He may grow into a fine hand, a useful barer of many crop seasons to come. If it were not for him being free labor, his death would come as no concern to me, but pure joy.

My night sleeps are restless. I am tormented by constant images of impending betrayal. If this child does not die, I am sure that he will brew a plan to kill me while I rest. I can never let my guard down and let his sly nigga ways get the best of me. When I call him, he will beat his feet about the plantation faster than a chicken in a cock fight. When I tell him to be gone, he will disappear like a hog's fart in the wind. If he is ever to blink twice in my direction, even with cause, I will surely take a boot to his face for thinking for himself without my permission.

Perhaps I will take him, with his flowery skin, as my sultry mistress to cook my meals, fold my clothes, and warm my bed. I will make sure that life will slowly be extracted out of him as he grows until nobody remembers his name. He will become one with the soil that he tills repeatedly, until he is part of the earth in which my tobacco blooms.

My wife, Shelby, tells me to remain still. God takes care of drunkards and fools; and here in the flesh is both. How dare she speak the words of the good lord and not stand in her place as the bible tells her to obey me. She too will succumb to my sharing if she does not tread carefully and watch her kind ways toward the niggas. Watch ye therefore, for ye know not when the master of the house cometh… at evening or at midnight or at the cockcrowing or in the morning. God is not the master here. I am. This hand of righteousness shall be laid upon all as judge, jury, and executioner of my own property as I see fit.

No man with such a thirst for blood is more of a drunkard, womanizer, fornicator, or sinner than the man who stands before me staring back from the mirror of truth. God says come as you are, and that, I do. God says we, the purebred whites of this rich land, are made in his likeness. That, I am. If I am to curse, it is because he cursed. If I am to walk with others as their master, it is because he does; and if I am to bed many wives, it is simply the will of God himself. Who am I to turn away from the continued work of God himself? I shall not.

Ruby

Been part of this land here for long as I can recall. Family is all that's left for me to look forward to as my candle's wick doesn't have much left on the stem to burn bright anymore. These old eyes of mine don't see too well, too far, nor too much of nothing anymore. These blistered lips haven't tasted the sweetness of good fruit since my heart dried up when he disappeared in the distance, swallowed amongst the tall brier bushes. None can survive starving prickles thrashing at every movement made to push forward and through. He was born of those bushes and to those bushes he returned. Those endless blue eyes drenched my thoughts on the day that I found him, wondering if the good lord had finally returned to save us wretched no-good niggas from this place that gags from hatred and the bastardly ways of mankind.

His image first appeared in my thoughts, as I was breaking from the fields, heat pushing me downward. It was just an image, but the light brightened my moment, allowing hope to fill my empty basket with new picked fruit. Avery was my fruit, my new-found life when all was departed, when life had stopped giving gifts and started taking them away.

That day in the briar patch, there was a scream of agony... pain like no other coming from deep within. Figured someone's pet animal had trapped himself within the womb of the scorned branches. Hesitantly moving closer and closer, I ever so slowly reached around the bottom of the bush. Quickly retreating from the reach of a rattle snake coiled upon the chest and shoulders of a white child, newborn and naked as a freshly picked pea, I shushed that child to be still. That snake wouldn't hesitate to attach itself to that precious face if he didn't quiet down immediately. Wasn't no time to dawdle! In one hard, worthless breath, before that snake had time to pursue its easy prey, I batted it off with as much strength as I could muster, trying my best not to harm the child. The leather would surely have come cross my own laced back if this white child had been harmed and they found out that I been the one to do it. My back and the Master's worn leather already had history together. We met in fierce battles many moons ago on the side of the house in order to settle my spiced tongue. No more these years, as the Master's leather and me are no longer friends; and my tongue no longer has the strength to whip words in defiance.

The Master didn't like the child no more than a free nigga likes old chains stained with his ancestors' salted flesh. Upon seeing the child and hearing how it was found in the bushes with a snake perched upon its chest, the Master cursed death on the child. He was beside himself like never before, stampeding all about the land, devouring everything and everyone within his path who even dared to flinch in his direction. I didn't understand what all the ruckus was about.

He summoned me to the side of the house. Thinking of making friends again with his leather, my knees remained stuck in the mud, unable to hold my fair weight. He then spoke in a low voice, close to a whisper, which panicked me even further.

He muttered "What will you name that bastard of a nigga child?" With no emotion toward the child, he refused to give the boy the last name of the land. He was simply property. He was simply Avery.

Avery

"Boy!" I flinch at the sound of Master's voice. Can't help it. It infiltrates my watery skin to the bare bone, feels like the crack of a steel whip, the boot's rugged edge in my ribs, the fist in my frequently damaged face. It was time for my lessons; and the lessons are many.

There was never a moment where there seemed to be fault on my end, but everything seemed to be my defect. Even when I was nowhere near the happenings, there was always a reason to bring the strap to my back, legs, shoulders, head... whatever was available for slaughter.

If only I had a hog's life, the possibilities would seem endless, as there would be relief from this life. Death would follow years of gluttony and bathing in the rays of the sun.

Thoughts of death often lulled me to sleep.

Freezing in winter with no blanket or cloth to shelter me and overheating in the molesting heat of summer without the benefit of foliage to rescue me, I lay in misery's breast, hoping to die. Too scared to end my own life, as I might miss out on what Momma Ruby says are my blessings to come, I pray that Master will no longer just send me to the edge of death but push me over to the other side. He calls them "lessons." I call them unannounced pure hatred of a lonely man using the devil's lessons as God's scripture.

He always says it is my eyes that tell lies, tell the truth, show my pain of being born of this earth and belonging to no race of this land.

My chance will come. The day will be mine, and freedom will release me of this life. I shall have my revenge in this life or the next.

Momma Ruby said that she stared into my eyes when she found me and she knew at first glance, though for years, she never told me what she knew.

One day, after years had passed and the crops lay in wait for harvest, I was staring at the sun, trying to blind myself, when she whispered in my ear to no longer allow myself the sight of a slave. She mumbled, "You ain't no child of slaves, you's a white child of purebreds. I have seen the children of whites by the raping of nigga girls, and you ain't one."

As far back as I can remember, I was a nigga… a slave like those around me, treated as invaluable property for profitable labor, yet meaningless as a mangy hunting dog.

Mondays are set aside for all us to get together and hear the words of scripture. This brings me great joy, as my mind gets a chance to wander off while barely listening to the stories of man. If there was a place for me in them stories, I would have the power to part the trees and lead my whole family and everyone like us up the way to a land where we are not hated, we are not slaves, and we are no longer human beings, but animals that freely walk with one another. We would be like the deer I see pass through our land, all with unique markings and the freedom to roam as they please.

Momma Ruby and the others sing together. They all seem filled with joy, with hope, with a reason for song. She always tells me to sing and sing loud. I yell as loud as I can, though I don't know the words, and I feel lost as a boy who sits so different than all who surround me. My voice carries over all, and Momma Ruby must hush me down. If she says sing, I sing. If she says hush, I hush. If she says I am of purebred, I tell her to mind her lips, as they speak lies. These words always fill my head out of spite, but I dare not ever speak them aloud to Momma Ruby. She is known for smacking a child right cross the head for back talk.

The lord tells the story of a man who was to build a boat to save all the animals and carry them to a new land. Would that man come for us too, to carry us to a new land? Or is it more of the story of the slave who terrorized the land with other slaves, killing all slave owners. It was told this slave longed for relief from slavery, from his life, from his owner, from his chains. Should my life take the place of his as he creeps into his sleeping master's room and bashes his head in until his brains color his pillowcase with a stream of blood and his floorboards warp from life exiting his body. This slave went from house to house chopping off all the heads of men, women, and children who owned slaves, anyone who ever raised a hand to a slave, anyone who was white and breathed life without his permission. He murdered with extreme prejudice. Maybe this man is within me.

Our day of rest ends with more song and retreat to the barren sticks of shelter running thick with bodies to eat a meal made with fatty parts from the leftovers of slaughtered animals. Some of the men bring caught squirrel and snake parts when they can. We eat like the house for a day. Nothing is left to waste. Even the bones will turn to useful tools, ground to powder for medicine. For the moment, for the day, we are alive, and so we sing.

Clarah

He is so precious, so fragile. His lips drained down in hunger, he suckles my kindling nipple for the first moments of life. Sloping in intimately to caress his face, the scent of mother's milk diluted about his tiny mouth.

It is quiet out now. The din has silenced, leaving only me and him to keep one another from isolation. This is the way existence should always remain, on earth as it is in heaven… pure.

A hymn, which my own mother used to hum to me, is playing over in my mind, and my lips form to create the same soft sounds for my child to enjoy. "We the people, the people of the land, search high and low to find our sands. Sands to fill our toes, walking from the shores. We are all heroes to God, the ones that he adores." Our song is interrupted by faint sounds of my name being called in the far distance. This jolts me back to my feet soaking at the creek's edge. My dress is muddied, my skin torn, my vagina still spilling blood thinned by the water. There it is again, getting nearer and more powerful. And again, and again, and again! I never thought I would detest the sound of my own name treacherously summoning me while sitting at death's edge. It makes me cringe with sickening terror.

I begin to vomit over the crown of my child into the water. I can't breathe. I just can't breathe. I cannot catch a quick breath to save my life. It is not time. It is not time for me and my baby to be found, to part ways. I hold him so very tightly against my breast that I almost suffocate him without notice.

"Shush now, baby, shush now! Else, they gonna find us." Rocking back and forth like a crazy old woman surrounded by four walls without protection, I pray, "Ohhh, Jesus, son of the father, savior of all mankind, save us from the wretched, from the wicked, from he who approaches with heavy hands. Give us strength to not succumb to man's wrath, no more, please!"

The steps are right upon us, but we lay still deep in the pyramid of leaves, unseen in darkness without uninterrupted light. He surely will find us, my Pa will. He knows these woods like he knows his name, even when drunk. It is only a matter of time before he smells my scent and gets to tracking me down. He will surely track me down. I am as sure of it as I am sure about death if he finds you in my arms.

There is a place for you, my baby, and there is a time for us, but it is not here, and it is not now. You shall lay placed beneath the protection of this brier bush, so deeply enthralled as if you were as one. Be safe, child, and be still, for you do not know when the master of the house is coming.

My Pa is here. I know it. He is no longer yelling my name, so I know that he has picked up my scent. His head is down, nose crowding the ground, slaying a direct path in my direction. I panic as old Doc Feeley's body lay floating in the water next to the creek. He will surely find his old friend, my old confidant, my grandpa. If he finds I killed my own flesh, the one who helped me most and kept my swollen belly a secret, declaring it an infection of my kidneys, my hide will be his.

Crouched deep into the shallow pocket of random foliage that holds me from perishing, I inhale as if my last breath is passing through me. The cry that bellows out of me comes from deep within, where lust, life, and destiny reside.

"He tried to push himself on me!" I screech. "Help me, Pa, please. He wanted to take me for his own, and he did!"

My Pa's eyes look as if he's seen a ghost. He stops where he stands at the sight of my shaggy hair, my bloody cloth tattered and torn, my bare muddy feet. He opens his arms to accept my pain as his own. No longer the source of my worry, he is now my protector.

My Pa peers over my slim shoulders to see the man he calls his Pa floating in the creek, disheveled within the blades of grass that sit high on the water. He howls like an adolescent bear who has lost its way, but I don't know if he cries for me or for his Pa. Does he cry out of anger or pain, hurt or joy in finding me alive?

Stifling his lips' movement, he struggles to form words to quarrel and says, "If he was not dead already, I would take what is left of his decrepit, soiled body and feed him to the wolves with my bare hands, piece by piece, for being the thief of my light." My Pa stood there in silence, just staring off in the direction of the darkening, slow-moving creek. Ogling the water as if it would bring him joy if it were to release old Doc Feeley from its grasp, but it does not. We waited and waited without the slightest of motion.

Sure of his Pa's death, he grabbed me and held me close, and we began our lingering trek home, side by side.

We didn't speak much as we sat in the cabin. Traumatized by the evening's happenings, Pa didn't say a word. He just kept mumbling under his breath something about a promise. I looked at him and he looked at me, but his eyes became more and more vacant with time. He looked at me again, up, and down. His head cocked to the left, then sluggishly to the other shoulder. It was a look I had not before seen. What had taken over my Pa? What demon had entered?

Sweat started to bead on the tip of his nose, then drip off to his tightened lips. His eyes widening with exactness, cut right at me. I had become his game. What did he know? What would he do?

"Pa, you alright?" Pa stands in complete silence. The only sound is of him rocking back and forth on the cracked planks of the floor, creaking with excitement. He seems to be stalking me with anticipation of a fresh meal, his eyes welling from beneath, his lip twitching with a grim smirk, hands shaking as he rubs them together. He stops where he last paced.

"Your trickery, your lies," he says in near silence. "YOU WHORE!" he bawls. I shriek in fear, falling from my seat. Retreating deep into the furthest corner of the room as Pa charges at me in fury. His pace is so vigorous that I haven't a moment to think, let alone react.

The beating is relentless and never ending. My already battered, bloody clothes cover me no longer. I am bare naked, completely exposed. Smothered in blood, the life I have is ending at the hands of my Pa. He whisks me up by the roots of my matted hair, dragging me kicking and pleading for my life, into the drab cellar. I am a prisoner of my own deceit, a captive of the war created by my own actions. It is all my fault, my burden alone. I suffer that God will forgive me and allow me into heaven once I have confessed and he has heard my pleas.

I sit in complete darkness, cold and hungry, weak and still bleeding from the beating and the birth of my beautiful boy. It's time to go.

I wish my mother was here to comfort me as she always had when Pa was beside himself with anger. She was soft and beautiful and, to me, the most beautiful and sweet women in the entire world. My ma left us a short few years ago, deteriorating at a rapid pace without cause. Neither old Doc Feeley nor the doc in towns over could find the cause of her illness. We found her at the edge of the forest where she loved to pick berries for her famous fresh, berry cream pie. Pale as fresh-rolled dough and stiff as week-old bread, the stains of berries covered her lips. The very berries that she loved to pick for her pies were the berries that took her from us, coated with poison that I had I placed there, knowing she would eat as she picked the vines clean. I didn't want to kill my ma, but I had no other hand to play. She was the only one standing between me and my lover... my pa. He is the father of my child, still lying helpless in the briar patch, waiting eagerly for my return.

He is the love of my life. He has always shown me love and affection... not affection of a father for his child, but affection known only by a woman, a real woman, from a real man. His hands gently caressing my shoulders as he walks up behind me while I am cooking on the stove, his gentle kisses in my hair, my neck, my back, all tell me that he wants me as I want him. I always give in. There is no other. He is the only one. Yet he fears that I have given myself to another... had another man's child. I have not, as he is my one and only, my first and my last love. There is no one or nothing on this earth that would ever make me betray my lover.

The thoughts of my child are vivid and real. They are changing me. I pull myself back into my body, and reality wrecks me in the back of my slumped body. If I die now, my baby will wither deep into the soiled roots of the briar patch, unknown to all, as if he never lived.

The foul, nauseating wooden boards holding the cellar walls steady are filled with rusted nails protruding from their sides. I begin scratching at each until I find one that is loose enough to tug at. With now bleeding fingertips, fingernails split open to reveal the flesh beneath them, I pull out each rusted nail, one by one, until an ample amount are gone and a space large enough for a child to exit emerges. Pausing for a minute

17

to take in all that I have done, I can still hear the sound of Pa pacing on the other side of the wall. He mutters as he paces, but I can't hear what he says. If I run, he will track me down, find our baby, and kill us both, no matter how long it takes. There is nowhere to hide and no safe end for me and my child.

There is lamp oil in the back shed under the tools we use for gardening vegetables. Creeping into the shed, I open the door hesitantly so as not to make a sound. The small axe with the broken handle that we use to cut firewood stares me in my face as if to say, "pick me." This is the one, the tool that I will use to kill my lover, my Pa. I am captivated. I am his, but no longer. My heart is torn. Returning to the deafening hole of the cellar to await my intended demise and then strike in the hope of reuniting with my child overwhelms my need to immediately run.

In silence, I sit and wait, and wait, and wait. There is no noise about the house, no movement of a single soul in or out. Did he leave while I was in the shed? Did he finally sleep to dream about how to rid my body?

I am curled tightly against the floor, hovering over my freedom, when the door swings open, slamming against all in its way. The realization breaches me that this is not my Pa, not my lover, not my child's father, but the guardian of death keeping me from returning to my stranded, helpless, beating heart. Springing to my feet with freedom in mind, my hands push with all I have, covering my Pa's face with a pouch full of blinding flour. He starts to yell profanities, all the while trying to clear his eyes to focus his rage back on me. I pull the small axe with the broken handle from its hiding place. With a full swoop of my arms, my hands become an extension of rivaled steel, splitting his chest wide open. The head of the axe crushes through all bone and flesh below his neck. I try to pull it out to strike again, but it will not retreat. It has found a home where it wishes to stay.

This is not the end. He is not dead. He whimpers in pain, pleading for me to rescue him. "Clarah," my lover sings softly, "flower," he says again, as this is what he would call me when we made love. He is at the mercy of the lord now, who will judge him for all he has done to me, and our little one.

What have I done? Who have I become?

My chest drops, and my faith moves away from me to not witness the truth of what must be done. The beautiful house that my family has built by their own blessed hands is now engulfed to burn at the tips of a scorching death flame, perpetrated by innocent lamp oil intended to light the hallways of our home. This was the home where I was born, the home that was to pass down to me in marriage and to my child in my death. My home no more. There is haste to make toward my awaiting heart.

My legs cannot carry me fast enough past the shed, past what I have done to my lover and my trusted confidant. Past the point of no return, yet I am frozen where I stand, teetering with the sight of my love being devoured by relentless flames.

I return to the destruction I have caused. There is still life inside; there must be. My love must not perish in the fire. He must know how much I love him. There is no other lover that I wish upon this earth to cherish. He must know that he has no worries. He will forgive me, as I am myself a child with good intentions and the maker of bad decisions.

The smoke engulfs my lungs, my eyes blister from the heat. I get down on my hands and knees, searching in blindness to feel the flesh of him. My fingertips touch rough leather,

19

hard, bound leather. It is his boots, but they are not lying near death on the floor. Rather, they are standing erect, sure as the tall trees reach toward the stars. My eyes wide open with bubbling tears from heat, his eyes meet mine. For just a moment, we are together again. His rifle barrels down as he hovers over me on my knees.

I cough, "I love...." everything goes dark.

Shelby

The man I married is not the same man appreciated by most nowadays. He was sympathetic and generous, thoughtful to the touch, and thoroughly kindhearted. A true God-fearing man from a good family, who was well known around these parts. If one is a Christian, it would be a feasible thought he came right off the pages of the good book itself, as if he wrote it with his own occurrence.

My family is from simple beginnings, where our imagination never allowed us the grand thoughts of owning land turned on the backs of slaves. Personally, there is no place for slavery in my mind. It is a god-awful business, but the reality of the life we live, it is of normalcy. Doesn't mean I have to like it. Never understood how one man could own another made at the hands of God. Just rubs me the wrong way thinking about it all day.

If it were not for the hard work of these men, woman, and children, this land would stay asleep throughout the many seasons, left to the elements to run wild. This land produces cotton, tobacco, and sugar, and it is quite grand. We allow the slaves to grow beds of vegetables and fruit about the side of the land next to their dwellings. They seem to like tending to their gardens after all work has been performed to my husband's liking. He has become a hardened man, almost a soulless man at the sight of any slave wandering about, dawdling without purpose. I say, "Leave them niggas be, and come over here to give me some suga." But my soft ways fall on deaf ears.

Truly, I don't believe he likes having slaves either, think he'd rather farm the land himself if he could.

The sourness started running through his veins when he acquired his first slave hand, a young boy full of strength, given to him as payment for a small plot of land at the rear of the land. He was a good nigga, a kind nigga, worked hard and kept his nose clean. We had no place for him to lay just yet, so he chose to sleep under the belly of the big back porch. One day, we were awakened by the sound of him screaming and hollering about something biting his face. We both come to run and see what was happening. Come to find out, he was bitten in the face by an opossum, so he grabbed the opossum by the tail, swung it against the ground until it was senseless, and bit its head off in return for biting him. Seeing his face all bloodied, I thought the small critter dug deep into his face, but it was the blood of the opossum that covered his mouth, not his own.

Realizing what he had done, I chuckled until I almost wet my nighty right there in front of them both. My husband even let out a tiny smile and laugh.

That day, the boy went from foe to friend to my husband. Years passed with only the two of them roaming and turning the ground of the land, choosing only a small corner of the grand property to farm. It stayed that way for a few years, until the land became too expensive for my husband to afford, and it was decided to sell more of the land on the backside, buy more slave hands to help, and make useful more of the property.

Didn't grow up reading nor writing much, but I know how to cook and clean and take care of my man in the bedroom. When we were younger, we happened to have sex like animals, anywhere and everywhere, three to four times a day sometimes. Surprised we ain't never had no children, not like we ain't tried, but sure would've been nice to have some running around these lands. Nope, it's just him and I, and now all the slaves. They all call him Master, he be Reginald to me, Reginald Ronald Reagan. He wants me calling him Reggie, but that sound like some little boy wetting his pants at night while sleeping with his mama. I ain't nobody's mama, I be the wife, his mistress, and his play friend. If he dares go looking anyplace else, it will be the last thing he do before I go frying up his peter in the pan and feed it to chickens.

Nope, times aren't what they used to be. He changed and changed a lot for the worst. One day, the boy and my husband were on a hunt in the woods for deer to fill our storage. Ain't nothing like cured meat throughout the winter. The day was getting long and cold, and the boys hadn't seen anything all day. They were hunkered down next to a cove where they know deer cross, when night comes looking on the ridge.

Leaning close to one another for warmth, they sat quiet as quiet can be without a peep.

A massive brown bear suddenly took hold of the boy's neck through the rocks where they lay. Reginald quickly reacted in fear, pulling his rifle up to shoot, aiming directly at the shadowy bear's figure clawing at his friend. Hesitating to not shoot his friend, he waited for a clear shot, which never came. The beast carried the boy off, screaming for help. The cries could be heard all the way to my front door and down to the quiet town below.

Carried off into the dense trees, Reginald followed to save his friend. Coming upon a small clearing across a light stream, the boy's head lay by a tree. His leg next, his hand, and in the distance, the bear standing on the boy's chest, eating him from the inside out.

That day, Reginald was left in those woods with his friend, and he from that day forth became Master. He vowed to never befriend another one of his slave niggas.

What's left is the crust of a man in years past. What I see there is the man I see today running them fields like a general running his war, hardened by the reaper, showing his ugly smile, grim with satisfaction.

No matter the thoughts of those around us these days, my husband Reginald is a good man, whose heart is confused and lost.

Now, around when the baby boy, now known simply as Avery, was first presented to him, it is told he saw something in his eyes. Something that told him this baby boy, found with a serpent atop his chest, was sent to our land to torment him, attack him for all the bad he had done. If only he had never accepted the first nigga boy as payment for the taking of his plot, the boy would not have met with such a death, one that should not be preyed upon against one's worst neighbor, who has imposed the most criticism, deprived of favor to another.

If my recollection is correct, the first sight of baby Avery, the white nigga child glared out like any other little nigga child, but those eyes were of no purebred nigga, nor one of mixed race that I had ever come to bear witness to around these shares.

Adorable he was, with such a minute smirk of ponderance, it was a blessing to have a fresh face about the place. It had been too long since a baby had been born here. The crisp air had become stale with repetition, a steady spoil of goods unsold, undusted for years. When felt, his flesh felt like the flesh of my flesh, when he cried, his cry was like the cry of all babies. That baby boy is like no devil I had ever seen in the bible, but a blessing sent down by God himself as a gift to uplift our lost spirits.

But in favor of my husband, he will not receive treatment different than any other hand raised around here to work. Long as he grows a strong nigga, an obedient nigga, and keeps his head down to work, Reginald may not take his appreciation out on his tender skin.

We can only pray a novel life comes to Reginald, or the devil will plague his humble mind.

Sitting about this old porch is boring as watching the rats carry away the grain from the feed bins blanketing my vision. Ain't never one to run amuck or complain about good living, but my ass has grown flat, as gravity has taken my floppy breasts in opposite directions of one another, down past my knobby knees. Would appear that my girly, slim figure which attracted all good-looking gentlemen's attention, is now round as a sheep's bottom, only attracting those with rotten missing teeth, bad skin, and dirty feet. God says come as you are, even if you used to be a giraffe and are now a roly-poly bug.

My, how times change, I just never know if it is for the better or the worse, but my favorite thing to do round here is eat. Will thankfully eat a wild chicken's ear to the gristle if they let me. When I was a little princess running about the house, eating more than a grown man with a humongous appetite, my momma would always tell me I was a cow in an earthworm's body. God rest her well in heaven, she didn't get to see me flourish.

Reginald likes me fluffy. He says he salivates at the sight of my big ole self without my nighty on. The dim lamps that ignite my path to the bed must be dulling his already diminishing mind into thinking I'm some haphazard floozy from the city coming to set a fire under his bedding. But we still make love like unconscious juvenile creatures in heat, even if the rabbit runs into its hole at the first sight of rain. It is speedy and over in just a passing few moments. Even still, that man can eat the skin fat from underneath my armpits, and I would love it, nonetheless.

"Back to work now, niggas!"

I hate when he spews such famine from his jaws.

When that white nigga slave was just barely old enough to stamp about the fields, he was set to work right 'long side them other niggas till night crept beside their shoulders. Ruby took good care of the growing child. Taught him to sit-put where he was told, listen when he was to hear, and always stay on the backside out the way of Master's good eye. It was nightfall when I witnessed the first sign of devastation at the cost of Avery's little arm. He wasn't no bigger than a peach in early bloom. There he sat on the finger's edge of a fallen paper tree, jarred in between the helps' shelter and the tall fields overflowing with sugar cane. Enjoying a fresh taste of new cane, the child sat with a smile on his face, chomping away at the tiny stalk of sweet goodness. I imagine he didn't seem to have a care of his surroundings, or the Master glaring at him across the backside of the house, as he struggled with his goodie stick.

The Master, with his keen ways of stealth that he has honed while approaching many slaves in the past aborting daily work, leaped from behind the shelter that hid his presence, and with a quick whip, he cracked young Avery's arm with an iron rod used to poke and prod at ornery hogs stubborn to move as commanded.

That innocent arm of his just about fell off to the ground, running from its place connected at the shoulders. The bone of his arm shattered in two, his skin gashed open, with blood hurrying from the wide opening, showing flesh. The scream from that boy made my hair lift from my neck, as I felt the pain in my own knees.

The Master walked away, looking back at Avery curled up with more fear than pain, with a satisfactory grin of accomplishment. He has made his mark; he has struck first blood of the child.

The Master embarked on his first of many lessons needing to impose on the child for being delinquent in the color of his skin.

Avery

Lessons taught since I was a child have turned me into the sour man I am today. It was those same lessons that leave me without feelings for the whites, uneasy feelings toward the niggas, and confused about the Lord's scripture. Never learned to read or write at the hands of other ignorant fools but learned to use my memory for all that came my way. Obsessed to look about my surroundings and pretend to read what's there, but all

I do is memorize what others say about it, word for word. One thing I have learned is to always act like I am learning something, or else I was going to have to learn it all over again, and again, and lessons hurt. Can't take too many at once, or else my young head might burst with knowledge.

The land is lush this fall with overgrown branches and leaves that grow fresh masks of vibrant colors, smiling about as they gather in a dance.

When I get to the clearing, there is the Master, standing there, blankly staring down at the wild grass freshly shaved by wild animals grazing on its moist blades. My knees halt me from another step forward, as Momma Ruby told me to always stay on the blind side of the Master. My breath disappears under fear. My legs stiffen from the sight of his mighty back and shoulders, draped atop—his head, with an ever so present filthy, brimless cover. His neck briskly turns to catch me looking his way, as if a sneaky bugger following his steps. I dare not look him in the eyes or else tempt my fate to be scorned and beaten, left in these unforgiving woods to make a nice supper for the animals that roam.

"Boy!" he slithers out. I shrivel and pee my pants. "You following me, huh?" I say nothing, just keep my head low to the ground, confused, as if my feet are not my own. "Come here, now!" he creepily growls.

Inching closer to his side, anticipating another lesson, he reaches out to gobble up my neck, but instead perches his large hand, roughened by years of drought, on my shoulder with gentle strength. Standing there for what seemed to be hours, a terrible anxious feeling compels me to hurry back home before trouble finds me. The trouble that would find me stands next to me in silence, so I fear not running back.

He stares at the ground, fidgeting with agitation, peering down at me every once in a while, to ensure I'm minding my lessons. Without notice, he says in a low tone, "This here..." he pauses for a long time, clearing his throat gently. His right eye wells enough to reluctantly allow a passive tear to escape quickly down his cheek to his chin. "Well.... Umm, this here be... new life. Life given to others of their own life... This here be your grave if you don't listen bout for lessons before it's too late."

Returning his focus back to the ground, we stand connected as the wind whistles with the breeze of night coming. My shoulder willingly accepts his final release, his tired hand left an ending squeeze to my arm. With an almost absent push, he nudges me away in the direction of home. Starting to run, I look back over my shoulder to see Master still standing in the same barren clearing that clenches his attention from movement. Running in ignorance, I look back no more.

Today, I see a mortal man, a man in pain, a man with a soul after all. I wonder if that man will change with the morning coming. If we are all so lucky, he will.

The morning is here. An anxious feeling of rebirth fuels my curiosity, for changes are among us now. I see it with my own two eyes. My bed releases me from rest with reluctance to liberate water from my middle, as happens every morning. My eyes barely able to focus, as the sun has yet to show its face. I am startled to attention to see the boots of a man settled directly in my footpath. There, locked in stance, threatens Master with his leather in hand, a blanked appearance minus any expression. Lacking movement, he nods his head toward me, carefully places his belt into each one of his laces that secures his pants, eyes still fixed on mine. Turning, he steadies off toward the morning fields' work.

He stops and turns back toward me standing in silence as he studies my movement. "Back at it again, niggas!" he yells, the sound of bugling alarms for all to wake. With no urgency as he shuffles away, kicking aside a rock the size of a potato, he begins to whistle a familiar song us slaves enjoy on our day of rest. Off, he disappears through the thick vines of high crops of cane. We never spoke of this moment again, and I take it we never will.

Ruby

Winter brings us the best time of year. The hawk chills warm bones into submission. Christmas is a holiday that conjures up visions of joy to eat and freedom to roam. There is family, for all us spread around close by. Some of us get gifts given to the ones who stay in good favor of the masters.

We walk around year-round with the same cloth on as the year past if we don't get cloth given this time of season to shelter us from the cold. During most of the year, we only get a chance to work, and work hard we do, until the sweat no longer coats our skin. The cloth on my back is no longer, and the skin on my feet stay solid to the touch.

It truly is a joyous occasion, the freedom offered to us, that the birth of Jesus lightens the heart of many who are constantly infecting us niggas with resentment.

All these years, young Avery has walked around with a simple stretch of rubbished fabric tightened around his tiny waste by jagged chords stripped from the loose bark of trees. There are many days he would work around the land with his happy dangling outside the edge of his makeshift britches. He didn't care if it caught dirt from the ground or pollen from the flowers pushing him around, he went on with his songs.

We all are getting ready for the day as it draws near. The Master and his wife prepare to leave for a short few days to visit family who are within a day's travel by carriage. They tend to give us a small pig to have to ourselves, allow us to have a kennel of flour to boil to add with our vegetables we grow on the side of our shelter.

Whispers chase the curiosity of us all, as a slave, a tiny man no taller than a fencepost cut to half the size, man colorfully known as Hoof, the Master's blacksmith, is set to ask Master to share in marriage with his dearest, Trita. She ain't no older than a lamb, nor smarter than a raindrop in June, but the width of her hips may have purpose for rearing many children.

We ain't never had a marriage around here, the Master don't believe in it. He thinks it is blind ignorance for slaves to marry. He says we don't have the right to hold another slave as our own, as we all belong to him. Property can't own property, even in marriage.

Fear intertwines with excitement for the unknown consequences of asking the Master for a wishful thought. Asking, or running away to elope, is the only answer. Either way, it can lead to a sentence of lynching or a loosening of the noose.

The day of reckoning is upon us, a joyful day we slaves long anticipate for a whole year. Today is the day Hoof asking Master to allow him and Trita to jump that old broom and be allowed to make a family. With midday approaching fast, Hoof sweats hesitantly with anticipation of his neck rolling along with his body. Never have known him to say much in the matter of conversation, but he can sure blacksmith any tool with precision and shoe a horse quicker than a pig knuckle is munched by a starving slave at sundown.

I just stare at him from the seat on my porch with a silly grin covering my lips, silently taunting him to get a move on. He doesn't budge an inch toward where the Master sits across by the corner of the house, sipping on his familiar glass of whiskey.

Hoof is nervous as a mouse in a snake's house. His normally steady hands, overpowering his desire to halt them from shaking, incapable to even shoe one tiny Jackass in what seems to be a half a day. Not looking at what he's doing, he grabs the pony by his erect penis. Quicker than lightening touching the ground, that Jackass sledgehammers Hoof right in the mouth, then again in his upper shoulder, sending him flying about fifty lengths in the air.

Screaming bloody murder, mouth bleeding, shoulder up in his neck area, Hoof ain't have no teeth left. Now, who in the right cotton picker, tobacco smoking mind going to have the gall to marry a toothless, short, fat head, purple and blue man looking like that? That child must be in love if she jumps that broom with a racoon like that. But she loves that man, she will make him feel much better later, I am sure of it. Those type of rangy hips can make any half-a-man feel whole again.

No sooner than his tossed little body plows the dusty ground with the bones of his back, his love Trita rushes over to pick his head off the ground, pulling his swollen, dusty head familiarly close to the care of her girlish bosoms. Taking a few moments to gather his thoughts and enjoy the comfort of a tragedy escaped, Hoof leaps to his feet, steadies them below on the surface of plain dirt, and charges the animal with a great stick he swooped from the fence's edge. He lays a heavy whack on the side of that animal like no other. Trampling to get away, the tether-bound ass lurches, avoiding Hoofs relentless revenge.

Not knowing what or whom was causing all the commotion in the barn area with stock, Master comes running around the corner in haste with a whip in one hand and a sly drink of whiskey splattering about in the other. Silence falls over the herd of slaves gathered around the happenings.

This is bad, very bad. Monstrous in nature, the Jackass is Master's work animal. The one who plowed the fields and carried the feed. The powerful broad back for bringing fresh water up to the house from the well far beyond the flat landscape. That ass is comparable to a child of the childless Master, purposed in remaining untouched and well managed.

Previously fueled anger for the animal quickly turns to fear of reprisal by the cowering plantation blacksmith, Hoof.

"Nigga! What the hell you think you doing to that Nag?" Master hollers. "Get your nigga as here right now!" he howls in a loud, strenuous voice.

Hoof scurries to attention at the feet of the Master, head slouched to never look him in the eyes.

"That there Nag is my property, I am the only one to touch my property in an improper manner. That understood, nigga?"

A scuffle of mass proportion ensues between Hoof and the Master, as Master clutches at his challenger's unclothed, sundried skin and sharply matted hair, slinging him about.

The year before, Master instructed men to construct a metal box, made to stew a man in the sun till nearly cooked from the outside in, baked in the dead heat of the hottest day at the outstretched arms of the sun's blaze.

Hoof stays right there in his toasty coffin, turning again and again as if he is trying to roast himself even for supper. There is no relief in sight if Master himself don't say so. He is left to pass away one minute at a time.

Night travels in, bringing a briskness with it that will drown any beast caught without proper shelter.

Little Avery eagerly tugs at my blanket that I use to keep the chill from this old, stubborn body, or else these knees won't act right. He can't stand the silence that surrounds the camp, filled with quiet moans of his friend Hoof dying in the distance.

"He gone die without water, Momma, he gone die."

I know for sure, if we get caught messing with Master's law, we gone die too. But if I don't do something this instant, this little boy is going to get himself strapped up to a post and whipped until he ain't got no more skin on himself to whip.

How are we expected to have a wonderful Christmas day with a dead man lying next to us all? There is no joy in death, except to know that one is finally free from a lifetime of torment and torture, leaving this God-forsaken place to rest in the embrace of the Lord.

It is the peak of night, Christmas is upon us, and young Avery and I creep on the side of our shelter, around the sticks of the roofless barn, making our way toward Hoof's prison. A noise startles us both into not taking another step. Still as the night, we dare not move an inch for fear of someone coming to see our rescuing deed.

There, by the foot of the cage, is Trita, grasping at the legs of the hovering box that imprisons her lover. Sleepless with passion, sobbing from depression, the young, scarred bride refuses to leave her lover's side. So, she waits with him, in hopes that death will come to them both. They will be together in marriage in this life or the next.

Avery moves away from me, advancing himself with caution toward Trita, mourning for her lover. He reaches his hand out to caress her hair hiding her face of tears. Her lips touch the cup he holds in his hands, and she takes a small sip of water.

He climbs the short ladder up to the opening where Hoof's hand rests just outside of the wooden shafts that holds him of full sight. His fingertips reach down just enough to moisten Hoof's fingertips. Retrieving just enough to rub on his lips, Hoof gives a small sign of relief. His fingers return four or five times more, each with just enough water to satisfy his lust for quenching his thirst.

Barely able to contain the strength to stand, Trita lifts her wilted body from beneath the stumps, releasing her grip on the short, wooden pillars just long enough to see Hoof's eyes looking back at hers. They both gaze at one another as the moonlight tips a short smile on their face.

"I will," Trita mutters ever so gently.

"I will," Hoof returns with manly pride. His bottom lip and chin shrill together, knowing this night may leave his Trita with only his statue by her side.

Avery begins to walk off into the dark toward one of the buildings holding feed. He reaches down to gather bunches of twigs and large, straight sticks gathered by a stump. He unravels the rope from around his waist and begins securing the twigs to the branch. When finished, he holds his makeshift broom to the sky, places it gently at the feet of Trita, and steps backward.

Trita glimpses over to see Hoof's bashed head sloped in defeat. She peeks down at the broom lying at her toe's tips. She, with pureness in her intentions, reaches to touch her fingertips to his. She takes a breath, pauses for a moment, and with a swift, silent leap, jumps the broom.

With a smile of satisfaction for the joy he has witnessed, bringing the two fouled lovers together, Avery whispers with delight, "You's married now."

Even with Hoof locked away from the rest of us, we now have grand cause to celebrate. Christmas is here, and the lovers have married in secrecy. It is our honor to collectively engage in the holiday that fills our cups until there is simple givings for us to share.

We must appreciate the ones still here, standing next to us in the living, appreciate the compassion and love we around here have for our family and loved ones, for Christ giving his life for the believers and the sinners.

We celebrate this day with a game we call "capture," where the children who have made gifts out of whatever they could find of scraps are chased around by their family and friends. Once captured, they are held until they reveal the location of the gift to be given to their captor.

With the Master and Miss Shelby now gone away on their travels to their family's home nearby, sharing Christmas with our clan begins with checking over the small pig given to us for the day's gathering. Can't wait to taste the succulent meat of the pig, as it has been smoking under the ground since two days prior. Oh, the joy of anticipation in touching the different meats to these old lips.

The men tend to the meat, and us ladies begin to gather and prepare all fresh vegetables grown from the land we till. We play games with pebbles, throwing for distance, we use them as marbles, click clacking the others, pushing them out of the drawn circle in the muddy dirt. Gathering in a crowd, we sing the songs of our days' rest, the songs of joy and freedom, loud as our voices will carry across the thin air. We have not a care to be given, no overseer to mind our manners, no harvest to see to, it is our day and our day to have alone. The joy I feel right now is like no other, it is an unspeakable spirit souring to the highest points of the heavens. Little Avery running around causing lots of trouble as he pulls and tugs to dance with anyone within arms-reach, dancing in a crazed spell like a madman. The sounds of our ancestors surround us, embracing us in their arms, letting us feel alive, knowing they are still looking over our physical being. We oblige their history with more dance, more food, more song, more of life.

The sound of music is momentarily interrupted by the clattering sounds of horses heavy with riders charging our way in the far distance. No one is expected around these areas right about this time. Everyone should be done with their travels, enjoying comradery with their distant families.

Drawing nearer and nearer, the sounds of horse's hooves clamoring about the road to the house gets noisier and more earsplitting. Gathering in the distance, along the tree-trimmed horizon, appears a troop of dark shadows approaching with tremendous momentum, one group pulling a large wooden wagon with rusted steel bars. In the front of the hustling platoon of men is Master Reginald leading the charge.

Frozen at the sight of the sudden return of the strict Master, we all cease to move. Frozen in the same places we once danced in bliss just moments before, our hearts heavy with fear, our minds confused with intrigue.

The dust seemingly endless with rage, the men come to an abrupt halt on command of its leader. The mood does not sit right, we are all stranded in time at the hands of many unknowns, filled with endless, mindless thoughts of prediction. Both sides holding their ground, neither crossing the imaginary line in the dirt.

Emotionless gazes from the other male riders to take a good look at the stock they have ridden such distances to purchase maybe?

Master yells for all us niggas to rush to the front and become seen. "All y'all women niggas come on here to the front. Come on now! Don't dawdle."

One of the men on the side of Master looks about the ones closest to him. Sweat dripping from his low, covering brow, tipping his filthy hat, he sighs a sign of exhausting relief. "Yup, these are some fine ones here," he yelps. "Just fine, I tell ya. You said they was sweet and ripe for the pickin', and they be right nice, uh huh."

Another man climbs down from his large steed without saying a word, just quietly spits out his jerky meat from his mouth and grunting as if releasing pain of his bottom from a long ride.

Unshackling chains clatter and click with drab excitement. The wagon doors creak open to release what is thoroughly contained within. Out of the darkness, with hands and legs free of binds, climbs out a never-ending slew of large, stoutly healthy, dark men, so perfect in muscular balance, as if themselves bred to perfection. The cluster of dark men, glistening from oil shared on their bodies for presenting, stand together in a straight line, fueled with unending pride. They do not look like mad dogs ready to pounce on its nearest victim but more as if well taken care of beasts who take pleasure in pleasing their owners.

The men all wait in silence.

Master, sitting atop his horse, begins to speak.

"Listen up! Here we have some very respectful traveling men of the south. They be traveling daily throughout the country of farms like this here. Unbalanced farms with more women than men. These be good, strong, healthy niggas, known to perform their duties with the highest of agility. These here niggas be the cream of the crop. The best of the best niggas sent here and hired by me for their proven bloodline. Champion niggas. They be here to breed with the ready women old enough to blanket. Those youngins that are virgin types and those with many children. These here... these here niggas you see before you be my guest. They will be allotted the same respect given to me. As you are my property, to do as I see fit, they will take the property of women stock I choose and bed them for the night, without defiance." There is a long pause before he begins again. "Now, this shouldn't interrupt your happenings at all... I come with gifts. Merry Christmas."

Avery

Once you see tragedy firsthand, you have a life of torment trying to unsee it. That night, when those men came riding onto our land, was the night my eyes changed colors. I wasn't nothing but a young boy dancing about with my Momma Ruby, satisfying my want to capture her knees and receive my Christmas gift. My arm never healed right from being broken, and from this night my head never mended from some things a child or no human being on earth should ever witness.

When those men road in on those horses with Master leading the way, Momma Ruby act like she seen the ghost of her ancestors returning, back from the dead. She just stood and stared, trying to form clear images of the dark figures approaching with her quickly fading eyesight.

I saw it was Master from way down far off. These eyes know the look of Master. I see him in my sleep, then when I wake, and all moments in between. I keep him in my sights now since he snuck up on me like a grubby, shifty snake while I was enjoying a sweet treat of freshly cut sugarcane. Father Time played a cruel joke on me. He beat me down day in and day out but never sped time up to hurry me along. He whooped me, and whooped me good, until all that's left in me are memories of the immense cruelty of human beings released upon one another. I wish I could go back and tell that little boy to stay strong, keep your head up. There will be times and moments when you want to give up and give in, but don't do it. I want to talk to that little boy and tell him to change his mind about hiding under Momma Ruby's shelter that night and run into the woods instead. That little boy is gone, and all that is left is this old timer, sitting on this porch, with memories of being hated all my life by niggas and whites alike.

The night those men came to us for our women was the night I started hating them too. When I notice one of the men is Master, I sprint from the hands of Momma Ruby to hide under the shelter where we sleep. She doesn't notice me disappearing from her side. She's frozen in fear, wondering about the sudden happenings unfolding in front of her old eyes. Shiftless, she dares not move a muscle, she dare not make a peep.

Seeing the Master on top his horse, lots of strange-looking white men surrounding him on all sides, I know this ain't good. Not one of these men has been seen around these parts.

Master picks all the girls to stand in front of him. Then he calls Trita to come over to him and move away from the feet of Hoof. She is slow in arriving, and he yells her name to come quicker. The scorned lover stops to look down at her dusty feet and quickly turns, bursting into a sprint toward the woods. The game of capture has begun, as the darkened men quickly give chase and apprehend her. The reveal of her gifts to them is what they desire. She too is now part of the bunch picked by Master. I know she will fight to keep herself pure from any other man forcing himself on her besides her new husband. She will hold herself pure for him and only him.

One by one, the dark men who were brought to the plantation for their seeds, to implant their filth into the wombs of our women, picks our nigga girls to their liking.

One by one, the women give resistance to the men's advances. We stay steady with shocked faces of discontent, as we are powerless to resist the wants of Master's gifts.

It is muddy and cold underneath our shelter, the sun has moved on, and bugs slither about my body, searching for embrace for the evening. We will keep each other company, as this seems to be my own resting place for the night. Not to arouse attention to my hiding place, I slow in my movement, shallow my breathing, hush my voice from painfully lashing out, "STOP!"

Surrounding me are the cries of the helpless, the wounded, the paralyzed souls of many I call family. I too am helpless, a child with a Master who I must obey and a discontent that I must bury. Covering my mouth, the door above the stairs that I hide under slams open with a loud cracking of the wood stopping against unstable walls. She is begging for her life, begging for the man to not do this to her, she is a virgin, she is married, she is the same as he, a nigga slave. This is not the men we see standing and working next to us in the fields, these are not of even the white men. These are nigga slave breeders, woman slave takers. Men who are spoiled by the whites for their breeding ability, their stature, muscles, perfect form, and virility. These men are the equals to nigga slave traders, Black Slavers hunting and trapping their own kind and selling them back into enslavement.

How are men of the same color given the awful right to rape our women, take our wives, sisters, mothers, daughters and in capture them as their own for the purpose of their own. Calling it giving a life, although it is taking the life, taking the power, taking the heart and soul of another without permission.

We are truly his property, to do with as he sees fit, as he pleases or takes lustful pleasure in our emotional demise. Abandoned by the safety of Momma, my fear seeps inside my thoughts on how much worse this will get before it ends. These men are no longer slaves, they are the inbred speared offspring of the whites, they are the devil in sheep's clothing, they are white niggas.

She flails her legs and feet about the room, everything within reach seems to be breaking about her. The door is left open for all to see what is happening inside the dark space, but the lack of light penetrating the sheltered cave, heartless to warmth from allowing anyone full view, simply silhouettes, and screams of pain from the depth of a virgin taken for reward.

There is no way to muffle the sounds that surround me now, almost as if the screams are inside my own head, tormenting my own thoughts. My ears swollen from the hammering of chastising voices above me silences my own pain from the cold that reeks in the blank space beneath my refuge. Never have I ever heard such sounds of desperation, such neurotic rhythms of agony. Unable to see anything above me, I can only hear discomfort pouring through the unsteady floorboards. It is the sound of Trita's whisper attached to the forced anguish. She is just a child herself; she is not of a woman yet, she is pure and innocent. Untouched by any man, her brow grows freely and unworried about perfection of the flesh, only of duty to self and family.

The traitor of slaves pushes and pulls her in every direction. The two are heard up top unconsciously thrashing for position around the room. Without notice, another one of the beastly men roars into the room, abruptly behind him another shackled to him in shadow. The two men enter with clear direction, as they have performed and mastered their duties on many occasions' past.

With a swiftness, Trita's arms and legs tightly bound at a distance, tethered, and spread apart to isolated sections of the room, unable to clutch herself, from protecting her unsoiled goodness. She does not want this to happen to her, not now, not ever. The men become more defiant the more she struggles. She remains helpless at the hand of such large, beastly men, focused on accomplishing their owner's commands.

Amid such mayhem at the hands of her captors, one of the men gently removes the little bit of ragged cloth that covers Trita's blameless skin, exposing herself to their anxious appetites. I don't want to witness what is happenings, I don't want to be here under these planks. I want a way out of the darkness, but there is no hope of light flashing me a pathway to escape.

Everyone knows when the moment comes, the exact moment of this night when Trita loses her fight with the men. Blanketing the dirt in which I hide, the treetops to the stars, the screech of a virginity lost to grown men, to vultures, pierces the night into the unknown. Cries of help are silenced by a painful howl, are quickly followed by chills of depression, as we all know the deed has started.

I cannot see what the men are doing. Her loud cries for help become muffled, silenced by the men who mistreat her girlish ways.

The Master knows not what he does in making this decision to spite us all on this day of Christmas. From where I lay, I can peer around the land and see to every corner where people congregate. It is at this moment I clearly see the difference, the massacre, the deceit, the betrayal, the love, hurt, pain. Obsessions of lustful wrongdoings possessed by men's needs to oppress those unlike themselves.

They take turns retightening the straps around Trita's arms and legs, ensuring the next man has his fill until completion. Only groans of unfiltered disdain empty the air. With each successive violation, Trita's cries become weaker, until I begin to wonder if she is dead.

Looking around, far to one side, men and women alike share in comforting one another as they weep in chorus. Some holding others' hands, some kneeling to pray, others standing in shock, while a small few comfortingly sing hymns, songs of freedom, hoping the wind will carry their songs to saviors.

Directly in front of me, at a not too far distance, sits the Master and all his white guests on top of the large platform landing, laughing and joking about the day's events while enjoying whiskey, smirks that shake a nasty giggle to their insensitive mouths, they mock the sounds of women crying out for their loved ones on different parts of the property, with multiple men attacking their bodies' virtues at will.

The men come and go, randomly visiting the areas in which the women are bound and waiting.

I look for any sign of Hoof attempting to break from the cave that holds him captive. Without expression, crying in silence, he blends into the background of his cage, not wanting to see his own shadow cringing with emotion. He is no man without the love of his Trita giving him the power to survive, the energy to fight.

Trita pleads for Hoof to help her, save her, come to her, but he silently refuses to motion toward her. Only the tip of his skinned nose glistens a peak of light glowing on tears drowning his darkened face.

Momma Ruby lays beneath his cage, flattened to full extension, closes her eyes in readiness for the Lord to take her, as she has seen enough hatred in her lifetime to carry her to the next. She awaits death as if a friend she has yet to see since childhood. I want to run to her side, but I am deathly afraid.

Seemingly having their fill of the day's treats, finished for now from playing with their ragdolls, the cowardly gang of molesters all gather together outside the shelters in a show of championing their accomplishments to their owners.

Master and the other white men on the porch, raise their libations in cheers to their warriors. Master yells for me, "BOY!" as he looks directly at my hiding place, points his finger at me, "CHOP CHOP, nigga!" With hesitation in my legs, I halt myself at a great distance to the landing and slowly inch forward until within distance of a whispering voice. I stand and wait for directions, afraid that I will be next for abuse at the hands of these other men.

The same man who released the beasts from their cage to wreak havoc on our women begins to laugh with hysterics. "This here sweet piece of cotton be your nigga? Who dat nigga daddy? You be dat nigga daddy?" All the men laugh except Master. He stands firmly placed with his eyes fixed on me in disgust, ignoring the men's banter. "Get some water... make it quick," he grunts. The well is deep, and the water here is shallow with vacancy. My pail filled, splashing about its edge, I carry a tin cup held at the bucket's rim with a tiny piece of loose rope.

The steps to my shelter have never kept me from entering, but this day, they hold me back in fear. There are only two steps, yet they move away from my feet every time I attempt to move forward. They don't want me here, and I don't want to be here, but Trita and the others need me now. Trembling with each step, I stop with my pail at the top of the landing right before the entrance to where she lays. Sitting the water at the front of the door, I turn and head back down the stairs.

Momma Ruby is there to shield my way out, "Go on now, boy, Trita needs you. She ain't gon get up and get it herself," she voices. "Go on now, you can do it, love." Turning to retrieve the pail, I don't dare rush in to scare her. I shakenly whisper, "T… r… i… t… a?" and creakingly enter the room.

There is no response from within the black holed room.

She lays in silence toward the sky, legs and arms spread far apart. Rope so tight it burns her skin around its healthy grasp. She is there, sprawled out on the far corner of the floor. Sweating from her battle, she pours blood from her area below, pooling beneath her, swimming in hell's watery stream. The men have had their way with her, have left her for nearly dead, bleeding, battered, and bruised. Diminished and soiled, impure. She lays in stillness, unsure of her existence, drained of all that is good. Traitors have taken her childhood and turned her a woman, as they say. If this is the method of madness to womanhood, then we should all remain children.

For hours, the men take rest amongst each other while sharing stories of their sexual escapades. Chuckling with exhausting anticipation, the men sit about the grounds relieving their thirst with our well's good water. Having rested well, they all stand one by one by one, take-in a good stretch, and begin heading back in the direction of our women to breed again. The thieves exchange friendly slaps about the shoulder for good luck in choosing their next.

My eyes well with dreadful anticipation of more seemingly endless ruin to come. Repeatedly stroking her soaking wet hair, I kneel at the side of Trita's lifeless body. Placing my fingers in the tin cup filled with water from the pail, my fingers rub moister on her lips, dried from screams. She does not move toward noticing it is me. Her eyes streak

46

tears that I wipe with my own cheek, her tears are mine to take with me.

My place is no longer at the side of Trita, nor underneath the shelter. It is at the side of Momma Ruby, far away from the happenings of more Christmas gifts to follow. God save us all, as we are held captive, helpless to our devourers.

The breeding goes on for two full days. It would appear there is no end in sight from the lulling about of the gifts that keep on giving us nothing to celebrate, there is nothing to lighten our moods.

The morning starts our day's work back in the fields. Our midday's rest fill our ears with more cries and screams throughout the area, as the men have taken rest till late, gathered their strength, filling their bellies to the top with our Master's provided feast, only to have their meals followed by chosen dessert.

A blistering sun melting our thoughts brings another day of unshielded stench from Master's guests, but as quickly as they came, this morning is still, quiet with vacancy. It is daybreak, and Master stands at the landing in front of his door to the house, yawning and rubbing his eyes from a long night of drinking. Two endless days and nights of feasting with the other filthy drunkards who are now gone, taking their vile men with them to inhabit their next position, has barely taken a toll on Master's unwavering gospel.

Ruby

Time moves on, and I have seen enough with these eyes of mine. Seen more than any one group of people should ever have seen in a thousand lifetimes. With every blink of light that I refuse to allow in, my eyes almost refuse to open back up again. I don't wish to see anymore, ain't no reason for me to test these old limbs of mine any further.

The ancestors are calling me home in my dreams, but I have refused to answer them in person. Always thinking that little Avery needs me to guard him from the others, I now realize, there is no protecting anyone from anything, including myself. I feel it inside me, my time is nearing, it is my time to finally have rest, to return home.

Walking about the marketplace in town allows for some pleasure from the day's work. Miss's Shelby has always sent me to town to fill her orders of foods and vegetables not grown on our land. Some of these foods I have never seen in my life, they are brought here from far off places for sell around here to mostly fancy people trying to impress their friends with imported goods. Avery gets to tag along with me if he minds his P's and Q's, stands close by my side. There is fear within me that he may become captive to wandering eyes and empty pockets if he doesn't walk closer to me than my own shadow.

We pick and poke at all the fresh goodies surrounding us on either side. Up and down, the town's road is filled with succulent fruit with vibrant colors and skins so appealing, one doesn't even think they could be real, too pretty to consume. We are without any money to try our own. The only money allowed is coinage given to us by the Misses for us to bring her food back for her cooking. We can't be gone all day, but the Misses Shelby never minds that we stay longer than expected, knowing I take my time visiting with friends from other areas, coming here to fill orders for their keepers.

Not everyone has bad living on their land. Devil masters who treat them with unease. Some have comfortable places to sleep, with bedding to cushion their backs, good clothes to make them presentable to outsiders and insiders alike. Some even live in the master's house, with their own rooms of privacy. None of us slaves on our land can ever imagine living in the same household as Master without wanting to slice the base of his neck with the same tool we bleed out pigs with before quartering them, and he know that too. Probably why he doesn't sleep to well at night. Scared we might do to him what he done to us; he keeps us niggas far away from his house. No matter that it's just a thought, it would never happen in my lifetime, us sleeping with him.

With my basket almost full of what Miss Shelby asked me to gather, me and youngin Avery, still a boy but growing just as fast as the fruit we pick, have a seat on the branches of a large fallen tree close to the end of town. We share in one of the fruits we picked for the Misses. She doesn't know it, but every time I head to shop for her and Master, I buy extra for myself to have a taste. She may see the juices on my shirt when I return, but she doesn't say nothing, just smiles and says thanks for fetching her goods from town.

We sit together and enjoy a few genuine laughs about what some of the white people are wearing, how they are walking and prancing around like royalty while purchasing simple fruit. We haven't a care while laughing together, nor have any qualms about where we sit, we have a note from Misses Shelby, allowing us freedom to roam in town and return before nightfall.

Avery just about kills himself running around the big tree. He runs so fast, round and round that tree he runs, just a laughing so loud he bumps his head right into that tree and rockets to the ground. Ooh, I laugh so hard! After finding his legs underneath him, and realizing where he is, he bursts out in a wonderful laugh that fills my heart tremendously. He ain't had a laugh like that in some years. It's good to know that little boy is still inside there, waiting to get out at every moment allowed. His crooked smile follows his thoughtful eyes in joy while he lays twisted in a mound of falling leaves and gathering twigs. Heaven is here on earth at this very moment. Although he is different from us, he is the same as us, he is a joyful boy waiting for his freedom, with much to offer.

A perfect day is at hand while we play together in the place we have chosen for our day out. Growing tired, I take rest back at the great fallen tree, which gives me a moment's peace. A shadow covers me basking in the sun, and I become startled. But then my heart fills with even more joy than I've had already. It is my friend from the next town over. We have met many times here at the marketplace, shopping for our keepers. She is a very tall, thin woman that dresses very well for her position. She is shared finer clothes than we are allowed, handed down to her by her mistress. She speaks with the lowest of voices, close to a whisper, and shy as a child to strangers. She brightens my day with a huge smile and a belated Christmas gift she has been holding to give me when we see one another again here. She drapes a beautiful colored scarf, made of the finest material in the world. I can only imagine where it came from. I am sure it was far across the ocean, across the world, handmade by those who take pride in making quality goods. Wrapped around my neck and shoulders, it is gentle against my skin, ambitiously tickling my cheeks into a schoolchild's giggles.

Catching up with the happenings around the land, we laugh and share stories for just a bit of time, as we both must be getting back before sundown. It is good to see my friend Chassy, she is a pure delight, refreshing of mind.

Suddenly, our overly cordial visit is interrupted by a rustling of falling goods at the end of the marketplace. A well to do man kneels down to help the woman retrieve her fallen goods, which were apparently displaced from her possession by a patron of the over-crowded place. The ruckus pauses Avery from his play place, and he stares in slight discomfort in wonder. My attention goes back to the well-dressed man, the amazingly beautiful, fair-skinned lady, and the child looking about without care for the fallen goodies feathering the ground. It is none of ours, and we turn back to one another, have a quick laugh about it, and decide to part ways.

I don't know if we will ever see one another again, Miss Chassy and myself, as my time is near, and my soul is weakening. There is nothing more here for us to enjoy today, our home calls us back with reluctance.

Whistling a tune, walking back with my full basket of goodies in one arm placed against my hip, the other hand playfully holding the outstretched hand of Avery, I hear a familiar crunch. With chunks flowing from his mouth and fresh juices running down his chin to his empty chest, he has picked his own fruit clean from a stand for himself, without payment. I look around to see if anyone has seen what he has done. He will get us killed if anyone is to find out we have stolen without payment. We must not be caught with something other than our own.

In one brief motion, the basket of goodies falls from my arm, and my hand slaps the fruit from his smiling face just before another bite. He looks up at me in complete surprise, gazing with his big eyes with sadness. He has never seen his Momma so angry with him for something without cause. I grab both sides of his arms with both my hands clinched tightly without release to halt all movement, looking him directly into his eyes for a silent moment.

"Boy, you ain't ever spoda take nuttin witout payin fo it! You get us both strung up quicker than Master and Miss Shelby can save our skin. You hear? YOU HEAR?"

Shakin' in disbelief by my emotions, he and I say nothing else. Bending down onto one knee, an embrace of forgiveness is all I have to offer for the scolding. His heart beats fast and hard, as if to burst out of his young chest. I feel him sigh and relax. He is back with me now.

We hold one another's hand and share a smile while continuing our path home.

Loving the day, "It sho be beautiful out here today, eh Avery?" I politely flutter with a giggle.

"Yes, ma'am," he replies in a small, cheerful voice.

Today, life is good, and for that, we are thankful.

Lipi

I spend an inordinate amount of time thinking about the things I can't have in this life. Things like my freedom, which was taken from me. Things like my voice, which I never had. Things like my family, which I lost. I serve my mistress well, without qualm, without quarrel, without question. But it is absence that truly fills my days.

Life could be worse. I could be in the fields. Instead, my hands tat the finest lace, sew the warmest quilts, and cook the tastiest stews. I spend what little free time I have with my dictionary. It was the last gift my master gave me. Who gives a mute slave girl a dictionary, you might ask? My master never treated me as a slave, but as a daughter.

My mistress calls me Lipi. My father didn't give me a name at birth. He sold me for a sack of rice instead. My mistress and her husband bought me for a considerably greater amount only to raise me as their own. They are the only family I've ever known.

As we move through the makeshift marketplace, heat blankets the day. The air sings. Dust turns to mud on sweating skin. My long dark braids and the slant of my eyes draw stares from free and bound alike, making me feel self-conscious. I am a novelty here.

The stalls lining the crossroads offer vegetables and homemade goods. The Africans who are allowed to shop here on Sunday morning are older with gray in their hair. Trusted elders.

All except one.

I never thought I'd see an English slave, but this white boy dressed in rags playing under the tree has never been free. The African slave woman with him hovers around him protectively, and my mind is filled with questions I cannot ask. When our eyes meet, I can see the same questions running through his mind. How did we come to this?

Two steps ahead of me, my mistress turns and calls over her shoulder for me to quit dawdling. She collides with a gentleman who is busy checking his pocket watch. I stop suddenly, and the packages tumble from my arms. With a flurry of apologies, the gentleman stoops to help us retrieve my mistress' goods. She smiles and, blushing sweetly, thanks him for his assistance. He can't take his eyes off her. I have yet to see any man who could, and even some women too. He doesn't notice me relieving him of his watch and wallet, but as I stand up the English slave boy is still watching me.

When her husband died of fever two winters past, my mistress decided to teach me the family business. We move from town to town taking a little here and there, not much, just enough to get by. I'm not stupid. I know that if we are caught, I will carry all the blame and the punishment. I have never spoken a word in my life, so my mistress knows that I will never give away her secret. Not that anyone would believe me.

We return to the hotel for lunch. My mistress is no lady, but we must keep up appearances or arouse suspicion. Upstairs, in our room, I set the packages aside and empty the deep pockets of my dress on the bed for her inspection. Four wallets, two pocket watches, and a man's onyx signet ring. My mistress laughs with delight. Seeing my face, she frowns and tells me to relax. We won't be here long. I can't tell her that the English slave boy saw us. I can only plead silently for her to be more cautious than is her want to do.

Despite my status as cohort, I still have my chores. Miss asks me to fetch water for the basin, and she washes her face and hands. She is small and delicate, like a bird. She hides her cleverness and determination behind sweet smiles and fluttering eyelashes. She has many suitors, and I wonder why she doesn't choose one of them and give up this life of crime.

Shelby

The years have gone on and passed without a sound. I see winters, spring, and summers fall year after year, and yet here I still am. This old place plays tricks on a person after so long of simply existing with nothing to do, nothing to show for half a lifetime of living. Guess I ain't done much with the time God gave to me. Ain't got nothing to do, really. My place here is to cook and maintain this old house that needs fixing from top to bottom, front to back. I ask Reginald why he don't have the niggas go ahead and fix up this old funky bucket of manure. But he always tells me that he doesn't want none these niggas getting nowhere near this house. Afraid they might take something or find a place to come into the house and cut us both in our sleep. I don't believe that at all.

Most everyone around here keeps to themselves for the most part. They work hard, do they chores, do what they ask when asked, and go on about they nights business when do. They don't have it in they bones to run around hurting nobody, especially the people who keep them with yearly cloth for they backs and allow them to grow they own food for their liking. Under the circumstances, they are living a good life. Most times, they food smell better than my own, so I go down to the camp area where they're cooking, sit down, and have supper with them. My lord, how tasty is it. I don't dare ask what's in it, I already made that mistake once before. One day, I sat and ate a meal, and said, "Oh, my, this here is of the mightiest flavors, tender and succulent! What it be made wit?"

Momma Ruby said, "It be chittlins." When I asked her what exactly was chittlins, I bout had a pure back slapping heart fit. She tells me it is that leftover insides of the pig. They clean them up real good, boil them for a full day, and they ready to eat. If I didn't ask what they were, I would have surely thought they was the tenderest part of a racoon's belly, dipped in oil and flavored with nothing but love. But no, it's the shitty intestines from the nastiest thing we have growing on this here farm. Who would have thought something so grotesque could taste so damn good?

Over the years, my husband seems to have the right to grow gentler in his ways. At least he tries to. I noticed the change in him a short few Christmases ago, after he left me for business, and I returned to the farm from a visit with my family in the next town over. He had a sadness in his eyes and even stopped drinking for a spell. I never thought he would put down or turn an eye up at the offer of a libation to moisten his lips and lighten his load, but he has.

Truly, I don't know how long this rest from his good ole whiskey will last, but I like having my old Reginald back here with me. Even if just for a little while, I will enjoy the sweet gifts he brings from the fields. Fresh picked flowers from the hills, shot squirrel for my stew, wild mushrooms from the base of the trees, and my all-time favorite—fresh wild berries to make my berry cream pie.

I love me some berry cream pie, but if my ass gets any bigger, I going to have to wear an elephant-size girdle just to fit inside my own house. Reginald loves it like no other. Every time he sees me naked, he starts clucking like a rooster in the morning, jumping around flapping his arms like he about to mount me like a fencepost. I ain't never safe around him without my clothes on. But I don't mind, he must love it that much, because I haven't seen him attempt to rubberneck another woman since way back before school. We were both young and dumb, just two ignorant squirrels trying to get a crumb. Them days are long gone now, and it seems we are all settling in. We have lost some and gained some, yet we are still stuck here somehow or another.

Master finally allowed Trita and Hoof to go on ahead and get married finally, since Trita end up with two new babies from Hoof. One them is a big baby like no other I ever seen around these parts. Same with a few other nigga girls around here, they just all ended up popping up with babies as if it was some new religion that came to town. Who knows who the babies' daddies these days are, they just hop from farm to farm in the middle of the night, hussying about like it's no tomorrow. Guess that's okay, because soon all these babies will grow old enough to work around here like everyone else, earn their keep.

Trita doesn't like when others touch on her, or even try giving her hugs. She flips out in a tiff, screaming and yelling profanities at the top of her lungs. She used to be a kind girl, gentle and soft spoken. Now she funny acting with those around her, but takes good, kind care of her youngin. Always looking after them, like she's waiting on something to come and get them. Her husband Hoof don't like talking too much to anyone anymore, he just stays in that old shed way in the back, shoeing them horses, blacksmithing new tools and fixing old ones. He proud to be a daddy, always showing his little one around the shop as if he going to be a great blacksmith himself someday. His babies ain't no bigger than the tools they trying to lift.

Avery is turning into a bright young man himself. He walks around here pretending to read the good book, knowing he don't understand a lick of them black words covering them white pages. Master gets highly agitated with him when Avery spurts out, "Without them black words, them white pages wouldn't mean nothing!" He is beginning to know that book backwards and forwards like the scars laid on his back for good luck, for lessons.

He learns the lessons listening to Reginald on the back porch, preaching out loud to himself like he used to do a long time ago. He could have been a great preacher if he wanted to. Everyone sitting around him would listen with intent in complete silence as he spoke the words of God, making us feel the pain then see the light all in one or two sentences. He was good.

I know Avery learn from Master, as I have peeked out my kitchen window on many dark occasions and caught him sneaking a listen, hiding in the bushes around back. Even though it is a small audience, I think the Master knows that Avery is there, listening, but I think he enjoys having someone listen to him.

Hearing him speak the word, always hoping for change, I believe in my hearts of heart that Reginald misses the Lord, and the Lord misses Reginald. The lord says, ask for forgiveness and you shall be received with open arms in his kingdom. Reginald has never asked for forgiveness. He says this slavery business, although cruel in nature, a brutal business, is the way of God. I don't think he really believes that.

He tries. He still pains over the loss of his friend, always asking God why he would take such a good man, an honest hard-working man who lived right by all standards of men.

He has yet to get an answer.

Now, with Momma Ruby passing away while resting on a fallen tree next to the fields, he just doesn't seem to want Avery to lean on any other woman nigga in their living quarters. If he sees him getting close to any of the women, he shouts for him to move on and get back to work. Reginald won't admit it, but he truly had a special soft spot in his heart for Momma Ruby. She was the one who kept everything together around here. Funny, witty, scary mean at times, and caring most of the time. That woman could surely cook up a mean storm and feed it to a hurricane to calm its belly. She wore her scars like wings of an angel.

Avery

Standing here alone, the only thing I have left is my thoughts, my dreams, my memories shared with Momma Ruby. She always told me to hush down and not be seen on Master's good side. Sometimes I listened, and other times I had lessons to learn.

These same lessons bring me here today, at the same spot where Master once gently held my shoulder, by his side. We never spoke of that day again, but this place that I stand must make men pure again, because that same day, I seen a hardened man soften to a tear.

Why do I stand here when no one is here to see me? I can run fast and far before anyone even notices I am gone. I know these parts like no one else around here. They don't know, at night while everyone is fast asleep, I sneak off through the trees and explore all that comes in front of me. Today, my legs stand in stillness, waiting for someone to command me to leave, be gone, move on, but no one comes near.

I miss my Momma Ruby so much, it feels as if one of my arms is gone, and I can't lift it, even with all my strength. She always told me that whenever I am down and there is no relief to help me on my way, to look to the lord above and speak to him.

Today, I speak from him, maybe people will listen. I speak as I have heard the Master speak on the back porch in his nights of blindness, and as he believed in every word he spoke, so shall I. But, for me, for my people, for Momma Ruby, for Trita, for Hoof, for... the truth...

"The path of the righteous man is beset on all sides by the inequities of the selfish and the tyranny of evil men. Blessed is he who, in the name of charity and good will, shepherds the weak through the valley of the darkness, for he is truly his brother's keeper and the finder of lost children. And I will strike down upon thee with great vengeance and furious anger those who attempt to poison and destroy My brothers. And you will know I am the Lord when I lay My vengeance upon you.

"And there were shepherds living out in the fields nearby, keeping watch over their flocks at night. An angel of the Lord appeared to them, and the glory of the Lord shone around them, and they were terrified. But the angel said to them, do not be afraid. I bring you good news that will cause great joy for all the people. A Savior has been born to you; he is the Messiah, the Lord. This will be a sign to you: You will find a baby wrapped in cloths and lying in a manger."

As I finish, I kneel to pray in the short grass.

I wander in silent pity, the only sound is of the wind meeting my breath, exchanging pleasantries. But, if Jesus was with hair of wool and skin of bronze, and if we were made in his likeness, then why do we not treat one another as if we are all brothers, children, and of God himself? We hate one another for the color of our skins, but we all bleed the same color blood. We hate one another for the color of our skin, but we all need the same air to survive. We are the only animals to walk upright on two legs, to speak in our spoken learned language. We are not the animals they make us out to be. We are not the beasts that roam the night searching to kill without cause. We hunt to eat, we wash to clean, we live for one another and for ourselves, we are humans, made in his likeness. So, why does man hate man for their skin color? I will never know. I am of the whitest white man, filthy and dirty to look darkened, enslaved since birth to reap the benefits of my Master and all who comes before him that are white.

White Christians speak the word of the lord yet use it against us to enslave us, capture us, hold us. Even a wild animal is not to be held at bay but left to roam free as he pleases. To graze on fresh morning grass silky with dew. Chase prey to feed its youngins, follow one another to new lands to settle a home. Animals roam free to be a family. We are no animals, yet we are also not free.

The life and struggles of Jesus are equal to our own. He died a vicious death at the hand of his abusers, those who did not believe him to be anything like them. Different than them all, just as we are now. Just as we remain, unlike them yet identical to them in man form. God cares for us, as we are the oppressed, the weary, the worn, the tired, the different.

I continue with my own words, my own lessons, as my lessons will now become his, his words will become mine, his torment will remain his own, my gifts will capture him, not letting go. They say that we are the evil, but I sit next to these same men, woman, and children, and they are not bred for evil. We are giving to one another, though we don't have much, but what we have we share in goodness. Our youngins are provided love when they are starving and thirsty. The whites share one big house for a handful of them, yet we share one small room for many of us. Bunched together to provide warmth and comfort when sick, compassion when beaten, hope when there is none, and life when there is death. We are not the evil kind unless evil is set upon us without reason, as is most of the time. Not lashing out in defeat, our mind finds ways through other paths for reckoning our woes.

Master has loosened the noose around my neck since Momma Ruby has returned home to rest. I am glad she no longer can see the torment brought on by men. Her eyes were always filled with so much pain.

I am not yet free to roam as I please as others are, but I roam into the edge of town under the cover of night, as to not be seen, but my white skin glows in the raise of the moon. Mostly, I try to travel when the moon is vacant in the sky.

Searching for scraps of food leftover from shop keepers, I see the happenings around town. Rowdy crowds of drunkard men drinking till they are dropping in the middle of the rocky roads, some using nearby trees as their waste area, ugly women exchanging coinage from men with blood-red eyes for sex in dark, covered corners, in filthy feed houses, in streets.

Under the fire torches lighting the streets of the bustling town stands a beautiful woman, the same woman me and Momma Ruby seen in town. The same woman who dropped her basket of fruits and vegetables in the middle of the road and gathered herself about the ground to pick them up. There is no beauty that I have ever seen that could compare to her. The light hits her silky hair, while the wind faintly blows strands of it into her face. Continuously portraying her ladylike portrait, she wipes her hair from her face, subtly pushing each piece behind her ear. She wears fine jewelry and colorful silk linens that perfectly sticks to her girlish figure.

What is a woman like that doing in a tramping hellhole like this? Maybe she is lost, but she looks comfortable where she stands, undeterred at the sight of random men coming and going. Passing by her standing there, men of different statuses gawk and whistle at her, and she stands without flinching.

Peeping around from corner to corner of each almost falling building, I get close as I can without her seeing me to get a better look at her standing there. Just under the broken window of the mail station, I step over a small crate with empty bottles for milk, held together with twine and ribbon to keep them in place. Startled by the sound of someone coming my way, I quickly tuck myself tightly against a wall, perfectly blending myself into the shadows of the flickering torchlight. She must not see me, or she will surely take me back to Master and have me whooped good.

Catching what is left of my breath after having such a close call, I relax back into my vision of beauty. She takes out a long tobacco-filled stick from her side pouch, slowly pulls it to her lips covered with bright red paint and flicks her light. Once, twice, three times she scratches her match tip, but fails to produce her needed fire. An onlooker standing close by, waiting, seizes his chance to inject himself into her space, providing an immediate light to her tobacco stick. Thanking him with a sweet kiss on his cheek, the man tries to kiss her but only receives a slap in the mug, followed by another one to the opposite side of his now brightly red, scruffy face. Grabbing his face in excitement, he smiles and laughs his way back inside the stacked business.

At last, we are alone again. I just sit and watch her for a long while as she finishes one tobacco stick after another, flicking them like bugs on a window ledge. We niggas ain't supposed to stare at a white woman in the way that I am looking at her now, or else we might get the lynching of our life, or maybe even death. Just a child barely able to release my water in the right direction, they may string me up and suck my eyes clear out of my head. But my eyes dare not change in fear of losing sight of her, to never see her again. So, I shall enjoy this night for as long as possible, to share this moment that we have, just her and I, together, at a distance but close in our hearts' unknowing love.

Lipi

Relax, my mistress said. We won't be here long, she said. Five years we've been here in this forsaken backwater of a town. She still has many suitors, but the love she gave up her life of crime for was a bakery. I suppose you could say she traded one kind of dough for another. I don't mind the work or the hours, and there's less chance of my neck swinging from a branch like I've seen around these parts, but it's hard staying in one place. My feet itch.

It's dark out still. The sun won't be up for a while yet. I have a little time before I must be at the bakery.

The moonlight turns everything black and white. There's a shortcut through the woods within an old bramble. There's an art to picking blackberries in the dark. My basket is nearly full when I hear a voice in the distance. I freeze like a frightened rabbit, ready to bolt. Slaves aren't allowed to be out alone at night, and I don't want my feet to dangle. Some people mistake my silence for stubbornness. Some people are ignorant, and ignorance can be dangerous. Listening closely, I can only make out a word here and there. It sounds like a sermon. Curiosity compels me to investigate.

It takes me a few minutes to find the direction the voice is coming from and longer to reach the clearing than I expected.

The moonlight shines on a white boy preaching to the trees. He's animated. Passionate. His hands won't stay at his sides. He moves with the rhythm of his words. He's taller than the first time I saw him years ago, but there's no mistaking the English slave boy from the marketplace. Keeping to the shadows, I eavesdrop on his moonlit sermon.

"It is for freedom that Christ has set us free. Stand firm, then, and do not let yourselves be burdened by the yoke of slavery.

"The Son is the image of the invisible God, the firstborn over all creation.

"For in him all things were created: things in heaven and on earth, visible and invisible, whether thrones or powers or rulers or authorities; all things have been created through him and for him. And through him to reconcile to himself all things, whether things on earth or things in heaven, by making peace through his blood, shed on the cross.

"You, my brothers, and sisters, were called to be free. But do not use your freedom to indulge the flesh, rather serve one another humbly in love. Once, you were alienated from God and were enemies in your minds because of your evil behavior. But now he has reconciled you by Christ's physical body through death to present you holy in his sight, without blemish and free from accusation—if you continue in your faith, established and firm, and do not move from the hope held out in the gospel.

"This is the gospel that you heard and that has been proclaimed to every creature under heaven."

Once he finishes his speech, he seems to shrink a little. His shoulders slump and his arms hang loosely at his sides. Then he heads off through the trees in the other direction, and I make my way back to the bakery.

Blackberry cobbler is always popular. It's still dark when I slip in through the back door of the bakery. My mistress is already hard at work, but she only raises an eyebrow when I pull back the cloth covering my basket to reveal its bounty. I dance a little jig in celebration. Miss gives me free time whenever I bring in foraged ingredients. She returns to kneading the dough for the day's bread, her voice filling the kitchen as she sings while she works, and I find myself moving in a rhythm like the boy in the woods. He remains in my thoughts as I go about my tasks.

After we bake several loaves of crusty bread, my mistress sends me out on her errands. First, I deliver the blackberry cobbler to the old woman who runs the hotel. She can read the excitement on my face before I show her the juicy cobbler. She exclaims that it will be perfect for tea, then gives me a small coin and a smile. I touch my chin and motion my thanks. My next stop is the general store. The small woman behind the counter with the hawk nose gives me neither coin nor smile, but she buys all the lace collars and scarves I offer for a fair price after a little bartering. As I hand over a note from my mistress ordering more flour for the bakery, my eyes snag on a small stack of bibles on the shelf behind her. Without a moment's hesitation, I point past her and raise my eyebrows questioningly. As much as she appreciates my beautiful lacework and my cozy scarves, this is the first time she has truly looked at me. She beams as she hands the tiny little black book to me. She wouldn't be so happy if she knew this heathen didn't plan on reading her pious scriptures. This book is a gift.

Returning to the bakery, I keep my head down so no one sees the sparkle of mischief in my eyes. I glance quickly over my shoulder before slipping between the trees. If I'm seen, I will just show them the bible and try to look God fearing. God gets you a pass around these parts. Not that I am burdened with an excess of faith. I don't see how anyone who has been bought and sold can believe in anything, but my need to give this boy a gift drives me on through the woods to the clearing where I had spied upon him in the early hours of the morning. The clearing is empty, and I quickly leave the little book of scriptures on a stump, hoping that no one else finds it before he returns.

I wish I could see his face when he discovers it.

My master gave the best gifts before he died, and I find myself filled with the same joy I saw on his own face when he watched me open my gifts.

With a smile of my own, I hurry back to the bakery.

Early the next morning, I make my way to the clearing, hoping to hear the English slave boy preach again, but the clearing and tree stump are both empty. I turn to leave, more disappointed than I expected.

Avery

It's her! The girl from the marketplace years ago. First, I see her mother in town, and now she's creeping through my woods as if they are her own to trample on. She looks a bit different, maybe a little taller than before, but not by much. She is not growing much at all. But what is she doing here, at the place I come to have time alone to myself? Could she be... No, she can't possibly! Is she the owner of the book left behind? Well, it's mine now, and mine to keep.

Wait, maybe she left it here for me to find.

But no one would give me a gift like this since I can't even read a lick of words.

Watching her creep off, back to the way she came through the brambles, my lungs can no longer take in air enough to breathe again. She is not bad looking, but she is not very cute to me either. She's skinny as a bare-boned skeleton and might disappear if she misses a meal just for one day. Her dress is just as colorful and beautiful as the one I seen her mistress wearing the other night.

With my eyes now off the creature who sneaks in the woods, I focus my thoughts back onto my book, my bible. I think, *there is nothing I cannot do without this book, and God.* This book is the key to all mankind, the actual words of God himself, saying we should all have freedom. Some don't know it yet, but we are already free, in our minds.

The morning break makes me tired enough to doze off for a quick second before I must head back to start my work in the fields. A large tree sits sagged over, hovering above my head, it keeps me company as if it watches over me. Always feeling as if this big tree was my protector, my worrier, I often confide in it, telling of my good and my bad days. As the days come and go, as in my usual routine, I sneak off into town to find the beautiful mistress standing out in the torchlit streets, puffing on tobacco stick after tobacco stick.

Flickering away into darkness, tonight she looks stuck in a trance, waiting for something, or maybe someone. If only I knew what her thoughts were, where her mind wanders, I could be right there with answers. How can she stand free as the smoke she loosens in the wind as it sways yet seemed trapped in a world that won't release her to lessen her weight? My eyes rest for a simple moment to control my own emotions. Her senseless thoughts are now my sorrow. My light dims with intrigue, and I doze off, pushed between where the crates reside nightly.

Without notice, "Waaa!" someone grabs a hold of my backside with a sharpened, tickling vengeance. Screaming out of my skin and back into it again, I quickly leap from my crouching space tucked between the high stacks of milk crates.

I fall over tools, right onto my goose-pimpled back. I try to shift up quickly to see if the beautiful lady is staring toward my no longer hidden direction, her statuesque stance interrupted by falling crates and a yelp of fear. Before I know it, a small hand muffles my mouth from further screams drawing attention to our position. Caught red handed, my tears start to flow over the outstretched hand smothering me.

I come face to face with my attacker, with my oppressor keeping me from viewing my new love. And feeling nothing else happening to hurt me, I heroically open my tightly shut eyes.

It is her, the one I seen in the marketplace that day with Momma years ago, sneaking the belongings off that well-dressed man helping to retrieve their goodies that had fallen. As I had noted in the clearing, she has grown slightly but remains petite in nature, though strong in her grip to shut my mouth. She is even more gorgeous than the beauty I have been stalking from across the road. Even more beautiful up-close than eyeing her at a distance in the clearing. She is not the same as them whites but exotic to these parts.

She pushes her finger against her thin lips and gestures, "sshhhh." Silently pointing to a man coming up the street, performing his duty to patrol the area as the law man. He is tall, a very large man in his uniform, a short top hat, carrying an extremely large nose and forehead on his face. I know he is a law man just performing his nightly duties of removing filth from the streets, but he looks like he could use a friendly hug for being so ugly his entire life.

We lay still in the shadows by the corner of the building walkway. The law man takes his sweet time passing us by, whistling with missing parts of his own tune.

Once he passes, the girl, who seems around the same age as me, stands upright and brushes her beautiful dress off from debris. Then the shifty girl reaches her arm downward toward me, offering me a hand to get on my feet. I share a smile with her, but she refuses to return my friendly request. Directly staring me in my eyes, keeping me intrigued as to what her name is. Now I must know who she is and where bout she lives.

In the distance, I hear a woman call, "Lipi!'…Lipi! Where are you? Come, come, now!"

Her name must be Lipi, as her mistress calls her back to her side. But what kind of name is that? I don't know what kind of name that is or who gave it to her, all I know is, I like it.

Minus any words flowing from her mouth, Lipi moves backwards in short steps, further away from me. Still covering her mouth for hush a whisper, she turns and disappears in the shadows toward her Mistress. Quickly, I position myself back into the mouth of the crates, where I was so well hidden, to get a last glance at the two.

They embrace in a warm hug for being absent from one another. The tall beauty flicks her final tobacco stick in the same pile that she has built all night. Holding hands, they carry on away from the bright lights of the torches and fade into the night. Before they fall to the darkness, she looks back in my direction, with a genuine last smile, she holds up her free hand to me with a wave, loosely clutching something in it.

"My bible!" I whisper in disgust, "she has stolen it without me knowing, like the man in the marketplace."

I will come to this same spot every day after nightfall in hopes to see Lipi again and get what is mine.

Returning night after night, there is no sign of the two in sight. Have they gone and left the area for good? Have they moved on from the god-forsaken puddle of smut oozing with the devil's offspring roaming the streets?

My thoughts overtake my senses that dull with anxiety.

Everything around me that is good seems to disappear from my life. First Momma Ruby and now my beauties and my bible.

The Master has ceased his ritual wrath upon me, yet the beatings remain in other forms. Life shows me flowers, but they all tend to smell like horse and cow manure that only grow poisonous mushrooms beneath them.

This is a waste of time; I will never see Lipi or my bible again. With a feeling of defeat, I turn and start my absent journey back toward the farm. There is a rustling coming from a small outhouse sitting alone on the far side of town near the well. Curious as I am, I begin to creep up close to the shack to see what the cause is. Inside the shack, muffled sounds of help come from the shaking walls. I sneak up closer and closer to the shack to try and catch a peek in the small, circled window opening. Stretching the full length of my body, unable to peer inside, I hesitantly start to crack the door open just far enough to look inside.

There, within is my friend, Lipi, the little girl who is the gifter and taker of my bible, a drunkard of a stranger hovering over her petite body, holding her against resistance.

Quickly, I close the cracked opening to not be noticed by either. He is trying to kill Lipi, but I cannot yell for help, for anyone to come, because I am not supposed to be here. She struggles behind closed doors; her silent screams are heard through her struggling limbs crashing about the tiny shack. I am nothing but a boy against a grown man filled with whiskey, intent on harming her.

Running as fast as I can to distance myself from the happenings, I hear Master's oh so familiar commands of, "Back at it again, niggas!" I flash the wrath of beatings at the hands of him, the gifts given to all the women on Christmas, the pain, screams, and foul stench of filthy, beastly men trampling about our land.

My feet no longer run in fright; they stand in command. Turning back toward where Lipi is held captive, a large steel pipe sticks from the ground where the train tracks run through. With a few heaves of my greatest strength, the metal shank releases its grip from the ground. The cries inside grow more faint as I stand outside the door, catching my breath to gather my wits about me. It seems like an hour has passed with me holding up outside the door, but I know it has only been seconds. My hands tremble in anticipation, the air shallows my breathing, sweat tumbles from my whisked hair to my shoulders, the moment is here.

Before I know it, the drunkard kicks open the door to see who shadows outside the shack. Startled by his sudden actions to release his anger on me for disturbing his violence against Lipi, I close my eyes and swing the metal rod in his direction. I continue to swing my rod at him until I see blood trickle from his brow, coming from his head and eye.

Lipi pulls to one side of the area, distancing herself far away from my manic swings. With grunts of anger running through my veins, I beat the man until he no longer moves a muscle. With the stranger now slumped down halfway between the outside of the door and the inside of the shack, Lipi shoves past us both, running toward the tree lined woods.

Dropping my death yielding rod, I stand to look at the man lying bleeding, gurgling, with fluid flowing from his mouth and ears. I take off in the direction of Lipi, as she runs faster than I have ever seen anyone run. Yelling her name, she refuses to stop or even acknowledge my chase. Upon reaching the creek, she stumbles across, falling to the shore. Tackling her with a great bear hug to let her know it is me and she is safe, she does not yell recognizable words, just kicks and screams, tearing at my face with her sharpened claws.

Finally realizing it is me, she loosens her grip on my sketched face. Both of us exhausted and scared, we look at one another, look back in the direction of the path we just ran, and just lay there. We are safe now, we are both safe, and the man is no more. We share a moment of silence to recover ourselves.

With no more strength in me, no more fight, I struggle to my feet with pride for what I have just done. Even though I was too small, too afraid of what might happen to me if I tried to save Trita from the beastly men in our camp, I did not let the same thing happen again to Lipi, my friend.

Reaching my hand out to her as she had done for me a few nights before, I help her to her feet. An object falls from her dress pocket. It lays on the ground perfectly still, alone, undefeated. It is my bible. The one she had given to me and then so gently taken away sits before us both, waiting for its rightful owner to claim it. Lipi reaches down to retrieve the book as I stand and watch. She is the true owner of this book, of the scripture, of the gift. She brushes the book off from its mud and leaves and sets a small smile on her face while tears drip the remaining mud away from the book. Grabbing my hand, she places the bible in my possession, pulling the other hand onto the first one. Taking a few steps back, she looks to run away to the comfort of her mistress mother, but she does not. Without warning she rushes heavily into my chest with a tightly gripped hug following her. Squeezing the life out of me, she holds ever too tightly, not letting go.

Sobbing with no end, she slowly releases her grip from around me. Lipi takes a few steps backward, puts her hand to her chin, and pushes it out toward me. She says nothing in words. With her thin lips, she mouths, "Thank you," winks a caring smile my way, then turns and runs away.

I want to give chase, but we have already chased once before. I just watch her run off down the dark pathway toward the end of town where her mistress usually stands gazing. With Lipi safely gone away, and the monster no longer a threat, I look down. She has given me back the gift she had taken. At last we are together again, just me and my little black book, my bible.

Pausing for a moment to reflect on our blessings for escaping the grasp of a drunkard's lashing, I speak aloud what I heard from Master's lips one night.

"God is our refuge and strength, an ever-present help in trouble. But he said to me, 'My grace is sufficient for you, for my power is made perfect in weakness.' Therefore, I will boast even more gladly about my weaknesses, so that Christ's power may rest on me.

"That is why, for Christ's sake, I delight in weaknesses, in insults, in hardships, in persecutions, in difficulties. For when I am weak, then I am strong."

With strength in my heart, and my friend Lipi safe, I relent. "Amen."

Mistress

Jezebel, hussy, tramp, whore, gold digger, these are all the words I hear around town from these peasant ladies who can't seem to keep hold of their gawking eyed husbands. It's not my fault they can't keep their men happy, that they must look elsewhere for comfort of their eyes. None of these God-awful name's suite me, nor are they to my liking, but I pay them no mind, as I am a pure lady in form and in habit. I do not fornicate with other husbands, nor look to take what is not mine, besides valuable trinkets that catch my eye.

I have traveled to many towns throughout this country, picking and purging myself of other goods to maintain my wealth. Since the passing of my husband many years ago, I am left with little to nothing of my own, due in part to his remaining siblings and children vulturing for a large taste of what was left of our vast estate. How it gleamed with beautiful champion bred horses from Spain and of the finest vineyards for producing tasty wines fresh from our own hands. We would sit out on our great landing looking over our land, having supper and talking for hours on end until our pallets were dry and worn with delight. We had everything our hearts could yearn for and more to share with others who we saw fit and in need of our help.

It took me a long time to find such a gentle man with a favorable heart for things more valuable than his own wealth to show. Money meant nothing to my love, my darling, my best friend. He always told me that money is a necessary evil, because those who have it make the rules even when they break them, and those without it break the law to get it.

It is filthy dirty with human excrement, vomit, and urine from one man's hand to another's.

Men, women, and children are bought and sold on the backs of coinage in the name of ownership and desperation.

Everything has a price, even him and I. I wish we would have hidden some of our wealth from others, or else I wouldn't have to do what I must to survive.

I was able to keep one thing, the only thing that was priceless to me that I could not produce for myself, as my womb is flat and without power to produce offspring, my love, my heart, Lipi. We've had her since three weeks after birth, given to us from a gypsy street merchant who needed money to solve a debt from his bad dealings. I don't believe in slavery or buying of the human flesh for ownership, but I am without child, nor does the future seem to want to give me one.

We dealt for this child, took all that belonged to her tender skin, and moved quickly away, back to our ship docked at the harbor. I have never told her where or how we acquired her for fear she will forever resent me for hauling her away from her family. For now, she will know nothing.

When the time comes, she will know the truth.

Like her father always smothering her with surprises, she too is a gift.

Ever since birth she has been mute, never making any identifiable sounds to form words. Only grunting and clicking sounds would she muster from her little body. Doctors said she would eventually grow out of the grunts to make clear words, but that day has still yet to come.

We have learned to form our own signs and signals for what she wants or is trying to say, it has become my second language and her first, even though she seems to read and understand words better than most. She is infatuated with words, and learning to write, although those same words aren't manifested to sound.

Lipi doesn't speak, but her eyes tell me everything I need to know, and one thing I do know is that she truly loves me, and I love her. If people were to know I taught her to pick the pockets and purses of ladies and gentlemen alike for their goods, I would not sit well as a caring mother. These things I teach is for her own survival. It is laying a foundation to let her know; anything you want, you go get it at all costs, and don't let anybody put you on the bottom of the earth's ponds and forget about you.

We have come to this shithole of a town in the hopes of hitting it big, grabbing what we can and moving on to the next town as usual. These people here don't have much in wealth, but what I have learned is all in all, they are wealthy with love and care.

Besides the handful of bottom feeders and slave owners carrying themselves as God-fearing people, the land here produces great yields of fresh meats and vegetables. Once a week, Lipi and I take a wonderful walk down the way from our small farm at the outer edge of town to the city square to gather our fresh fruits and vegetables from the marketplace. There are so many exotic foods, unseen around these parts by most. We have seen and tasted mostly all of them. Picking through the most beautiful of fruits, we find the ones we like most and grab some for home.

Most of the ingredients from my finds go right into my baking shop. The fresh pies and pastries made there are desired by all, with even the evilest of spiteful woman desiring my friendship to get a chance at me sharing my famous recipes with them. Try as they may, my friendship and sharing of my recipes doesn't even come at the offer of a hundred coins.

My Lipi has a chance to roam here, freely and without worry. She doesn't roam far, but I have taught her to take care of herself and always look around for trouble brewing. I trust she will keep her lessons close to her.

Today is a busy day at the shop I have opened in the middle of town, baking goods since the before daybreak. This is work that is honest, and it can make Lipi hold her head high and not have to run again. It is time we set roots someplace, and this place feels like home, for now.

She is usually running in and out doing her chores and running errands for me, but I have not seen her in quite some time. I don't have time to worry about her, she is more than likely up to her mischief, sneaking about, being nosey, in everyone's business. She will soon show her face, and when she does, she will clean the entire shop for lagging the day away.

Once three o'clock comes around, my baking of all goods stops, and all is done for the day, except to finish selling them all by the time the shop closes after dark.

The bakery sits in between a busy brothel and a saloon. One filled with the ugliest ladies from many towns over, the other with the filthiest drunkards to walk these lands from far and near. After my days' work is finished, I love standing out in front of my bakery shop just under the torchlight, decompressing from all my hard work, smoking my tobacco sticks, and feeling the breeze in my face. I stare down the road, where the tip turns north. It is darker the further down the road you head. No torches to light the way, no people loitering, just darkness within darkness. I call for Lipi, but she does not come to me as usual. I call again. "Lipi. Come, come, now, little one!" again there is no answer, and she refuses to come to my side. She must be just out of reach of my voice. Or maybe she is running amuck,' gathering berries for tomorrows pies.

"Lipi, come, come, now, little one, it is time to retire for the day!" I repeat with a louder tone.

She is nowhere to be found. The night is unusually silent, not many ladies of the night nor drunkards clamoring the streets. In the distance, I can barely make out a small, lightly colored figure, shuffling in the middle of the road, slow as a turtle. Clearing the smoke of tobacco from my vision, I lay focus on the small figure struggling up the road. As it comes closer and closer, I can still barely see with clarity. The first light of the roadway brings clarity to the now clear figure in the shadows, it is my Lipi. But why is she taking her sweet time coming to me?

"Lipi... Lipi... get over here now, child." I see she is trampled, her beautiful clothes dripping off her thin shoulders, completely disheveled from her person. My precious baby girl. What has happened to her? Who has done this to her?

Dropping my tobacco stick, running to her side, I catch her before she falls to the ground. She is soaking wet from head to toe, hair in disarray, filled with leaves and garbage, feet smothered in mud and soot. Falling into my arms, she says nothing, makes no gesture, only breathes a heavy sigh of relief. She is safe in my possession again; I will never let her go.

If only her father was here, he would know what to do. This place is supposed to be safe, supposed to give us security, a home, a place to finally settle. Her father would find whoever imposed this tragedy upon our blessing and wreak havoc on that heathen until he is more than dead.

The air pushes past her thick, jet-black hair blowing in her face. Carrying her up the pathway and toward our little farm, her limp body doesn't shift an ounce in discomfort, just falls to the side with ease. She is weak from her fight. Whoever did this have taken the life out of my little Lipi. They will surely pay for this blasphemy, this blatant disrespect of my only child, the one I have cherished, the only thing I have left to remind me of her father.

Someone is following us, I feel it. The crumpling bushes alongside the road alert me to their presence. I fear they will come for us, follow us home to do harm to us both, but I will not allow that. They will die trying, as I will die protecting my Lipi. There it is again, the same crumpling noise, drawing closer and closer as we walk up the path.

"Who is there?" I yell. "Show your face, so I can rip it off at the skin!" I continue with my rant. My contempt goes unanswered by the night stalker creeping in the shadows.

Holding her tightly, I hurry to make my way into the safety of our home. If I have learned anything in my days traveling around the country, it is how to take care of me and mine. I don't need any man to take care of me, my independence will fight a good fight, and they will know not to come around here anymore.

Quickly placing Lipi's limp body onto the mattress, I grab my loaded rifle I keep tucked behind the stove for uninvited guests prowling about my land. Slamming open my front door, I let off two fiery shots in the direction of the intruder. "Show your skin, asshole!" I scream. But nothing comes back in return, the land seems to fall asleep, only echoing my gunshots. I stare out into the dense landscape, trying to focus on any movement, but there is none. I wait with anticipation for any sign or sound, ready to exact my revenge on even the innocent if placed incorrectly on my land this night. Waiting and waiting, I stare. There is nothing but my empty gun shells smoking about the ground that shows life. Stepping back into my house away from the dark, I pray they come out from the shadows and show their face so they can taste my thirst for revenge for doing this to my sweet Lipi.

Morning brings new life to a new day. There will be no bakery today, as I have stood guard all night long waiting for whomever did this to come and finish us off.

The night came and went without even a peep. My eyes droop in exhaustion with the rise of the sun pushing through the cracks in the walls' wooden planks where the mud is vacant. Warmth of the sun overtakes my senses to want to set out and search for her attacker.

Her precious face sleeps without worry. Holding onto every dream, she sleeps. I want to dream what she dreams, see what she sees, through her eyes.

She stays resting close till noon, as I stand guard, leaping from my chair by her bedside at every crimping sound.

Falling asleep on my watch into a deep exhausting trance, I am awakened by a slow movement of my hair brushing across my face, tucking it behind my ear.

It is my Lipi, she is awake and softly gazing at me with care. We exchange smiles and a soft touch to one another's face entangled with hair. Such a strong, relentless, precious girl, she is not concerned about herself, but more concerned with me.

The sweet smell of bacon, grits, toast, and eggs permeate the noon day with a delicious fragrance to make anyone's empty stomach dance with joy. Setting our places at the table, built by the hands of a lost suitor, there is a rap at the door, heavy in nature. We look at one another, startled from the sudden noise taking us over. Another knock comes in secession with the one previous, and more like a banging. Pushing Lipi under the breakfast table for her wellbeing, and once again grabbing a hold of my long barrel rifle, now placed directly behind the door, we stay completely silent.

A voice comes from behind the door, "Mistress Bella... it's me, Sheriff Douglas." Relieved to know it's the sheriff, I set the gun aside back behind the door and open the door ever so slightly, as to get a simple peek of the sheriff standing there with another man to his side. Never seeing this strange man who accompanies the sheriff, I am wary of his presence.

"Is there something I can help you with, Sheriff?" I question. He explains, there has been an incident in town at the outer edge next to the outhouse. A man has been murdered. Beat to death with a metal rod at the violent hands of a vagrant. Surprised by his information, I encourage him that I know nothing of the incident, as I have been in my home all night taking care of my sick little girl.

The man next to him, a tall, scraggly, scarred man, face hardly recognizable as human, with a long grainy beard and not many teeth left, claims to have seen my Lipi down in the area around the same time of the murder.

I inquire as to who the man is that has been murdered, and why. Apparently, the man was the mayor of the small town just next to our own, who had come for a visit.

Without provocation, the stranger next to the Sheriff belts out, "It was your slave girl, I seen her down by the outhouse. I see her walking up the street past nightfall. You know your slaves ain't supposed to be out without permission past dark!"

Glaring widely into the Sheriff's eyes, I profess with all my subtle emotions that it could not be Lipi, as she has been in the house all day and night, deathly ill with chills running through her body.

As the Sheriff insists on seeing my Lipi for proof of her illness, screams of bloody murder come to my lungs, "Get off my property! Get off!" The door slams shut, and the two men stand stunned in silence for a few moments before finally relenting to leave my porch. But not before yelling profanities at the face of my door by the stranger.

There is nothing left here for us. Just like the last place and the place before that. It is time for us to move on. We have worn out our welcome.

Our things are just simple things, our lives have no place here nor there. We are valuable, but they just don't know it yet. They are vile men without honor, without pride, without... justice. A man calling himself mayor of a town, voted in by the people to represent the people, violated the rights of the same people he is meant to protect.

It's time to move on.

Sheriff Douglas

"Yup. He's dead alright. Dead as can be, poor fella." Whoever did this to the mayor is going to have to pay with their life. There is a white man, a mayor, dead in my town, and this ain't going to go over well with his townspeople, not without bloodshed. This isn't a good way to die, all curled up with his head all bashed open, laying in an outhouse with his pants around his ankles.

Looking around at these folks I know as my neighbors, friends, there is clear fear written on the faces of these people. Chattering of the happenings fuel the urge for justice. This just isn't right by any means.

Look here, this old steel pipe laying bloodied and used, popped his skull wide open like a watermelon at a nigga's birthday function. Can't say he was a good mayor, or even on the straight and narrow, but no white man deserves to die like a lame dog in an open pasture. We were just in the saloon sharing a glass of whiskey not long ago.

The good ole mayor stinks to high hell, I would say he been dead for at least a good day. Awful squirming maggots crawling about his blood, making it move around like a rippling in the water. Flies forming a blanket over his body, making me squeamish by the sight of it. Whoever did this to the good mayor is trying to send a message, but what kind of message they're trying to send, I don't know.

He ain't have clean hands, but he is well known around these parts as a good white Christian who takes care of his family. The mayor sure doesn't ever pass up a chance at having a good lynching to keep his niggas in line, but I be damned if a good white man is going to get killed in my town without retribution.

This is definitely not the work of any white person I know, this here is at the hands of a darky, one of them wild blacks roaming about the land, killing good white folk, like that nigga rebel boy Nat Turner. That boy killed men, woman, and children alike for even looking at holding a slave.

"Anyone around here see what happen to the good mayor?" I plead with folks standing around to speak out so we can bring this to a quick resolution. I hear the gossip forming around the crowd already. My request to bring the perpetrator to light falls on deaf ears. If there was ever a moment in time, when it was time to put my foot down and own my authority, it is now.

"You say you seen what? You see a little skinny nigga girl running off into the distance?" I ask, responding to a young lad standing at his momma's side, hushing his mouth from speaking out.

A stranger in the distance shouts, "I see that little China slave girl walking around here, I know she know something. She doesn't like us normal white folk anyway. She thinks she and her mistress is better than us, walking around here all high sadity, with their nose in the air. Looking down at us hardworking folk!"

I sit and think for a second about nigga girls who would have it out for the mayor, but none come to mind. Our blacks around here are good people, hardworking niggas that keep their heads down and nose clean. We treat them good around this town, unlike many towns close by. All our blacks are treated like good pets, almost like family, when they are well behaved, and most of the time without incident, they are.

Elections for a new mayor was just around the corner, not far in the distance to run. There came a time quite a few years back when the mayor's popularity around town started to falter. The townspeople didn't believe in the mayors building of a ring of the best built slaves, brought together to travel from town to town, breeding farmers' nigga girl stock for a nominal wage. This tragedy can be the will of God reaching out at the hands of one of his faithful followers to right the wrong imposed at the will of the mayor. Or the will of one of the nigga slave girls exacting revenge for the taking of their virginity.

As I sit and ponder who could have done this to him, the list of potential suspects grows larger and larger by the moment.

The growing crowd of townsfolk form something of a mob, looking to head out to every farm within walking distance to produce their own justice, with just the idea that it was a slave girl who killed the mayor, tiny in stature.

I must maintain the law around these parts, people cannot take justice into their own hands with just the words of a small child as witness. This will not become some wild witch hunt at the blood of our good blacks living in this town. I have never been one to care for slavery, nor have I ever owned any myself to work my land. Most of the people around here can't afford to own even one slave let alone an entire plantation full to work from sunup till past sundown. Growing up here in this same place my daddy and my daddy's daddy were hardworking men, owning their land and growing our own. I have never once seen my daddy, or my pa act ill-willed toward any black. They just never had any close to them or befriended any either. They were always taught to keep their distance from the blacks, as they had nothing to do with us, and we don't have nothing to do with them.

Being the Sheriff of this here town for over twenty years, I don't let no one outwardly mistreat the blacks for no odd reason. Respecting the fact that they have the right to own property and do what they wish with their property. It is not my cause to interrupt in disciplining their property as they wish, just not in my presence. People around here have grown to know that about me, so they do their business behind closed doors, in the safety of their own homes, and on their own land.

The rolling wagon arrives, setting itself just at the side of the outhouse where the mayor's body lays crumpled against the ground. It takes three men volunteering to lift his overweight form. Hesitant to grab ahold of the mayor's rotting corpse, it is hard for either of the men to find a clear place on his body to grab onto.

The men lift with one big heave after the count of three. All the maggots that once feasted on his body without disturbance now lay in various mounds of fluff, spreading out, desperately seeking the sanctuary of their next meal.

Covered with a blanket and off to the morgue on the outskirts of town, the wagon rolls down the bumpy road, clearing the trees. With a look of disgust in the midst of a scream permanently scarred onto his face, a remaining whoosh of the blanket hides the horror from nosey onlookers. The stale smell of death relentlessly clogs the air trailing the wagon. The stunned crowd walks beside the casketed wagon until it moves on faster, toward its place of preparation, its resting place.

The stranger who spoke up claiming to see Mistress Bella's China slave roaming free toward the dark around the same time we suspect the mayor to have met with his untimely demise, takes a ride up to the house with me to ask her some questions. Normally an extremely friendly woman, she doesn't take too kindly to our presence on her land. Refusing to answer any questions or to let us inside to talk with her slave girl, that door slammed in our faces so fast, I didn't even have time to apologize for interrupting her noon day or wish the slave girl my best in getting well soon.

She too is a stranger around these parts, as she has only been living around here a short few years. I've had some complaints of people suspecting her and that little China child of having sticky fingers but never an ounce of proof. I just figure people are being a bit skeptical of newcomers, as they always are. But those pies and pastries she makes from her bake shop moves from her shelves quicker than a tick torched by a flame from a dog's ass.

If I don't follow up with information given to me about the mayors' brutal death, then these good people around here that support me as Sheriff might decide to hang me from a tree by my own pretty white neck. Satisfied that the China slave girl had absolutely nothing to do with the death of the now late mayor, I move on back to town, gathering volunteers to march

89

along as escorts throughout the town to investigate each farm that holds nigga slaves, especially nigga slave girls.

Right along with me, remaining close by my side, the little boy who claims he witnessed a little skinny black girl running from where the mayor's body was found rides along with me. If this boy seen what he claims he seen, then, he shouldn't have any problem identifying the black he saw running away from the area. Putting together axe picks, sledgehammers, machetes, rifles, rope, and anything at hand to defend against an attack by blacks or owners of the land, the unsettled crowd of volunteers grows more restless as we get closer to our first property. Coming upon the large gates blocking the entrance to Doc Feeley's old house.

Doc Feeley lived around here for as long as I can remember. He raised his family in this old house. Had one boy he kept busy with chores to keep him from getting into any trouble. Heard he was found dead in a creek, beaten to death about the head, his son and granddaughter was never found. They suspect they both perished in the fire along with the house they lived in far up north. The property now is owned by some uptight, rich, oil man and his family.

As we approach, we are met by a line of men holding rifles while standing guard at the property. While everyone is yelling profanities at the men standing fast without movement at the gates of the property, the owner and I have a small talk on the side by the fence post. I reassure him that we mean no harm while searching for someone suspected of killing the mayor from the next town over, respectfully requesting to see all his nigga slave girls. That we have a witness to a little skinny slave girl running from the area. With great resistance from what is expressed to him falling on defiant ears, he finally relents for fear of the impatient bunch turning thugs set behind us. One by one all the nigga girls from the farm line up to be seen. They are shy and scared as to what is going on. They do not look any of us directly in the eye for fear of identification from the mob, and the boy.

I tell the boy to take his time and look at every one of them girls closely. Make no mistake in who he saw out there last night. The boy is shy in coming forth to get close to the shaken slave girls, but he does. With his head and face to the ground, my two fingers give his young chin a lift in the direction of the women awaiting his decision.

"Go ahead, boy, you see that nigga girl standing here?" I encourage him, while asserting my command of the law. The boy looks up and down the line of women, then back and forth again three or four times, before he says, "No, sir... these not them" In a lower voice, I encourage him to look again, "Look again there, boy... you sure ain't none of these nigga girls the one you saw?"

The boy hesitantly looks over the line of slave women once more and politely responds, "I'm sure."

Satisfied of his decision, I apologize and thank the man for his cooperation. The slave girls, who look well taken care of, release their tension-filled shoulders, stiff with anticipation, and quickly scatter back toward their dwellings.

This is one of the most difficult hunts for me today. If we are to find this mysterious nigga girl, there are no courts to attend, no judge nor jury allowed for a slave to profess their innocence. The revenge of justice will be immediate and swift. This crowd of townsmen will exact painful lynching upon her soul, but at what cost? Will the cost grow to an insurmountable, irreversible forfeit of trust between our good blacks here? Knowing I will not control this many angry people once finding the girl, I encourage all young men and women under the age of eighteen to return back to town, go home, and wait for further instructions. We will need eyes and ears everywhere now to assist in leading us in the direction of the murderer.

A few of the volunteers hesitate to go back, others stand fast without budging. In a much firmer voice, I demand the younger ones to return home immediately. Slowly, they filter out and back toward their homes. This hunt for our town's killer will see no distractions or get off course at the mad minds of too many. I am the one in charge of the law, I am the law around these parts. We will have order, even at the sake of my death.

This is a beautiful part of the country, as I have traveled the better part of it throughout the years. Freely as I travel, I would not like it if someone was to take my freedom from me and not allow me to enjoy the gifts that God has given. Besides finding the mayor's body fermenting with death, the day is one of solace and warmth. Birds give chase through the branches of tall trees lining either side of the road. Unlike the center of town, these estates that employs free labor at the hands of slaves are of great distances apart from their neighbors. There is time to ponder what I will do when this girl is found.

We don't even know if this slave girl had anything to do with the mayor's death. She could have run with fear from whoever as to not get noticed or fallen into the arms the grim reaper himself for bearing witness to this ungodly crime. Maybe I can question her as to what she has seen if anything. It's possible she holds the key to our murderer's identity.

We all continue rambling together up the road, chatter of what is to come of the person once found compromises level heads. If the nigga girl knows who the murderer is, will that suffice for the mob to digress in their search for revenge and direct their attention to the real person in need of coming to justice? What are the consequences of a nigga girl confessing to have seen a white man murdering the mayor? She will surely get strung up for lying.

If she claims it to be her, she will die a painful death at the hands of the towns people.

Ever since I was a kid, I have had my eye on being a law man. When younger, I would pretend to be the law man with my daddy as my deputy. We would sneak up on my pa working in the fields or the barn and arrest him for working too hard. My pa didn't like it very much when we interrupted his days' work, but he always played along with me. He always said a man must work hard to take care of his family, but a man must also take time out from work to enjoy his family. Both my pa and daddy were good men, hardworking and honest men. At a crossroad, where I stand at this moment, they would know what to do.

Crowding across the road filled with anxious bodies awaiting their turn to pounce without hesitation, an angry mob of the mayor's followers is coming directly in our path. Some atop horses while others trail behind brandishing weapons, thirsty hounds pulling at their collared leashes, barking, and howling with angry intent in their eyes.

We come face to face.

Weapons locked and loaded, prepared for a fight, I explain to the angry bunch of misfits we are in no need of any further assistance from out of towners. I am the law around here, and we are only seeking one little skinny nigga girl who might be a witness to the murder of their good mayor. Continuously reintegrating the fact again that this young girl is in no way suspected of killing the mayor, she is only wanted for questioning.

Having a heavy desire to get to the bottom of this by those who smother me with their taunts of justice, common sense escapes me without return. The group hears nothing I say over their chants of justice for their fallen mayor. I explain there were no witnesses to the murder, only assumptions flying around about who might have seen the murderer. Growing larger by the minute, more and more townspeople begin gathering together from towns nearby, all coming together to volunteer their services in the search for answers.

Surrounded by anger oozing from the pores of grown men, women, and some small children egged on by their family, they are after the blood of their first nigga kill.

Slowing the angry group of people swarming with a hundred folks from neighboring towns, confused as to the purpose of our hunt, destabilizes our direction, and I am now powerless, with no control.

Searching for a mysterious little nigga girl is quickly gaining unwanted steam, momentum without direction that only creates unorganized mayhem. An unrecognizable older man, large in size, kneels down to what looks to be his young son, standing only three feet tall at anyone grown man's belt line. He is teaching him how to tie his first rope noose, knot by looping knot. With sharp precision, the man sitting in silhouette performs his task again and again until he hands the unfastened rope over to his son to try.

94

"It's your turn, boy. You make that noose nice and tight now, ya hear?" he tells him. Tightening and loosening the noose with every completion, the man tells his son to repeat it again and again, until it is done perfectly. Unable to complete the perfect noose for a good lynching, the boy's father cursorily snatches the entangled rope from the boy's hands and shows him again how to hook and loop a good noose.

My father has never been a man of bad character to stoop so low as to instill lessons with the deadly intent to harming or maiming another in pleasure, nor an animal for sport. These are people, not animals hunted for sport. We have lost our way and have taken the path of the unrighteous. To see a man so proud teaching his son the art of noosing makes me sick to my stomach. This is not a nigga lynching fest; it is not a teaching ground for the capturing and killing of niggas. These people seem to take lightly the life of those simply for the color of their skin, negating any spoken evidence of guilt to a crime.

As the mob and us continue up toward the next plot of farmland, reaching the property line closest to where the house sits by a live river, I halt all the men and women accompanying me. Feeling defeated for carrying an unruly crowd of now misfits to perform my appointed duties, I reflect to the crowd.

"Everyone listen up now. This here town belongs to me. I am the law around here, and that's that. We have no witnesses to who the murderer is, only information leading us to believe someone might have seen the face of the murderer of the good mayor. Now, put these dadgum rifles and weapons away, and let me do all the talking from here on. We don't need no one getting so scared they don't wanna talk. AND SHUT THEM DAMN HOUNDS UP, ALREADY! I can hardly hear myself breathe, let alone pissing on a rock."

Settled from my abrupt speech, followed by firm stares of my authority, the mob is quiet for now. We are refocused on the task at hand, tracking down the little skinny nigga girl witness.

A scream interrupts the silence, "Over there! Right there, that be the one I saw right there!"

Immediately becoming unruly, the unrestrained, thirsty mob breaks their necks to catch a glimpse of the little boy's pointing position. The shadowy figure moved way to fast, slithering effortlessly into the cracks of dense shrubbery lining the fence at the end of the property.

Heading toward where the shrubs split, the group bursts past the area where we saw the figure disappear.

There, standing high on a great horse, Mr. Reginald Reagan, owner of the land. He is a well-known man around here. This is his home, his land, and we all know him by his great words from the gospel he speaks. Or rather used to speak when he was younger and more fit to speak honestly. The steed he sits upon rears high and roars with anger, his harness and reins clinking at one another, fighting for position. It turns in circles as Mr. Reginald holds to steady the excited horse. With a click, click of his tongue and a 'whoa girl,' the horse steadies in place, stomping its feet as if ready for battle. A warrior standing its ground on a prideful field of battle.

Halting all at once, we stand waiting, staring, panting like a pack of hungry animals stalled from pursuing its meal. Mr. Reginald questioning the reason for trespassing on his land, the bunch all tries pleading their case at once. Perusing over the ramped crowd itching to continue their pursuit without any further resistance, the now irritated Mr. Reginald directs his questioning of our presence toward me.

With an informative, commanding voice of authority, I tell him, "I am sure news around here travels fast, Reginald. We here looking for a little skinny nigga girl who might have seen something. Something like the face of a murderer. This here boy claim to have seen that nigga girl running onto this here property." Looking off into the distance, scanning over the bodies of the many gatherers carrying loaded rifles and weapons, Reginald just sits on his horse trampling around. With a small smirk of disgust, he finally replies, "Ain't none of my nigga girls," as he leans back into the spine of his horse. He continues, "but to satisfy your curiosity so you good people can move on, I will show you my stock of women. Not all y'all are welcomed to come trampling my blessed land, only you, Sheriff, and the boy who claims to have borne witness."

Leaving the rest behind to look on from afar, I agree to his condition to eliminate any of his stock. Like the farm before that and the one before that, he demands all his nigga girls to come up and be seen. The boy steadies himself once again, still shy but more forthcoming with eyeing all the girls. One side to the other, he skims over their faces one after the next and back again. I grab ahold of his shoulder and walk him down to the first one, a little skinny one, frail in her own right, looking tired at the end of a day's slaving. With their faces drowning in shame, the boy looks up at them, then the next and the next, on down the line. He stands in silence as we wait for his answer, but he does nothing but stand, shaking his curly head of hair in doubt. My patience begins to run short as I spat, "Well, boy! Any of these niggas the one you seen?" The boy says nothing. Turning his head toward me, he says nothing. Silence and hard breathing by the lined slaves overtake the interrogation.

The boy responds, "No, sir, none these standing here be her." He looks off into the distance, then whispers, pointing with his eyes wide open, "That be the one I seen." Stunned by his denial of all the slaves in front of him, identifying another off in the distance sitting with her backed turned, Mr. Reginald and myself string our necks to imagine who else he could be speaking of. He claims this is his entire stock of nigga girls. Is he hiding others out of sight? Is Mr. Reginald, the ex-preacher of God's scripture turning a blind eye to the murder of a good Christian white man, a mayor of a town? Mr. Reginald squints his eyes and turns away from his horse to get a better look at who the boy has surely identified as the possible witness to the mayor's murder. Standing beside him as the moment of truth come to light from the shadows of the unknowing, Mr. Reginald lets out a small chuckle. "Boy, that be my nigga slave boy, that ain't no nigga girl. He ain't no bigger than a flea, so weak he can't even do harm to himself if he tried."

He chuckles again.

Alarming the restless mob gathered in anger, the boy shouts, "That be the one there, the one I seen in the shadows running from the mayor!" With one passion fueled burst of relentlessness, the group charges past the three of us standing there, raging towards the boy, intent on serving justice with their own hands.

"Get that puny nigga girl!' the stranger from before, yells. The other man, who was once showing his son how to tie a perfect noose for hanging, encourages his son with an anxious tone, "Bring that rope with ya, son, we bout to do a hangin!" I am left powerless to withstand the barrage of angry townspeople with a grudge to settle. The boy, paralyzed at first from the sight of eyes peering him down with lust, bolts from his sitting place and directly into the mouth of the barn. All the slaves that were looking on retreat backward into their houses, horrified of seeing the devastation following an angry, unruly mob out for bloodshed. Doors close to protect their younger ones from the onslaught, as the boy hides in the barn, where Hoof normally shoes horses for his master and some of the townsfolk.

Cowering on the backside of Hoof, standing guard at the front of the door, the boy refuses to come out of his corner, blanketed by stacks of hay and piles of broken wood.

Swarming to every cornered edge of the barn, the crowd takes up positions, guarding every possible way out for the terrified child. Unknowing of what is happening, Hoof continues standing at the entrance of the barn, facing them mob with hammering tool in one hand, a fiery piece of metal in his other. Hoof stands in silence, chin to the sky, head held to its highest point. He doesn't move a muscle in retreat as the stranger walks up to him. Standing eye to eye, knowing it is the death of a slave to look at any white person directly in the eyes, he does not bow his head. The stranger moves forward, brushing past Hoof. Keeping his eyes on the stranger as he moves past, Hoof is blindsided by another man following directly behind the stranger. The hardened club pounds the head of Hoof, making an echoing, loud, thumping sound, the crack of the wood heard all the way to the main house.

Rushing out of the front door, window screen breaking against the chafed railing of the porch, Shelby sprints, pushing people to the side to get to the front of the barn. She is too late. She arrives at the moment where Hoof's attacker draws his wooden club back over his shoulder, where is rests with pride.

A drawn-out scream of pain bellows from behind us, "NO...!" Trita fights to get to her husband's side, only to be held back by the others, fearing for her health. Her legs flail, her feet stomp dirt with frustration of held revenge. There is nothing she can do for him now.

The man calls for the boy to come, but the boy refuses to budge. Repeatedly telling the boy he will not be harmed, the man entices the boy out with promises of just talking, but the boy stays put, eyes closed, holding himself as if he is the protector of his own body, his own life. Kicking all blanketed debris from the boy's hiding place, the boy is grabbed by his long locks of stringy hair clumped at every reaching edge by the stranger's massive hands and yanked to his feet.

I yell, "Hey! Let's stop all this madness. This here ain't no murderer. STOP with all this here, it's unnecessary!" I pause for a second, shoving my way toward the stranger. "You ain't the law here, and this ain't your nigga!" Looking at me with utter disappointment, the stranger grabs the boy's hair tighter in his clutched fist and with an undermining mutter, shoves the boy on the ground, falling to his face.

Hushing the crowd, I lean down to where the boy is laying and quietly ask him, "Boy, did you see who murdered the mayor?" Avery shakes his head with quickening lefts and rights to say no. I ask again, "Boy, no don't lie to me, now, understand? Did... you...see... the person... who murdered... the good mayor?"

Looking up at the faces staring down at him, surprised to see a white nigga boy as a slave, he says, "No," once again.

The crowd of angry onlookers draw closer, squeezing the circle around the boy, almost smothering our position on the ground. "Boy, if you seen who did this, you better tell me now, or else these people here gone burn your body and hang you dead at the nearest tree, then kill every other nigga on this here farm, hear me?"

Waiting for his answer, a woman raises her heeled foot to kick him in the head. Seeing the heel coming my way, I instinctively cover the boy with my upper body from the damaging stomp. The mob grows angrier.

Pleading with the boy to tell me something, anything to satisfy this crowd, the white nigga slave boy, says, "Yes" in a barely understandable whisper of a voice. Bending down closer, I place my ear close to his lips and tell him to tell me who it was. Who did this to the mayor? Who is the murderer we seek? Laying on the ground, almost flat on his back, with me hovered tightly over him, he starts to speak, "Yes, I know who killed the major... it, well, it..."

Interrupted by his master Reginald imploring his white nigga slave boy to tell them who it was, Avery tired of his life here on the farm and wanting to join Momma Ruby, starts to divulge that he himself is the murderer of the mayor. He closes his eyes, tearing up, petrified of knowing these will be his last words, that he will meet a painful death for murdering the mayor, an unspeakable death at the hands of this angry mob, he hesitates. "It was m..."

Before he could get out his last word, a deafening screech comes from the back of the crowd, "ME! I DID IT... IT WAS ME. I KILLED HIM!" With necks bent back, breaking to see where the confession had come from, the sea of people slowly parts way to reveal the voice, the maker of such a confession, sure of death. The savior of Avery.

With the loss of her virginity, the loss of her soul, and now the loss of her husband Hoof, Trita eagerly confesses to the mayor's murder.

A deathly silence comes over the entire farm. With that moment of silence quickly passing, all hell breaks loose, and the once crowd that rested with anticipation of the boy telling who the killer is, to perhaps confess it was him, now rage uncontrollably at the body of Trita. Tearing and beating her about her head and body. The crowd muffles her cries with stomps of their boots and heels. She gives no resistance to the onslaught of beatings at the hands of many.

Held back from getting to the girl, I cry for them to stop, that justice will be done, but not here and not now. This is not the way to handle justice around here. I am the Sheriff. I am the law around these parts, and this is not how we treat our blacks around here.

Minutes go by, and the crowd seems to grow tired of exacting their beating onto the girl. They eagerly stand back to admire their handy breakdown of the girl's flesh and bones. They step back, then back some more, as to let their children appreciate being included in their first nigga kill.

Letting go of my arms and shoulders held at the imprisoning hands of a shady few, I make my way to where her body lays in death's chamber. I see nothing or hear nothing around me, it is just her and I there. At this very moment, time stands completely still. Slow motion seems to move us backward as I see everything happenings all over again, from the start to now. Here we are, missy, this is all my fault, my fault alone. This should have never happened to you or anyone. I know in my heart of hearts you did not kill this man. You did not murder this white man.

With the hunt coming to an end, everyone thinking they have caught and killed the murderer of the mayor, satisfied of their justice, I bow my head in shame to start my way back to town. Closing to the gates of the property, I stop and stare out into the darkness, with the town lights way off in the far distance.

Clusters of crying starts up again behind me. Turning to see, I take off back toward the house where the group is moving away from me. "No. No, no, no, no… no… NO!" I scream in great agony. My eyes cannot believe what it sees. There is nothing on this earth that can take away an image once it is imbedded deep into the mind.

Pushed up against a fence, pinched between ties of barbed wire atop the fence, her neck twisted in the clamps of sharpened wire, with her neck lodged tightly within the barbed wire, two men pull at her feet, trying to dislodge her head from her body at the wire's razor-sharp edge.

Angrily, I raise my rifle and fire two shots in the air to stop them from this horrifying attempt at a full lynching of an already ravaged body. The men turn quickly in the direction of the shots. Themselves now in fear for their own lives, they begin to scatter about the property. Leaving evidence of their torment behind, a child yells, "Nigga lover!" back at me as he is hopping the fence ending the property toward the road.

This is my doing; this is my burden alone to share and to be forgiven by only God and no one else.

All of us stand there, appalled by the girl's body laying intertwined in barbed wire, unrecognizable from the beautiful face she was blessed with. Standing with both my arms almost dragging to the ground, I hear a voice start to speak.

"Do not be amazed at this, for a time is coming when all who are in their graves will hear his voice and come out—those who have done what is good will rise to live, and those who have done what is evil will rise to be condemned.

"My Father's house has many rooms; if that were not so, would I have told you that I am going there to prepare a place for you?

"And if I go and prepare a place for you, I will come back and take you to be with me that you also may be where I am."

The boy's words only deepen my sorrow as to why we do what we do, as to why we are here to witness what is unwanted, unfathomable, unreal yet very real.

The way back home couldn't hold my heavy feet long enough.

Avery

First Momma Ruby, then Hoof, and now Trita, and if I stay idle, death will soon hunt me down, taking me to join them in the afterlife. If I take my own life, I take the power out of death's hands and put it in my own hands.

No one on earth should hold the key to life or death besides God himself, but they do.

Drawing tired and weary of all that gravely slides into my rhythm of life and interrupts it, I wish to die but cannot yet. He will know where to find me, but he does not know that now I welcome him. I do not fear the coming of death, as he has become my companion, now he will become part of me. The flame inside me has burnt out. What I have seen should not embed the mind of anyone and yet becomes the normal for people to witness.

We are expected to simply move on as the day moves on, as the night moves on, as the time never slows but tics away with us in it. I wonder if they would care enough to even search for me, to hunt me down, track my steps. If my feet will carry me, the wonders I could see, the places I could go, but there is no place for a slave. Pale as the purest flour, I am still and always will be a slave. It has been told that free slaves aren't really free. They are constantly on the lookout for kidnappers stealing their free papers and forcing them back into slavery, forcing children into households of men who want a young toy to play with, a mistress who wants a slave for her domestic duties she refuses to claim as her own.

What is out there I do not know, but what is here, I have already seen.

While everyone remains in turmoil over what happened to Trita and Hoof, Master, and Mrs. Shelby retreat to the house, leaving Trita's tormented flesh for the rest of us to turn to ash, releasing her from her wiry grave.

Dragging Hoofs body by his rough ankles closer to his love, the darkness constantly tugs at me to follow close behind. Emotionally relieving himself from the moment at hand, the good sheriff lumpingly turns off in one direction, herding the remaining townspeople away from the cycle of death that continues, and it is my best option to walk in the opposite.

The loneliness overwhelms me, maybe the whispers of the others is true. Not like anyone else, they always talk about me disappearing into the woods, walking until my legs can no longer move, carrying me far away from here.

But this is my family, this is all I know. I am not of the whites, nor am I of the blacks, I am nothing, no one, I don't belong anywhere.

It is a freezing kind of chill in the air this evening, and the night slows to a crawl, then stands still. Is this what it feels like, caught in between life here on earth and readying yourself to return home into the awaiting arms of your loved ones who moved on without you?

Creeping into my shelter, no one notices I am no longer present, but vacant. In age, I am old enough to train the elements in my favor, but I have nothing to cover me, to keep the elements from holding me hostage at night, to keep me from the freezing cold. Mainly my thoughts are with Lipi, wondering if she will be alright. Will Lipi recover back into the gentle, giving person who shared a gift with me?

My moment is now. The time has come for me to travel on my own, take my chances, as I am sure to die an unhealthy death if I remain here.

This is my resting place, the spot where I have remained for hours, sharing my spoken words at the mouth of the sky without an audience. This is my last visit for now, or maybe forever. If I am to return here one day, I will return a free man, an unwanted man with a life that I am proud of. Shackles will not accompany me back to this place, only death or freedom.

Momma Ruby would have my bare skin if she knew what I was thinking, or maybe she would encourage me to go on, see what happens. I am old enough to brave the elements on my own now, a young man without hair on my upper body.

Since I was younger, my mind has always remained curious to what is beyond our land, what is beyond our town. With only stories from other slaves coming for a visit on special days with their masters from next towns over, Momma Ruby visiting with Miss Chassy in the marketplace on days Mrs. Shelby sends us for goods, or Master and his visitors having talks about their travels, I have nothing or no direction to guide me. Maybe Lipi and her Mistress can lead me far away from here without bringing attention. Maybe they are angels and not devils who will trap me, sending me back to a warranted death for even thinking about running.

Without motivation, I will not move from this place, from this very spot, until I know there is a sign for me to run. God will show me the direction he wishes for me to take, for the place he wants me to go, or else I will remain here until they come for me at dawn's end.

At first, I was standing remaining strong, then I kneeled, but with the piercing cold cutting me down, I now sit in complete silence, curled within myself, feeling utterly defeated, waiting for a sign. My lips quiver uncontrollably, the leaves push past me and over my feet, resting before moving on, allowing another to come again and again.

My ears no longer have feeling, my hands cover them to give some sort of small comfort. My bible rests in peace at the base of my feet, just below the fallen leaves. If I am to leave this place, my eyes cannot be heavy, I must have my wits about me to spot danger that seeks me at every passing.

Wiggling my toes, insuring they are still there, they hurt while I cannot feel them moving. Between my knees rests my head, lowering itself like the weight of a bale of hay in the prairie for cows. My heart beats faster, my lungs are tight with anticipation, I must run and must run now, but I cannot. It is too late for running, my body will no longer allow me.

I will rest until the sun warms me again, by then I will surely have a sign. Exhaustion overtakes my will to survive, and my dreams turn to nightmares, occasionally jolting me from my slumber. Thinking my life will end where I sit and ponder, a blanket of warmth comes over my shoulders and down my back. An amazing thrust of hope refills my body, overtaking my will to rest in my dreams, to fall asleep knowing I may never wake again.

Is this the sign I have waited for?

It gives me strength to move my hands and toes again, to feel them beneath me. My quivering lips come to an abrupt creep on my face, still at intervals, just enough for my body to relax. Pulling my head from the comfort of my knees drowning my sorrow, my vision becomes clearer.

God's shadow hovers over me, keeping me from the elements, holding me in his warmth. My eyes focus on his shadowy figure, I must see the face of him, he has come for me in my time of need.

Becoming clear of the shadowy figure, it is not the face of God I see but the face of an angel. It is my friend Lipi. She blankets me with her arms and shawl wrapped around me. She has rescued me, as I have done the same for her. We are equals.

Why is she here? Why did she come for me? Did she feel my presence, knowing I was abandoned, in dire need of new life? She has come to me, and for this I am grateful.

Reaching out with both arms, barely able to squeeze with any strength, I hold her closely, not releasing her for a long period of time. She doesn't seem to mind.

This feels good, it feels right, but best of all it feels warm. With only a smile, and never saying anything, she grabs ahold of my arm and gestures with a wave to follow her toward the opening just on the other side of the clearing from where we stand. I know this path, as I have traveled it many days and nights, but where are we headed? Where does she take me?

Before daybreak, she leads me quickly down the path and through the back of our farm. Crossing the creek that runs along the side, dividing the farm from the town, we skip across the large rocks making a walkway across the creek, lit by the light of the moon that dims quickly with the sun following behind it.

Straying off the side from being seen, never letting go of my arm, Lipi leads me through patches of wiry limbs, thorns, and brush, slapping at every inch of our skin. I do not notice my cuts bleeding from the deep scratches received at every brush of the limbs, and I do not care. As long as she is touching my arm, I feel safe.

Crossing into the path, a distinct voice echoes past the greenery, "Back at it again, niggas!"

He is awake, Master has started the workday. It will only be a matter of time before he notices I have gone. His voice traps me in my steps for a moment, yanking Lipi backward.

In a jarring moment, she turns to see what I have stopped for. Her eyes open wide, she shakes her head and gestures with her eyes to keep on moving. We continue in a hurry off the path, then back on it again to hurry along. Entering the town, we stop at the same crates where she once found me cradled behind.

Making sure all is clear on the dark, early morning streets, we rustle ourselves around the back to where the baker's door stands slightly ajar. She turns to shush me, putting her hand up to tell me to wait. Entering the back door alone, she quickly returns to where I stand outside the door, opens it wider, and hurryingly pulls me in by my shoulder. It is her; she is in front of me, closer than my own eyes sit in my head.

Face to face with her Mistress, Mistress Bella. I dare not make a peep for fear of disrespect. I do not want to say anything to offend her, not even a hi. She might punish me or Lipi for allowing a slave into her bakery. Not even moving an inch, we stare at one another's eyes, trying to gauge one another like a warrior sizes up his opponent.

"Hello, Avery."

The Mistress knows my name? I say nothing in return. "Well, hello, Avery. Aren't you going to even say hello?"

Putting my head toward the ground, looking at my worn feet, I mutter, "Hello, Mistress."

With a gentle kindness, she places both her supple hands covered with fruit and flour mix from the morning pastries she was making onto my shoulders. Her smile is like a mother happy to see her child for the first time. Rubbing my shoulders and arms as if trying to shake the cold from them, she says, "Thank you... I know what you did for my Lipi... I am grateful and thankful she has a friend like you. I know you are a slave, so I cannot offer you much but small coinage and some of my fresh baked bread, but you may take as much as you can carry back with you to the farm." Mistress shuffles me over to a counter area by my shoulders, hands me a small sack, and shows me her fresh baked bread. Placing one in the bag, then another, I look over my shoulders back at Lipi. She is smiling.

Grabbing one more loaf of bread to have my fill, my stretch is interrupted by the sounds of whistling and callings of my name. It is Master, and the others come with him, looking for me. They do not know I have changed my mind about running, but now they will hurt me good thinking I was running anyways.

Mistress sees the look in my eyes, and she turns to Lipi for understanding. Her look tells the same horrifying tale as mine does. Terror is coming for me and anyone who holds me safe. Panicked, with bag of bread in hand, I thank Mistress for her kindness. Shuffling past Lipi right out the door, I stop and turn. Quickly, I thrust a hug that was deeper than my understanding of the bible, and with a swiftness, I lay a kiss on her forehead. Our hands interlock as I try to escape, but she does not let me go.

With one rough yank of my arm, she releases me away from her grasp.

Running into the distance, I turn in my last step before I can no longer see my past, her silhouette stranded in the lighted doorway of the bakery buries into my mind.

Pushing aside the bush's limbs, my body is secluded from the Master's and other's sight, desperately searching for me. The whistles and calling of my name seem to come from all over the town, from every direction, one end to the other. I cannot tell who is who or where the voices come from. Confusion sets in deeper; the voice's calls get closer, I am trapped. The end is near, my heart hurts, as no one will remember my name, no one will come to help me from what pain Master will impose on me.

The sheriff has denounced standing for something that divides his beliefs in half. He will not come to my aid, because I am simple property, to do with as the Master feels.

Crawling on my belly to go unnoticed, my bag of bread drags alongside my slithering self, scratching my side with its rough texture. Hidden within the belly of the shaggy bushes next to the town's road, I am rushed backward by a horse attempting to trample me as I lay close to its path. I dare not move when the turning wheel comes close to running my head into the ground. Two men sit deep atop the wagon, gearing it to a halt at the place I lay covered. This is not where I wanted to be, where I wanted to lay to only get discovered by two filthy men just hanging out, happening to stumble on me without searching.

The men sit and chat for a long while. All around me are the calls and whistles of my name, shaking me to the core. Becoming impatient, my body rolls closer and closer to the wagon until I am completely underneath it, lying out of sight of the two men. if I lay here too long, the others will find me here.

They come closer to where I lay. Crawling on my knees in the shadow of the wagon that hovers above me, I barely stand to peek into the cargo of the men's wagon. There is bottles after bottles of moonshine in the back, covered by a huge tarp. I'd know this kind of drink anywhere, as Master's friends bring over cases of it in trade for their fill of some of his good whiskey drink. This is my chance to hide. With the two men embracing one another in deep, meaningless banter, I lift myself into the back of the wagon, and cover myself with the tarp. Laying still as possible, knowing that I may be discovered at any time, I try to hold my shuffling down, becoming still as the cargo I lay next to.

Voices are right on me, I hear them talking aloud to the two men sitting on the wagon, still yapping about nothing. "You see a little filthy white looking slave nigga boy round here?" Master's voice reeks out. The two men chuckle at one another at the Master's unusual request, inquiring about the whereabouts of a white slave nigga.

"A white slave nigga huh? HA! Ain't ever heard of such a thing, that's an abomination if I ever heard one!" one of the men responds. The two men chuckle again at Master's presence. I can only imagine Master standing, focused on the two strangers who continue their yapping toward one another. Angered by the men's disrespect, I hear the swift whistling of wind passing as Master abruptly raises his rifle. Hearing the gun cock-back, the two men sit stunned in fear of their lives. "You strangers ain't here for no fancy soiree?" The two sit without response. "Well then, I suggest you be gone, and quick. Now, BE GONE!" Without hesitation, the two men straighten up their goods sitting next to them and gather their coats laying on their laps. With a quick snap of the horse's reigns, the wagon takes off toward the end of town, carrying me unnoticed along with it.

Lipi

Such paltry gifts we had scraped together for Avery. He lost everything and now we sent him out into the world alone with

113

barely enough coins to rub together and a single loaf of yesterday's bread. I feared for Avery, but I couldn't hold him here with me any longer. As I watched him disappear into the lightening gloom of sunrise, my throat ached with words I couldn't find the feelings to express. I never wished I could speak so much as I did right then. I would tell him how much his friendship meant to me. I would tell him how much I enjoyed the stories he would tell me from the Bible. I would tell him that freedom is something you carry in your heart, whether you wear shackles and chains or not.

I took two steps towards the door as if I would follow him, but Miss Bella put her hand on my shoulder, and I sobbed. My heart felt too big in my chest, making it hard to breathe. I had left friends behind before, moving from town to town as we did for so long. Why was this any different? What was this boy to me that I wanted him to stay every time we parted?

Miss Bella took me into her arms and rocked me gently, whispering soothing sounds like she used to when I was small and I had scraped my knee. After a time, she dried my tears and set me to making the dough while she started the ovens. She hummed an old lullaby while we worked, and soon the bakery was warm and smelling of freshly baked bread. The work brought me some comfort, but my mind was with Avery as the sun rose and my Mistress opened the storefront for the day. From time to time, I heard the tinkle of the front doorbell as customers came and went. She knew them all by name, and I enjoyed listening to them exchanging pleasantries. It almost felt like any other day. But for me, everything had changed.

As I slid the first apple pie of autumn into the oven, the bell tinkled again, and I heard Sheriff Douglas' deep voice say good morning. He told Miss Bella about some nasty business that had happened yesterday at the Reagan place. There had been a lynching, and the blacksmith had lost his life trying to stop it. He said Miss Shelby was beside herself, and now young Avery had gone missing. The sheriff was going door to door asking if anyone had seen the boy.

I froze at the sound of Avery's name. Anyone caught helping slaves escape would be punished. Women were less likely to be whipped and hanged than to go to jail, but there were no guarantees this far south. I held my breath, waiting for Miss Bella to speak. I knew she wouldn't give us away intentionally, but Sheriff Douglas was a lawman, and he prided himself on his ability to read people.

My mistress was unflappable, and she soon sent the sheriff on his way with a warm pastry.

Word of Avery's disappearance didn't take long to spread. Not long after Sheriff Douglas left, there was a commotion in the street. My mistress and I went outside to find several angry people marching down the street. Suddenly, a woman in front began shouting and pointing. It was the owner of the general store. She'd seen me with Avery many times.

Miss Bella read the mood and told me to run.

I turned and went back into the bakery while my mistress blocked the door. There was no time to stop for anything. Out the back door and into the trees I went. The branches snagged at my dress, slowing me down and scratching my face and arms. I had no destination in mind. The best I could hope for was distance. I slipped on fallen leaves, and exposed roots clutched at my boots. It felt like the forest was against me, but I kept my feet under me and made it to the clearing before I

115

heard the barking. The baying of the hound set a panic dancing in my soul and lent swiftness to my feet, but I could never outrun a dog. I had almost reached the creek when the hound caught up to me and bore me to the ground. I went down hard, hitting my head on a rock.

When I came to, someone was dragging me through the woods by my hair. Twisting my neck, I saw a mountain of a man. I tried to bite his wrist, but he might as well have been one of the trees for all the good it did. I began to panic. Just yesterday these people had killed two other slaves. They wouldn't hesitate to punish me for helping Avery escape. Death comes for us all, but I was not ready for that final freedom. I thrashed and grasped at the passing trees, but the man's grip on my hair was strong, and soon we reached the bakery. The angry mob was waiting for us. One of them tossed a rope high up into the air, and it fell over the big branch they grew out into the road.

I caught sight of Miss Bella. She lay unmoving on the ground near the back door, and I groaned inside. They had killed my mistress, the only mother I'd ever known, and it was my fault. Everything was my fault. With this thought, I ceased my struggles. Perhaps my death would put an end to this madness.

I had always been so careful. I never let my rebellious nature show. I never acted out. And now I would dangle because these blackhearted men couldn't find Avery.

So be it. I wished I could say goodbye to my mistress, my mother, but it was too late now.

As they slipped the noose over my head, I wondered if I would see my old dead master in the afterlife or if I would just cease to be. I knew what Avery would say and, for a moment, I could almost understand the comfort he takes in his faith.

Then, suddenly, the men pulled the rope taut, and all thoughts of comfort left my head as my feet left the ground. They hauled me up slowly, hand over hand, laughing and joking amongst themselves as they worked. If I had hoped for a quick ending, this wouldn't be it. In spite of myself, when I couldn't get any air, I began to struggle. I didn't want to die. I tried to get my hands under the rope around my neck, but it was too tight. I kicked my feet as if I could still run away, but the noose bit into my flesh all the more tightly. Stars floated in front of my eyes. Darkness began to claim me. Then, my eyes flew open at the sound of a gun blast, but all I could see were dark spots across my vision.

I heard men's voices raised in anger, and suddenly I was on the ground. Sheriff Douglas was frantically trying to loosen the hanging rope from my throat, and suddenly I could breathe again. He stood and turned back to the angry crowd and told them to go on home now, that no man should take the law into his own hands, and I wasn't their property. For a moment, I thought they would turn on him too, but they just glared at the sheriff, knowing the law was on his side since they had no proof.

Denied their justice, they departed grudgingly. When the sheriff turned back to me, I lay shivering in the dirt, scratched and bruised, but alive. He took me gently into his arms and carried me back to the bakery. He set me down at the table and left out the back door again. He returned shortly with Miss Bella's lifeless body in his arms. As he laid her on the floor, I ran to her and threw myself down next to her and wept.

It was all too much. This wasn't how I wanted to gain my freedom.

Sheriff Douglas returned with water from the well and tried to get me to drink, but I pushed the mug away, spilling the water over Miss Bella's face. Suddenly, her eyes flew open, and she tried to sit up, but he shushed her and told her to calm down, that it was over now.

When she saw me alive, we both began to cry.

The sheriff went back to the well and filled a bucket with water. He began to clean the cut on my forehead, and before long, the water turned the color of rust. He took one of my Mistress' aprons and tore it into a long strip that he wound around my head, talking while he worked, telling Miss Bella that I would need to see a doctor and soon, but we couldn't stay here. The townsfolk could return any time with weapons, and he couldn't guarantee our safety. He put us both on the back of his horse and took us to our house. He helped Miss Bella pack a few essentials, and then he went out to the shed and fetched the horses. He hooked them up to the wagon and brought it around to the front door.

Miss Bella brought the quilts out and made up a bed in the back of the wagon for me, Sheriff Douglas carried me out and laid me down gently. If the townsfolk had taken justice into their own hands once, they could do it again, and she wouldn't risk losing me. I gestured urgently that I wanted to stay. How would Avery find me again if I wasn't here?

Miss Bella was firm, though. This town had a sickness in its heart. It was time for us to leave.

My mind was empty of all thoughts. I lay staring up into blue sky as Miss Bella climbed up onto the wagon seat and drove away.

Shelby

We have before us an ordeal of the most grievous kind, many years of struggle and of turmoil that will follow. The suffering is not of only the slaves but of those impacted by slavery and the awful business that is founded on monstrous tyranny. It is a mistake of the most revolting kind. Never have I witnessed death so extreme at the hands of so many, who know so little. This here land has remained my home for so long that I have become numb to what is bred on its soil. It bleeds from the ground and taints the waters that flow here, they have become stained with resistance to what God knows as the wicked.

This is not happening to us on our land, where we supply ourselves and many towns over with fresh crops. We have lost help, we have lost family, we have lost ourselves, but most of all, we have gained nothing in return for our losses. The children now have no mother or father to tend to their needs, help them grow to learn their place here.

Poor Hoof, who is the best blacksmith we have ever seen in this town or any town around these parts, has perished at the hands of selfish fools commanding devious attention.

What have we come to? We have moved forward in life, yet we remain still, silent to social understanding, corpses to our undug graves.

Restless on my front porch, staring out across what has been built here over years, happenings from nights before will forever shred my mind to pieces.

Returning to the house after witnessing the beatings and lynching of both Hoof and Trita, having all that he could fathom, Reginald wept uncontrollably. Curled up in my arms, sobbing with no end, his meltdown eventually brought anger to the surface.

"This was a mistake," he kept repeating, while securing himself further into my breast pocket, muffling his words that grew louder and louder with every plea. Holding his head close to my beating heart, hoping my words will bring him faith, I murmur, "There, there, my love… This slave business ain't for good folk like us… It has changed our spirits. It has changed your spirit… The gently caring Reginald that I once knew has gone, and all that is left is this man sitting here, waiting to grow his spirit again… it's time to let go. God has shared his wrath with us, his angry thoughts about owning people as property, and he is not happy. Rest, my love, tomorrow we will live again, the right way, the Lord's way."

We lay entangled in thought and silence, holding one another captive. The moment of change in near, I can sense it. He is with me, and I am with him again.

As if just another day, before the sun rises, my love set out for the fields to work the land right alongside the slaves. I have never heard him yell so loudly for a slave as he did this daybreak. Commanding Avery to come to him now, but with no quick response, he continued his rant about the land, determined to locate the boy, who is often known for being mischievous.

He is nowhere to be found.

Taking a few slaves with him out into the woods, through the clearing where he is often known for visiting, Reginald returned home without finding him. Thinking that the boy must be gone forever, he expresses to me the boy must have succumbed to the mob while journeying out at night on his own. If that is the truth, then there is nothing more we can do for him. It was for the best, as he has only found unrest since the day that boy came to our land.

With Avery having the outward appearance of a purebred covered in soot, I always wondered why that boy never just up and walked away. He never tried to run off. He just stayed put like any other slave around here, never looking for a way out. Maybe he stayed around for his Momma Ruby or simply because he knew no other life since birth besides this one. This life of slavery.

Posters of rhetoric drape the walls of towns found in the morning hours, posted in the cover of night by Abolitionist groups who condemn slavery here in the south. They speak about the freedom of all people, the equality of all people, including the blacks. But where is the equality when losing our workers desperately needed for laboring in our fields? Who will repay us for the oppression set on us for the actions of the mob, killing off our slaves, our property? Who will reimburse us for our loss, our family members? Who will now help us supply the townspeople with blacksmithing tools, shoeing our horses, helping to provide for the mouths of Trita and Hoof's children left without a mother and father?

We have suffered a great loss at the hands of chaos and a town sickening militia. Now, Avery is nowhere to be found, either run off or as my Reginald considers, succumbed to the wily mob for putting himself in the dark without permission. Wherever he is, freedom is not far behind, and neither should all the other slaves be either.

Sitting here the last few days allows my mind to contemplate vows spoken to my husband. Till death do we part. Is my life more meaningful than anyone else's? Do I not breathe the same air as everyone else, whites or blacks, wealthy or poor?

I come to the evident conclusion that I most assuredly do. If this is my life, and my faith is unchanged, then I am no longer worth the air that I breathe nor the life that I live.

I am here for now but feel the life within me slowly slipping away, slowing my blood to a minimum.

The air is sweet with pollen from the honeysuckles surrounding the outer portions of our land, wishing to cover it in its entirety. These birds are free, whisking around without a care, floating in and out of the rooftop rafters, where they find good nesting for new birth. We used to sit here in peace for hours on end. We loved it here, and we loved one another. sometimes that love is no longer enough. We must give in; we must let go.

My tiny fingers rub the rim's edge of my fresh glass of lemonade with a sprig of mint from my window garden that I love so much. Unlike us, the garden grows to maturity, it is picked at its peak for freshness, dies, then returns each season. Continuing to rub my rim, ensuring I have filled the glass with all I can fill it with, my lips softly circle the edge, moving back and forth before I drink. It will not be long now, and it will not be painful.

I only wish to sleep until the next life is given to me. One without hate, one without slavery, one without us.

The sun that shines on me begins to dim; my eyes begin to heavy themselves on my round face. My eyelids shake to open themselves to catch one last glimpse of this beautiful land, once so gifted with life that we have singlehandedly dispatched off.

This feels like rest, feels like peace.

My arms fall from the table where my cool lemonade lays still, hands releasing its grasp. As my head becomes cottony, it tilts to one side, coming to rest along my top shoulder, arms dangled to the ground, touching my fingertips like a soft brush.

I shall rest now.

Avery

Having left all that I know behind me, there is nothing more to think about besides my friend Lipi.

I have been traveling for hours underneath this smelly tarp on these bumpy roads, to where, I do not have any clue. Feeling every bump, hole, rock, and sway of the wagon, the pitch-black fills me with an almost calming sensation. The rattling of the moonshine-filled covered jars' bumpy rhythms start to play like music in my ears.

My mind has nothing to do but float off, giving in to the moment, remembering songs we sang on our free day. I can hear Momma Ruby's voice singing in chorus with the jars tapping side to side, sounds of clinking and clanking, almost like the clapping of our hands while enjoying the gospel.

Rocking back and forth, pressed against the floor of the wooden wagon, the metal brackets holding it together has nails that scrape against my skin with uncomfortable consequences.

It has been an extremely long ride, and I do not know when the men will stop, but I am more than positive they would not be happy to find me part of their cargo when they do. I will wait for my moment, then jump out as quickly as possible to head for more protection. Peeking from underneath the covering every so often, the only thing visible to me is trees, streams, and a never ending rocky, dirty road that falls further and further behind me.

Leaving all I know behind me has become the scariest of all, yet the unknown is even scarier. At any cost, I must keep moving and hidden from sight. Master and the others will surely come for me, track my steps to wherever I land.

My life is now in my hands, I must depend on me for my own survival, or else all that I do from here on out will be for nothing. My sack filled with bread sits around my waist, but I am too afraid of making any sort of movement, drawing attention to myself from the two men driving the wagon, who seem to never stop drinking or talking. If I didn't know better, I would think they are a married couple who have become sick and tired of one another from too many years of traveling these back roads.

I am left to my own thoughts. My hunger pains me, cramping as my stomach starves for the bread that lays so close by in my sack.

A trickle of rain interrupts my thoughts of hunger, growing louder than the clinking of moonshine jars. My cover grows more and more soaked with every moment that passes. Hearing the men in a panic, they give a loud heave to the horses to hurry along. A quickening pace drives the horses to move swiftly to find shelter and get out of the coming storm. Roaring of lightning and thunder coming together one after the other frightens the horses into scurrying even faster down the rocky road, now transforming into a muddy surface acting like quicksand to slow the horse's movements.

Feeling the wagon finally coming to a stop, fear overtakes my entire body. Stealing another peek out to see where we are and get an eye on the whereabouts of the two men, I come face to face with one of the men hurrying alongside the cargo. I remain still, and he doesn't notice my presence as he runs past in a desperate search for shelter.

That was close.

With the two men gone away from my place, I peer around for any direction to travel that is clear. I quickly gather my sack of bread, making my way underneath the wagon once again. We are in another small town. This one is even smaller than my town, the shacks here only glow with very little lighting.

Pouring in rage, the rain blurs my vision from seeing too far ahead of me or around me. With every strike of lightening, I catch a small glimpse of shelters in the distance. They surround me, but if I choose the wrong one, I can run directly into the hands of wrong doers, who are sure to return a slave for a small reward.

Lightning strikes again and again, and then again, lighting a way toward shadows of men gathered in the distance between buildings. Quickly, I shuffle through the rain-soaked darkness, feet sinking into mud. With every step, the mud layers more and more on my feet and ankles, until they are heavy from its weight. Finding a small strip of roof hanging over the edge of a small area, I pull myself underneath, holding myself closely against the wall to give me relief from the downpour.

Lightning strikes again, followed by more booming, crackling sounds of thunder. Fueled with the thought of capture, I know that shelter is my savior, and I must find it at once. Walking alongside a wall, before taking one more step, a pair of eyes sharpened by light stairs directly at me from below. I dare not move another muscle. Waiting for lightening to strike again, frozen, I wait, and wait.

Focusing in the same direction I had seen eyes staring back at me, I see them again looking right at me. Many eyes, many faces, arms, legs, large and small. It is a grave of men, women, and children. Old and young, healthy, and frail, they are all here. Bodies piled on top of bodies in a bed of overflowing corpses, minus large patches of flesh ripped and torn from bones, left to rot in their own feces, massacred.

With the coming of rain, the soil releases a disorienting stench of decaying flesh, overtaking my sense of direction. Footsteps of people approaching sends me retreating into the shadows. They come near me. Lanterns glowing just beyond the grave on the other side. Blank in thought of what to do next, I leap into the field of bodies and begin covering myself with handfuls of mud, pulling from the sides of the grave. With people closing in, I wiggle my legs between the space of bodies closest to me, pulling the body of a small child on top of me. The smell, the stench of flesh, all overtake me causing me to vomit with nothing in my stomach. My insides spill over into my face, my throat clogs trying to stay quiet.

Lights are above me now, the rain does not let up even for a second. I shut my eyes tightly, hearing voices claiming they saw movement in the area. Minutes pass by, and the men seem to loiter at the same position, waiting to see where the movement came from, but I remain solid in my position. Tears from my eyes blend with rain flowing over my face. Never would I imagine stumbling upon a massive grave, filled with pain, filled with bodies, with me in it.

With the men retreating from out of the storm to the safety of their shelters, I slowly open my eyes to take a peek above where I lay, making sure it is safe. They are gone, no longer hovering above me with their lanterns, and I am able to push the body lying on top of me off to the side. Wiggling my legs from between the grasp of other bodies, I free myself, pulling up to rest on the side, before making my way out. The rain starts to freeze my bones, the lightning telling of my position as I move, but thunder stifles the sounds of my movements.

Getting my bearings about myself, the noise of a fueled crowd cheering rips through the pounding rain. Looking around, there is only one building out of the few that is well-lit with life. Cheers overflow my senses, raising my curiosity more than my determination to run. I draw closer to one of the lit windows closest to the side edge of the roaring building. Coming from deep underneath the side of the window, I raise myself high enough to look inside. My eyes wide, my breathing shallowed, my heart fluttering, I take a quick look, then hurry back down again, wondering if anyone caught me looking.

I sit for a minute, waiting to see if a shadow or figure comes to look for me. When nothing happens, I gather my thoughts to take another peek at what's going on inside. Rising to one lower corner of the window, I notice lots of men are gathered inside, laughing and joking with one another, money exchanging hands. The room overfilled with excitement, but for what is unknown. In the middle of the large room sits a large black and brown dog, barking, surrounded by the large crowd of bystanders, held back on a chain by a tall thin man, grasping tightly with both hands. As many of the men gather in bunches, chattering loudly amongst their smaller groups, the dog handler continuously taunts the beast into fighting with a huge human like doll made from heavy fabric, dyed of the darkest ink. It looks like they are training dogs to attack slaves.

In an instant, the once bustling crowd comes to a complete, silent standby. Then, without notice, erupts in a raging frenzy, upping the level of bets and chatter. Above the crowd's head stands a very large man, a size greater than any other man I have ever seen in my life. A very dark-skinned man whose head seems to touch the top of the roof from the inside, he just stands there doing nothing while the crowd yells profanity at his face and toss debris toward him. Standing tall and mighty, he does not seem to fear any man in the room, nor the large dog pulling at his owner's chain, ready for war.

The dog owner taunts his dog more and more with the large fabric doll, then tosses it aside to focus his dog solely at the huge man slave.

We have always heard stories of these dog fights, snarling beasts pitted against men, women, and children, slaves to the death, but we only thought of them as stories made up to keep us slaves from running. I am a witness to how real they are now. Not made up. Not just stories.

Alongside the swarming men, another slave is pushed forward, thin, and scrawny, and next to him another, then another, all roped together at the wrist and neck. Focused with deep, dark eyes, bloodshot red, snarling and foaming at the mouth, the animal yanks, and tugs at the chain to get at the men. growing more and more rowdy by the second, one of the men is released from his ropes. He too looks focused, unbothered, like a warrior. Any man in his place would appear to fear for his life, but not this man, he stands there looking into the hungry beast's eyes.

With a swift push from behind, the slim man stumbles forward, directly into the mouth of the beast, who is released from his chains. The animal tears at his skin, ripping at every part of his body, tearing all flesh from the bone piece by piece. Screaming in agony, he sprawls on the ground, grabbing at any part of the animal he can grab onto. With beast-like precision and razor-sharp teeth, he has no chance at defeating the animal.

Before long the man quiets and goes limp. His neck is tightly locked onto by teeth shaking his lifeless body from side to side until he no longer moves a muscle. The once healthy, warrior-looking slave has quickly become a bloody, unrecognizable pile of mushy flesh at the cost of exchanging coinage for sport.

The men cheer and ready themselves for more. They chant for the next slave to enter, to challenge the hungry animal, to die a heroic death.

Before the disorderly wild pack of men have a chance to settle themselves, bursting forward with a loud growling roar, the oversized, dark-skinned man I first noticed enters. Lunging at the animal, the man grabs the snapping beast by his bare throat, catching it off guard. Turning his head toward the man, the animal latches on to the man's large forearm, ripping the flesh from it like a sharpened knife skinning a wild boar.

Wrestling the large man to the ground, the beast mounts the man, snapping and ripping at his face and flesh. Coming face to face, they are caught in battle, the big man losing his battle to survive. Wrapping his legs around the animal from below, the man squeezes down tightly, taking one hand to the side of the face of the animal and the other large arm pulling the crazed animal tightly into his body, not allowing the animal to bite at his face. The two push and pull at one another, the animal fiercely trying to wiggle out of his gripping hold. Laying on his back, moving frantically to keep out of the death grip of the animal's jaws, he reaches his arm out as far as he can, grabbing ahold of the dog's chain laying below the surface of the trampled dirt covering the room's floor. Still holding the animal with one arm tightly, without even slight release, he wraps the chain around the dog's neck with the other. Holding with his back hand for leverage, he wraps the chain round and round until no more length is left. Then, giving all his strength, he pulls both end of the chain tightly around the animal's neck, lifting the animal backward away from his face. Whimpering, the dog begins to pull off the large man, his eyes begin to shut, his breathing begins to labor.

Seeing what is happening, the onlookers start to quiet. Stunned from the turn of events, they become restless, knowing the inevitable is near. The unruly heathens begin yelling out in disbelief. Never has a nigga slave defeated one of their animals. They have never bet against the beast. Only, how long it would take the animal to kill its opponent. This time, they have all lost their bets against man. The will of one man alone has overcome all who opposed him, who thought him dead before he even walked into the room.

Strangling the animal, the man turns the dog to his side and rolls over top of him, crushing down on the limping canine. As the life now flows out of the animal, the man takes revenge on the dog's furry skin, ripping and tugging off the flesh of its ears, nose, and neck. With one last bite, he rips the inside of the animal's neck, lifting his bloody face to bare his brutality within his own jaws.

Disappointed at the sight of the animal's demise, the crowd sieges onto the wild man, beating at him with closed fists, chairs, and hard boots. The others join in beating the remaining, previously untouched slaves waiting their turn to die. Now they are dying at the hands of the diminished crowd.

I stand outside the window, shocked at what I am witnessing, unable to comprehend seeing a man defeat a large beastly animal with his bare hands, with his own will to survive, with his own courage.

Guarding my position at the window, stuck in one place, knowing no one is paying any attention to my standing there, a crashing whips past my ear, shattering the window before my face. A fiery ball tears at the room, then another and another.

Cringing, I jerk around to see where it came from but only see flames floating in the air, coming right at the shelter where all the people are inside.

Looking back into the room, the inside door flies open with a crashing boom, quickly overflowing with men thrashing about with wood pieces, branches, clubs, fists, and field tools at the crowd of attacking onlookers. Stunned by the sudden sneak attack, the betting men immediately meet with death at the hands of rebellious slaves bringing a halt to the ring of brutal fighting.

Without knowing which direction to run, my mouth is covered, and I am slammed with the ground from behind. Looking up, I am face to face with a black face, forceful white eyes barely inches from my eyes, sitting nose to nose. To my neck rests a large knife, cutting at my skin. He says nothing to me, only looks at me as if he is stealing my soul right from inside me. I lay silent for a second, then let out a scream for help that falls on deaf ears. Still without flinching or saying a word, he slowly grows a deviant smile which spreads across his face. With the pressure of his blade bringing blood pouring across my neck, he jumps up, running off into the night, toward the flaming building.

Turning to crawl on all fours, I make my way to the corner of the building, watching the rebellious group going from one structure to the next, they set a flame to each one after taking all that is inside, heading back into the woods with their stolen goods. They are not after me, they only seek revenge on those who have set out to do them harm. They do not know I am one of them, a part of them, far away from home.

Observing the mayhem all around me, I feel a sharp thump to my back and another to my head. Everything goes black.

I don't know how long it has been since I passed out. The pain to my back and head is unbearable, like when Master crushed the bone in my arm when I was little. My eyes refuse to gain focus back, trying to catch a glimpse of any light shining in pitch-black surroundings. I can hear voices coming from somewhere, but I cannot see from where or from who. It is many voices chatting amongst themselves, some whispering, some deep and methodical.

The land I am used to seeing is all twisted up, unrecognizable. I am feeling tremendous pressure in my head, and blood drips from my chin back to my head. Realizing I am dangling upside down from the base of my feet, I begin to struggle, reaching for the rope tightly binding my ankles together. It is a long way down for me. If I am to fall, my head would crack wide open.

Strapped upside down, bleeding out like a stuck pig, I grow weaker by the second. Rolling in and out of consciousness, I start to believe I am hanging at death's door, waiting for him to answer, and let me in.

Feeling myself being twisted around, played with like a child on a wooden swing, I know there is someone here, next to me. What is it they want from me? They don't want me dead, because if they did, I would have already been killed back at the dog fights. But I am here now, but where, and with who? Who are these people that hold me upside down, playing with me like food?

Twisting one way and then the other, but never all the way around to see who does this, I finally come to see light setting behind a very large figure of a silhouette pushed right up against me. Continuing to tug at the rope closest to my ankles, the man gives it a twist, just enough to keep me moving side to side, faintly disorienting me. Whistling, all the while twisting me, the man takes a few steps backward from where I dangle. Calmly bending over for his face to meet mine, he has the face of a monster. His nose lays where his mouth should be, his eyes playing on his chin. From this angle, he is, without thought, the ugliest creature I have ever seen.

He continues his whistling in my face, not saying a word, just staring into my eyes, curious as to what kind of creature I am.

I am not creature, I am a human, I am Avery, I am a slave just like you.

Stepping backward, still whistling his creepy, slow whistle, coming into focus while standing straight up, it is the large man slave I saw in the dog fight who defeated the beast with his bare hands. The same man who ate the face off the snarling dog trying to kill him in sport.

He is going to eat my face off!

With my rope still twisting me side to side, round and round, the figure comes in and out of my sight. Turning makes me even more dizzy, trying to catch a glimpse of focus of the towering beast killer.

As he watches me, I see the flickering flame of fire dancing behind him in the distance, figures of others gathered around the fire, sitting, and staring my way. Having stared intently at me for a long period of time, having me hanging and twisting, the man's whistling stops, then starts up again, then stops. Seemingly a man of few words, he speaks to me, commanding an answer, "Who's boy are you?"

Not understanding what he means, and getting dizzier from the turning, I say nothing for fear of throwing up in my own face again. He seems to stand event taller in the absence of my response. Still looking into his eyes as they roll around, gathering small pictures of his face, he speaks slowly. "I am Richard…"

Shocked, I do not dare tell him my name, he might have already heard of me running away from the farm. He might look for a reason to return me for coins. Calmly, the man turns and walks away from me. Reaching the fire, he bends down, reaches his hand into the fire, pulling out a branch burning with embers and a flame at the tip. Taking the burning branch in his hand, he taps it on a rock, pulls it close to his face, and gives it a heavy blow of wind from his mouth, exciting the redness to burn hotter.

Turning to look over his shoulder directly at me, he starts his way back toward me, the branch in hand, starting up his whistle once again. Dangling from this high tree, strangling my ankles, I am helpless to do anything but wait for whatever is to come.

Slowly fading in at out of consciousness, but not wanting death to come for me while my eyes are closed, I refocus my eyes on the man, who is now set right upon me again. Putting the flame close to my face, my head runs from its heat.

He asks, "What kind of creature are you, boy? You don't look of the whites.... You don't look of the blacks... but your eyes are like theirs, like the devils." The man waits for my response.

With great fear of what will happen if I don't speak soon, I tell him, "Avery, my name is Avery." Waiting for me to say more of who I am and where I come from, I continue, "I am... well... I am a nigga slave just like you!"

At once, all the men around the camp burst out in uncontrollable laughter, joking and poking fun at how my skin is pale and only darkened by filth, masking my true color. Still laughing, Richard returns and pokes the hot stick at my body, sending flaming red ambers about, burning at my skin. Screaming in surprising pain, I wiggle uncontrollably, trying to keep the burning dots away from my bare body. Richard laughs as he continues to do it again and again, laughing harder and harder with every dance as he performs his ritualistic torment over and over.

Suddenly, a hush comes over the men. All the laughter immediately stops as the men bend close to the ground, ducking and scrambling to put out the flames. Kicking dirt onto the fire, Richard takes the burning stick and penetrates the ground's surface deep enough to no longer see the red on its stem. He grabs my face, putting his hand tightly over my mouth, aggressively whispering, "If you make one sound, I will make your insides hang!"

It is silent, darker than any night I have seen. My eyes can no longer focus from the sudden turning from flames lighting the night. His hand is so large covering my face, he does not realize he is covering my nose, suffocating me. Starting to pass out, my grunting becomes louder and more panicked. Darkness gets darker and darker, coming closer to the end, my eyes rolling back in my head. If he only knew he was killing me, or maybe it is his intention to quiet me by taking my air from me.

Unable to breath, or have a clear thought, no words appear in mind for God to get ready for accepting me into heaven. I burst out, gasping for air that eludes me, that feeds me life, as he realizes what he has almost done and releases his grip from my face. Shushing me with his finger, I barely have time to catch my breath, when he puts his hand over my mouth again, not covering my nose. Unable to fill my lungs, and only through my nose, my face feels like it will explode off my face.

In complete darkness, Richard stands as tall as he can and quickly cuts the rope that holds me in suspense. With my legs free, he wraps his arms around my waist, keeping me from making noise falling to the ground. What are they afraid of? I have witnessed the destruction and warrior mentality of these men, as they are beasts amongst beasts, able to kill with their bare hands. What do they hear that I do not hear? Who dares comes to threaten these men slaves?

Besides hearing with shallow breathing of men all around me, the trees are silent, the woods stand without rustling. Quiet as a resting baby. Then the deafening screech comes out of the dark, and it will not stop. I hear what sounds like a hundred men all fighting one man as he screams in pain. Within seconds, the screaming stops, and silence is restored, followed by more laughter. Pushing dirt aside, uncovering the redness from where the flame once burned, one of the men blows hard at red sticks, igniting the beginning of flames once again. Blowing more and more, gentle at times, harder at others, the flames begin to flow, poking their heads out, starting to dance, lighting up the darkness.

Releasing my mouth from his large hands trapped around me, Richard frees me from his grip without bothering to check if I would run and makes his way over toward the group. Patting one another on the back as if congratulating one another for surviving, I realize they have not killed an intruder, a wanderer, another white man. They have cunningly set a trap for a large, wild, male boar. He is even bigger than the dog whose face was ripped off; larger than most pigs I have ever seen on the farm. Impaled from field tools made to hunt with like weapons of war, he lays with his mouth wide open, bleeding out from his ears and eyes. He too was a beast of the wild, and now he is a hefty meal for the wily hunters, a gift of death to provide life.

Throughout the night, men take turns tending to the portions of meat that have been cut up in smaller portions for easier cooking on the fire. Amid men taking turns in devouring their prized hunt, standing at the base of the fire in the middle of all the men enjoying, Richard speaks out. "Merci, seigneur de nous avoir fourni ce repas du sang de la terre de nos ancêtres afin que nous puissions nous nourrir pour donner à notre corps la force de combattre nos ennemis."

Stunned at his ability to speak another language never heard around these parts, all the men sit holding their meal in hand without taking another bite.

Sitting outside of the group of men still close to the tree where I hung by my feet, Richard speaks in English. "Thank you, Lord, for providing us with this meal of the blood, of the land, of our ancestors, so that we can feed ourselves to give our body the strength to fight our enemies, amen." He finishes, then grabs a well-done piece of pig meat from the fire. Splitting the hot mess of flesh with his own hands, he takes a huge bite from one piece, tearing into it with his teeth, then tosses the other half in my direction. Starving from having not eaten in almost two days, devouring the meaty, well-cooked piece was all that stands between me and choking on death.

Eating my meal, turning my back to protect it from any sudden assault by others, I keep look-out while snarling at it for being a much-needed treat.

Walking over to me and sitting at my backside, Richard elbows me in the back, telling me to slow down when I eat, or I will choke and die without any help. Taking in all that surrounds me, I start to realize I am in no immediate danger, so I slow down, and we share a few moments of eating without saying any words. Thoughts continue to run through my mind even though no one has tried to attack my any further. I am sitting here without shackles, without ropes, without anyone keeping me from bursting into a sprint, but am I a captive? Am

I free to leave as I please, or am I their slave to keep hold of and do with as they wish? Right now, this freedom does not feel like freedom but more like a temporary thought of freedom.

Sitting just a few steps from the fire, where most of the other men are still gathered, deep into the night, I wonder where and how did this beast of a man come to this area, to the ring, fighting killer dogs, growing so large, being a beast himself. How did he come to lead these men? These men who are willing to risk their lives to save his life by killing all that put him in the position to die at the hands of a wild beast for pure enjoyable sport.

Clearing my throat of all I have consumed over a short period of time; I build up enough courage to let my thoughts come to the surface and out of my filled mouth. "Richard, are you a free man or a slave?"

He does not respond, simply keeps eating and staring out into nothingness. Hesitating while waiting patiently for a response, I start the question once again, "Richard, are..." before I can finish, he hushes me with a piece of meat to his lips, takes another bite, then starts humming. He doesn't seem bothered by my question, nor does he seem very interested in answering it too quickly, he just continues to hum while slowly chewing his meal.

Richard lays his head back and gazes toward the sky and the stars, "They are beautiful, yes?"

Not saying anything, I look at the stars to see what he sees. I guess I never really took the time to look at them while free. They do seem different now that I am not waiting for a call from Master. My eyes see more of what is there instead of what is not there.

He starts up again, "These lights in the sky guide us to places, they see what we don't see, light up what we cannot light up. They are not man or of this earth, nothing to control or hold back. They are free. Free to roam, free to shine for no reason at all, just because they can. I am black, and I am not free, but the white man is white, and he still is not free either. If they hold us as niggas, hold us as slaves, they will never be free of us…. or themselves. You ask am I a free man? No, none of us are free. We will be, but for now we serve one another in life and in death. We stand together in secrecy to right some of the wrongs of others hoping to squash what remaining life we have in us, our people, our ancestry. Mr. Avery, I see something in your eyes that I did not see in my eyes. I see fight, I see there is fear, there is hurt, pain, anger, and there is will. Although your skin is pale and your eyes are blue, you are more like me than some of the men surrounding us, but you are not nigga, you are worse. You are a white posing as a nigga, and that… Well, that is dangerous to us all. More dangerous to the whites than to us niggas. We already walk in the dark, in fear, without homes. We have nothing more to lose, besides our lives, and that… we are all willing to give freely for one another to live." He finishes for a moment and rubs his face and head. Something else seems to bother him, but he hesitates to speak.

Finally, after a long, starlit moment, taking a deep breath, speaking in a low, slow tone, Richard continues, "As a very young boy, I was given to a man who lived in France, and we moved around a lot. I was his caddy boy, everywhere he went and everything he did, I was there to help him with whatever he needed. I fetched his clothes, his water, drew his water for his bath, and even made food. He taught me the language of the French but also taught me better English-speaking ways. I have seen many places and many faces, some I liked and others I despised, but I was never to speak of any of it in a foul manner.

"He was a gambling man. Nd when he ran out of money in one town, we would move on to the next and the next, until he came into more money from gambling, then we would stay, eat good, and sleep well, at least until he wasted all his money away again. Sometimes when he was desperate, he would have me work for other people for a day or two, sometimes even longer, until my wages were enough to gamble some more with.

"One day, as I am standing in the corner of a small room where the men were playing in a card game, waiting to serve anyone who requested something, another man noticed he was a cheating man. He held more cards that any man can hold for any one game. The man pulled out a pistol, and my master, always carrying a slick knife in both of his sleeves, pulled the knife and stabbed the man at least a hundred times until the man lay bleeding to death. No one went to help the man, and my master took all his winnings and what was left over in the man's billfold and coat pockets. That same night, we got on a ship headed for the states, and that is why I am here in this land. Having never visited this land, I have only heard stories of it. Stories of death, stories of how the French enjoy clothes and sweet treats, tobacco and other goods all made on the backs of black slaves, beaten, and killed at the hands of their owners.

"Upon getting on that ship to come here, every bone in my body surrounded by my skin seemed to weaken and fall apart at the thought of arriving to the land people called, "the bloody land." Being here, I have seen the worst things that men do to other men. I have seen where the cotton, sugar, and tobacco grow from the blood of the blacks. I have sat in the streets of France and watched people wear the finest clothes and eat the goodies produced by our people.

"One thing I know is they do not taste the blood of the sweet treats they put in their mouths, up against their lips. They do not wear blood on their clothes, knowing they were made of blood. With every puff of their tobacco, they do not realize they are releasing the souls of our ancestors who cured the leaves they take for granted by throwing it unfinished onto the road. They squish it with the bottom of their filthy, worn boots, as if with every turn they are trying to stomp us out of existence, one by one.

"Sometimes I would sit and laugh to myself when I saw one of them struggling to put the fire out of one and it would just keep coming back. That is our people you are trying to take the fire out of, but all it takes is that one to refuse to go out, it just keeps coming back.

"My master could not afford his debt any further, his gambling grew too big for his pockets once we got to this bloody land. The only thing of value left was me. He lost that too."

Though not wanting to interrupt his story, as he seemed to perk up a smile in between thoughts, I ask him, "Did you run?" Richard let out a small, quiet chuckle and replied, "I should have." Taking a moment, he starts to reflect on the day his life turned for the worse.

"It did not matter what it was, my master would bet on it. I once saw him bet on whether or not a prostitute's big toe was larger on the left side than the right side. The group of men coaxed the woman to take off her shoes to see which one was larger. Upon taking off her shoe, some of the men began to laugh hysterically, as the others who were disappointed at their loss threw their hands in the air in disgust at losing the bet. Even though my master won a simple few coins in comparison to what he would normally bet or win, he cheered the loudest of all the men. I do not know if he did it to get rich or just for the challenge and thrill. Whatever it was, he should have stopped a long time ago.

"He has given me up for his own debt. Since then, I have done many things that I am not proud of, many things that I know are not right and shouldn't be done to any man or woman. I have been taken a hold of by the mayor of a town, and he has put my size and strength to the test. He has made me beat other men to death in contests to fight. Giving me weapons to smash their faces in, pull out their teeth, gouge out their eyeballs until they screamed in agony. These are my own people I must kill for his enjoyment and his greed for coinage, for the entertainment of his guests. The moment I thought to take my own life was the first time I killed a man with my own hands. My hands wrapped his neck so tightly, his life slowly went away. He gurgled from his throat, gasping for any kind of air that would be allowed in. His eyes rolled back and forth uncontrollably; his urine flowed out of his front while his hard matter leaked out the other. No one can imagine the filthy stench of death until it is done with your own hands. I wanted to die right along with him.

"Later, as I would continue to be forced to kill our own men, I would imagine it was the white men who sat around laughing, joking, encouraging blood to spill, betting on our

143

lives like fish on a hook for supper. They would die quick and with vicious intent."

Sitting here listening to his words makes me reflect on how he was able to kill that dog in a fight with his bare hands. He has squeezed the life out of many who have tried to take his life. He, himself, wanted to take his own life, so why did he not kill himself? There is nothing to live for when we are constantly fighting for our own lives. Or maybe there is... fighting for the lives of others.

Richard grabs some of the soil from the ground and sifts it through his hands, washing his hands with the earth before continuing. "I do not know why I sit here and share this with you. I do not speak about my story to anyone, knowing the devastation our people here have gone through and continue to go through. They used me against my own. These filthy controllers led me to believe that I was doing good. They told me my size and strength were to be admired and revered for such perfection. They told me I would no longer have to fight for my food but would eat the finest meats, drink until I pass out, rest in the warmth of a fire on cold nights, and sleep under the stars on hot ones. For months, they did exactly that, as the group of slaves that were all chosen to be special arose in the morning to exercise by running and lifting anything and everything in sight around the land for strength. We laughed and told stories of our past, making fun of how we are slave kings, eating, drinking. Never told what was expected of us, this went on and on without question. We were free to roam if we remained on the land itself, which this land seemed never ending.

"Then the day came when all of us men were gathered up. The controllers lathered our bodies with oils and scents of lemons and oranges. They loaded us onto a wooden box wagon with small, barred windows pulled by many horses. We traveled so long, we were able to sleep, wake up, and sleep again. Once we stopped, we were once again fed like kings and given warm places to rest for the evening. I could have never imagined what we were there for. I could never imagine how they would use them revering us for our perfection, with claiming we are doing good for our people, and turning that into what we had to do, what I had to do.

"When morning came, the controllers came to retrieve us. They walked us from where we slept to get another fresh meal. As always, us men laughed and enjoyed the comradery of one another, as we had gotten to know one another's stories. After eating, we were led to an open area filled with green grass and beautiful trees. It was calm, it was quiet, as we all stood with anticipation, wondering why we were there. In the distance, walking our way, was a crowd of beautiful young women. They did not have the look of a normal slave but that of well-kept ones. The kind you find inside their master's house. These beautiful young women did not seem to be of a woman's age, but they stood proud, giggling at the sight of us men, all oiled up. We were then told, we are to have our way with all these women as many times as possible in one night, as the owner could not afford to pay or provide more food for more than that. Upon hearing we had full permission to have our way with these girls, most of the men started running and grabbing at any woman they could get their hands on. Making their way with them right there on the ground in front of everyone.

In shock I did not move, I just stood still, hoping no one could see me. But I am very large and cannot be missed, even at a distance. One of the controllers pushed me to go ahead and

145

choose one, but I did not. After all was done and the screaming stopped, I realized that we were chosen to produce babies of great health and stature. We were told that we were…"

"Breeders… Slave Breeders."

Listening to his story and realizing he was one of the breeders that came to my farm and raped our women, I heard nothing else Richard had to say. Before I knew it, I leaped to my feet, wrapping my arms around his head and neck, trying to pull it from his body, kicking and clawing at him as he remained seated.

He quickly stood up with me around his shoulders and tossed me into the mouth of the fire. Surrounded by the burning pain of fire, he grabbed my head and shoulders and yanked me out of the coals before I burned. I can feel the scars grabbing a hold of my skin, beginning to scar my back, arms, and legs. Stunned, I calm as he shakes my body to settle me down.

"Stop it, stop it now, boy! I am not one of them. I refused to take part in what they had made for us. Some of the men loved what they were doing. Other men, like myself, despised the thought and the sight of it. We are not animals meant to breed for man's purpose but meant to love and nourish one another. The night I decided to run away, the men and their dogs came after me. They chased me until I could no longer breathe, I could no longer run. The only reason I got away is because I passed out and fell from a cliff into water and washed down the river, ending up in mud, filled to my neck and covering my entire body from being seen or smelled by them damn dogs. I was lucky. From that day forward, I made a promise to myself that I would never be forced to hurt another one of my own but hurt all those who hurt us, who hold us, who turn us into animals for their own pleasure. I will make that same promise to you here today. I promise, we will kill the controllers and all who made us hurt our own. All who are responsible for keeping us.

"In time, we will rid this land of every single one of the breeders who like what they do. They will know how it feels to have the pain of another that is unwanted. But, in time…"

Agreeing to what Richard promised me, that we would have our day to see the breeders and those who controlled them die one day, he told me about the men's plans to travel the land, helping those in need as we went along. We could not stay in one place but for a night, as we always knew we were being hunted. Whoever was coming was always just right behind us, picking up our scent, nipping at our heels, hoping to track us and kill us.

The years went past, and I joined the men on every adventure, learning all that I could on the way. I told them the story of how I killed a man who tried to hurt my friend Lipi. How I beat him about the head until he no longer was able to move. How they killed my loved ones, Trita and Hoof, and how I came to see Richard fighting and killing the beast. I know I gained the respect of all the men after telling my story, because they stopped teasing me for the color of my skin, stopped sending me on wild chases for things that did not even exist, for not belonging to any race or home or clan, for being white. I was one of them, and I felt at home. I was right where I was supposed to be.

Sneaking across lands in the thick of the night, the group would get ahold of whatever supplies we could. Picking from the lands that produced fruits and vegetables, we ate pretty good most of the time. Other times we would try to hunt for our meals, trap animals, or gather whatever was close by, always trying to avoid being detected.

If we caused too much trouble at once in one area, a large price would have to get paid. We would be in trouble and chased down by all they could gather and send our way.

We helped many people on the way. Mostly, we took along those who wanted to run away, leaving behind all those who had no desire to leave or were too scared to run. We moved from town to town without being seen or noticed, sometimes traveling what seemed to be five days travel in just one night. There were many times when we ran further and faster than the night before just to avoid capture. This life we live is not the life expected by anyone. We are the hunted, the hunter, the gatherer, the warrior, the runaway slave.

On occasions where Richard and the men figured we were far enough away from any danger; they would have me take my bible and share God's words with them. They claimed it gave them hope, it gave them inner strength, it made them feel loved, and most of all feel free. Sitting by the fire, receiving word that we will be attempting to rescue a slave girl who is being held deep in the belly of a water's well, lowered into the dark to keep the secret of being with the master's child from his wife, I give prayer.

"Vindicate me, O God, and plead my case against an ungodly nation; O deliver me from the deceitful and unjust man!

"But this is a people plundered and despoiled; All of them are trapped in caves or are hidden away in prisons; they have become a prey with none to deliver them, and a spoil with none to say, 'Give them back!'

"When he found her in the field, the engaged girl cried out, but there was no one to save her.

"So that we confidently say, 'the lord is my helper, I will not be afraid. What will man do to me?'

"Amen."

Richard

He is a good young man, this Avery. Strong and mighty in his ways as if he was raised with sound values. I like watching him turn into a soldier with the other men close by. There are those who despise his presence, but most of us like him being around, he will be useful when the time comes.

Over the years, I have shown him how to hunt, how to fish, and how to trap, not only animals but people. He is a quick learner but hard in the head, strong-minded to go about doing things his own way.

He is anxious to get to the Slave Breeders' main camp to revenge what we have done to his farm, his family. But I cannot take him into a fight that he is sure to lose if he is not yet ready. He does not realize I am grooming him to go to war with his mind and not his feelings. He must set all his anger for revenge aside to attack his opponents using their own weaknesses as leverage to defeat them on their own land at their own game.

We have traveled this land through the thickness of the trees, the darkness of the valleys, the sides of the hills, always moving in a quick pace to avoid capture.

Many times, we have come close to dying, yet have survived.

Others have abandoned us, only to allow themselves to get captured and killed. Some have tried to give away our positions or predict where we would travel to next, but once we have gotten word of their trap, we immediately change course. When they thought we would travel north, we would travel directly back at them, sitting directly under their noses, watching them as they were trying to find us. The hunter becomes the hunted, while we leverage against our enemy to fall into our trap. Always trying to avoid the chase of large militias, I am sure they will catch up to us one day, but not until we have made our way throughout these lands, silencing the voices of those who oppress us and the gifts they wish to impose on us. Slavery.

They call it the underground railroad, a chain of pathways and hidden corridors, places to hide. Those slaves who seek their freedom move from place to place in secrecy from those who wish to capture them and take them back to their masters for reward. Working with others allows us to move around freely and forward without being seen while on our way toward the camp. Once we are there, we will bring the fight directly to their doorsteps, to their fields blossoming fruit, to their necks, throats, and heads. They will know what it feels like to have control of nothing more than the air they breathe now.

Avery will have his moment, and I will know what it feels like to remain free of harming my own people at the hands of my own brothers. They are not all bad men. We are not all in agreeance with roaming from town to town and farm to farm, seeding the land. But, when there is a choice of working the fields, carrying heavy loads from place to place, turning land that has been turned a thousand times over, in comparison to eating, drinking, and roaming freely, some are more than willing to sell their souls to the devil to taste the ripened fruit of a small kingdom.

Sickened by the sight of wrongdoers, we do not set out to rebel against everyone in our path, as we would have more men at our heels than we can run from. We must pick and choose our forums to fight, to kill, to help, to change courses. We must stay to the shadows and keep our path erratic. Survival depends on all of us working together, making sure we are our brothers' keepers, even at the sight of death staring us down.

We must not fear what is in front of us but embrace what is to become of us.

Under the cover of the night with just the moon to guide us, we had to put our differences aside and our minds back in place for us to rescue a nigga girl slave abandoned in a dry well far-removed off the land of her master's house. Others knew she was there but were not allowed to go near or send food her way. Left to wither away at the hands of nature's elements, the torture of dying a slow death from starvation and dehydration kept me from resting easy at night, knowing she was there.

The elements would soon swallow her whole.

With everyone who works her land and the surrounding lands knowing her master is the father of her unborn child, he sat her deep inside the well to waste away beneath the surface to hold their secret from his wife and mistress. If either were to catch wind of his indiscretions, he would become a victim of their scorned hearts. Our lives have remained the least valuable of all livestock, yet the most valuable of nothing more than indulging pleasures of flesh. Why are we so easily disposed of, so easily forgotten, so easily erased without the ability to seek justice? Because we do not fight against those creatures who seek to devour us.

She was there at the bottom of the dark well, sobbing in exhaustion, barely able to shed anymore tears. Her swollen eyes hardly able to catch a glimpse of us sending a rope only inches from her face. Startled by our sudden presence, she clambered backward at the side of the moistened walls filled with hundreds of years of tree roots pushing through its sides.

Reaching the top of the well's opening, rope still wrapped ever so tightly around her waist and legs, her belly showed the end of a full-term birth waiting to happen.

Warming by the fire back at the camp, the woman tells the tale of being bitten by a snake that had fallen into the well just a few nights before. Frightened for the safety of her and her unborn child, she petrifyingly stomped the snake's head until it only squirmed about and finally stopped moving. After a full night, starving and thirsty, she decided to eat the body of the snake. She claims it was the devil in the form of a serpent sent to take away her child.

Avery speaks to us men in the words of the Lord. I don't know how he can remember everything he hears and repeat it back in return yet cannot read or write. He speaks with the passion of a full-grown man, but he is still growing. He has no clue what this world has for him. All the suffering, the pain, the disappointment. Growing up as a slave himself, losing all his loved ones, beaten and tormented, running and hiding, but none of that will prepare him for his own death, especially if he is afraid to live.

Today, I sit here, underneath this shady tree with the rattling of broken leaves, birds cheering us on, the animals smelling our scent, refusing to come near, but I sit right here, a free man, caged by what does not let me move freely. This earth beneath my feet lets me wiggle my toes in the dirt where my people have walked before me. The air lets me send messages without sound to those behind me, as the water gives me life that moves through me. At this moment, it feels good to be alive.

Watching the men gather their senses about them, I am hearing the whispers behind uneasy feelings that some wish to move faster and further north, where there are free men, free land, while others think about giving a deadlier fight to plantations across the land. They think dastardly deeds to all the whites is the only answer to freedom. I say it is the only answer to an immediate and sure death.

Their actions are without true purpose, without validation as to the consequences. Some of the men are made of pure ignorance, but they fight with the hearts of lions and the quickness of snakes. I would gladly lay down my life for any of these men who walk with us, as they are truly my brothers not only in arms but in blood. Sometimes listening to Avery speak his words rouses the others to want to fight harder. I must remind him of what we are here for, but sometimes I am unclear in what are we really doing, what our purpose is.

Reminding myself of the inevitable, that death will surely come, it is our responsibility to do all we can for our people. What that is, I do not know. I am hoping there will be a sign from the heavens guiding us in the right direction.

For now, we head in the direction of the breeders while helping all those we can on the way.

One man has my heart out of all the other men. He has walked by my side since the day we met, never leaving it. He says he has always had favor with his master's wife and daughter, but I don't know if this is true, as he tells the most farfetched stories known to any man. He brings smiles to my face with his stupidity, yet his heart is filled with the blood of his ancestors', ancestors. Telling stories of his family coming from Africa, the prince of a kingdom, who was captured and sold to traders for good sandals and strong alcohol. My friend, Cheeks, as we call him, because he is always smiling, raises hell like no other when it is time, all the while smiling at his enemies. Appearing to enjoy killing others, he is always a soft-spoken man waiting to explode. He is my friend, as I would never want him as my enemy. Unsure if Cheeks' stories are made of whole cloth, his scars follow him, masked by laughter.

If it weren't for the relentless bravery of Cheeks leading the men to come and rescue me and the other men from the dog fights, we would have all succumbed to the boots of those men, angered at me for killing their prized fighting dog.

He was never happy that he let Avery live when he had Avery on the ground with his sharp knife directly on his neck, so he simply keeps away from him now. His thoughts are that all those who are fair skinned, who are white, who are mixed, still have the blood of purebreds, and a purebred's blood coursing through you is like being purebred oneself. He says he has never met a good one with kind intentions, only good ones until it was time to make a choice, and he knows what that choice will always be.

Knowing we need all the men and tools available for the fights ahead, there is respect given for my wishes to keep Avery around for when he is needed. Cheeks claims, ever since Avery has been around, there are things coming up missing, men running off to the north no longer willing to fight, and spirits following us.

It is no fault of Avery, those men running off were cowards, those things coming up missing is because we did not hide them well enough in the ground, and those spirits are the souls of our ancestors keeping watch over our group. This boy is no traitor, he is a soldier for our fight, and he will be quite useful in the very near future.

It feels like we are being followed. Many eyes from deep within the woods and hills seem to peer at us from every angle. Now that we are slowed with a slow-moving woman carrying a child within, there is much to think about. Of no use to us in our fight, we must scramble for a place to hide her, find someone to care for her and the child. Trying to keep our position secret will find itself difficult once the baby is born. It will cry our locations away, drawing our enemy right on us. If she wishes to stay, then the baby must die, a sacrifice of one must come to life for the future of many.

Cheeks

I never met a person so white yet claim they are a nigga. If I was born a white, I would just go ahead and kill myself. Or maybe if I was born white, I wouldn't even know that I was black. Well, maybe in that case I would still kill myself, because looking around at all these black folks around me, I would think, *Damn, they skin color sure is beautiful, and my white skin sure is plain.* Welp, might as well kill myself for being ugly.

Black is beautiful, and white is just not that bright, put a little darky on that white and it might turn out alright, might. I ain't never met a white man that I liked, but ain't never might a white woman that I didn't. It is the forbidden fruit, not even to look toward for too long without repercussion. There, in the streets, holding bags of food on the city streets might be a man, a woman, and their child. That man will look over at me in complete disgust, while later that white woman will look at me with curiosity. Well, I am curious too. Curious as to why she is so curious.

I won't say that I am the handsomest man, but whatever it is, it seems to attract the white women into tracking me down and inviting me to the comfort of their beds while their husbands play around town.

I stayed in good favor with my master's wife, and daughter. With his land being vast, and his business always carrying him out of town for long periods of time, that left a lot of time on his wife and daughters' hands to fill, and boy was I willing to fill in. When it came to exciting themselves into a frenzy of passion, they were like animals in heat. Many days, I found myself thirsty and tired, exhausted from having to perform many times in a day, going from hiding with one to running off and hiding with another.

To see my dark skin against their fair skin brought me joy, knowing I have taken a part of what the white man holds so precious to him, his white woman. Leading all us slaves to believe they are the purest of snow, the mothers of all that exists, the angels sent directly from God himself to keep watch over us all. Well, who is keeping watch over them when the master is away? I am!

The other slaves around me know what happens when the master is away, and sometimes when the master is still close by, but they dare not say anything for fear of death at the hands of lies placed upon his precious angel's reputation.

When the lady of the house took a liking to me when I was just becoming a boy, she made the master give me work as the water boy. I carry water to and from the house from the lake, the stream, and sometimes the well, depending on what it is used for. That's all I do all damn day, carry water around. Doing this keeps me close to the house most of the days, which allows the lady and her daughter keep close eyes on me, working without much clothes on. Always calling me to bring them water, while they smile and look at me like they going to eat me up right there. Half the time, they don't even need any water, just asking to be asking, because they can.

I might be a nigga slave, but they my slaves for the short moments when I take control of their bodies. Just like every other white woman around these parts, I know it is just a matter of time before I am invited into each one of their beds, one by one. Just like it is surely a matter of time before their husbands notice they no longer desire them in their beds, because I have already been there. I think in one day, I had bed at least thirteen women in three different counties. They all chased me down the river, claiming they wanted to have my babies. Little black babies just like me. I had to climb a tree just to get away from them, waiting up there eating fruits of the tree until it was dark, then I crept down past the sleeping women and off into the woods.

Oh yeah, they love me like no other. If I decided that I didn't ever want to leave their beds, they would probably tell their husbands to never come home again, it's my bed now.

It's not because I don't like these whites that I ran off, it's because I hate these whites that I ran off. Well, that and they were going to kill my black ass when one found his wife had a little nigga baby that she claimed he was the daddy of. Lord, they sent out a posse looking for every nigga slave within an hour's walk of where they lay. They held that baby up face to face with every nigga around to see if he was that baby's daddy. It was just a matter of time for them dogs to get a strong hold of my scent and lead them right to me. This neck is too pretty to be removed from this perfect body, because then this head of mine would no longer exist above my shoulders, and I kind of like it right where it is.

I remember one time, I was sleeping with this big ole girl, and she let out a mean bit of air. It was so damn loud; all the slaves woke up and went to work in the fields thinking it was the master sounding the alarm for work.

I tell you this, they don't really call me cheeks because I smile a lot, they call me cheeks because that's what I get. My bloodline is that of kings, queens, and princes, reaching far back to the great motherland of Africa, where my peoples' people respected the land, and the land respected them. My thin build and high-pitched voice was apparently a defined trait in all the men of my tribe. Powerful warriors who refused to be imprisoned by any man, by any boat, by any master. All but one it would seem, or else I wouldn't be here today, in this foreign land.

Although I call it foreign, it is the only land I know, and the only land that I have hatred for. One day, a thousand boats will come to this land and carry us all away from here and back home. When that day comes, it will bring unspeakable joy to us all. We will finally be free to return to where we came from. Until that time, I will do what I can to eliminate as many as possible, so when they come for us again, there is less of them to kill.

Maybe I should start with Avery. He walks around here proud like a black, but he is not one of us, he carries the blood of a purebred. With those eyes, he looks around too curious for his own good. Too curious to be one of us. I keep my distance, as just the thought of him sometimes makes my arms twitch. I hold myself from reaching out to his pale neck and slicing it right off his shoulders.

My good friend Richard says he will be useful to us one day, but a white is only useful for one thing, and that's gutted like a pig to scare off others from following too close behind.

Sitting here watching this pale boy, my arm twitches, and my hand straightens for the want to slap him right across his face, making his nappy, matted up hair fall right off his big head.

He preaches to us men at night when we gather as if he himself spoke the words of the Lord, as if he himself is carrying the blood of our black ancestors.

He claims to be a slave, raised by a woman named Momma Ruby since birth. Looking and sounding like a slave don't make you a slave, especially not a nigga slave, but all I know is he is willing to fight with us, willing to die for us, for our people that he claims are his own. If he is not who he says he is, if I see one flaw in his bones, one lie from his lips, I will cut them off, hold them in my hand and make them kiss my ass before throwing them in the fire to become ash.

His stories may be even louder than mine, but at least mine are true. I watch him for an opening, while he loafs around, speaking with the pregnant slave girl named Zhara. They have become thick over the past few days, but they will soon have to part ways, as she and that unborn child must go. They can no longer travel with us, but we still have a few more days before we are to meet up at our new location with the railroad, who will take her from our hands and lead her with the others to safety.

Richard reminds me, all whites are not the same, there are different levels to their madness, but I say the only difference to their madness is there are just different levels of stupidity.

Waiting for the others to arrive, we have hunkered down near a stream, covering ourselves in the water's mud to keep us from detection of the unwanted. Hours come and go as we pass the time in beds of ants and critters surrounding us. We must not move in the face of a predator, it could as well be a hunter's dog sniffing us out, the hunter waiting for us to stand and run.

This time, I am set high up on a ridge overlooking the trees to look out for the others coming along or for our enemies attempting to sneak up on us. Shifting my position to achieve a better view of the known path used by the others we wait for; I hear a snarl. Stiffening in fear, I hesitantly turn my head to see what has snuck up on me so crisply.

I come face to face with a mountain lion, breathing at my backside, hair on his back standing so high he looks larger than ten men.

Attacking me faster than a white girl in a group of niggas that look like me, I do not dare scream for fear of giving away our location, scaring the others from meeting here. Wrapping my legs around the animal, my knife finds its way through the front of the animal all the way through his spine. His tongue falls from his mouth, and his eyes look at me in surprise that his meal would not be eaten today. He will not fill his empty belly with the meat of man today, or for never.

As the night grows long and cold, looking at the animal laying in silence, staring back at me as if he still wants a piece of this dark meat, I take my knife and gut him for his skin, and wrap it around me for warmth. Holding both of his eyes in either hand, I twirl them in my palms until I get hungry and eat them for better sight into the night.

Waiting here, laying inside this beast, I guess Richard was right. All that appears to carry the blood of evil, at some point can become useful, can become a gift.

Throughout the night, I have kept warm inside the skin of this beast who once preyed on me, until morning. Hearing the rustling of leaves in the distance, I slowly come to stand to see what approaches us. It is the others, making their way through the land, getting closer and closer to where we are to meet. With a call like that of a small bird, I subtly alert the group of the others' presence.

Shedding my new friends' skin, I emerge like the king that I am, discarding the shell of my fallen enemy behind for others to find.

161

All my enemies be aware, their skins will become my shelter if they dare follow too close.

The others are made of plenty of men, women, and children, carrying hardly anything for warmth or food. We share what we have with them before sitting for a while, trying to explain what a white is doing amongst us. It is hard to say he is one of us, but he is, and he has been for a while now.

It is time to release Zhara and that unborn that breaths inside of her with the blood of her master, so she will no longer slow us down.

Speaking with others as to the direction they will travel, we decide to move in the opposite direction, splitting our groups and onward to the next in hopes of dismantling the Breeders' camp. We are at least five days' walk to their camp, and unsure if they will occupy the camp when we arrive, but if they do not, then I am sure we will wait for their return. When the time comes, I will cut the manhood of them away from their bodies and stuff their mouths with them. Even in death, they will be unable to speak of the massacre they have witnessed.

Looking around, waiting to part ways, Zhara and Avery sit in the far distance, whispering closely. There looks to be a fight brewing from the two, who have always spoken closely but now with a lot more emotions.

Walking over, they stop what they are doing to pay attention to me standing over them.

"You two are wicked. Always plotting in secrecy. Tell me what you both speak of in secret. If you lie, I will cut both of you in half and make you whole again with one another's parts," I grumble intently.

After they ponder in silence for a while, I clear my throat and pull out my knife from my sheath behind my back. This prompts them to sit up straight and begin telling me of the future.

Hearing their thoughts, I immediately shut the mouth of Avery, who's presence already has my arm and hand twitching with excitement for his face and allow Zhara to tell me the rest. She does not wish to travel with the others underground, instead she wants to stay and fight, give back the life she has been given for escaping the well.

"This is not my child, it is only my body that carries it," she cries to me and Avery. "I did not ask for this to press upon me. I did not want him to share himself with me, as I am a child, no bigger than my mother when her master pressed himself against her. How can I ever be free when I am with an unwanted child of another who left me to die in the dark, in the cold, far away from all I have loved dearly? I will be constantly reminded of my death, not of my life," she explains while rubbing her overgrown belly.

Knowing exactly what she is saying but not wanting to appear heartless, I ask her, "So, what is it that you discuss with Avery? He is of no use to you."

In response to my harsh questioning, looking directly at him, she explains, "He will take the blood from my body and wash it down stream. The child will be no more, and I will be me, in life or in death."

I am not shocked, and this is nothing new. I have seen many women abandon the birth of children, unwanted at the others of others. The possibility of them both dying, of neither of them surviving the task, will always come to mind. The death of a child can mean the death of the mother that holds it.

Avery does not know how it feels to take a child's life, I cannot let him do this deed, something that I would ask no one else to do. I will do it myself.

While Zhara speaks of freedom, her eyes show hope, her voice shares freedom, her posture bares strength. Balling my fist by my side, I release a grunt and thrust my fist deep into the core of her swollen belly. Collapsing to the ground in groaning agony, Avery jumps to his feet in surprise. He is ready to become her protector, her angel, but he is not ready to fight me.

Hovering over her body, I tell him, "It is done. I have taken your place as her death dealer. You might have taken a life of a man who deserves it but never of a person you cared for. Never a mother and her child. It will take a few days to make sure it bleeds out of her womb, or if she will die too. I have done my part, now you will watch over her until she passes the child or until she herself dies in your arms."

Walking away, I stop to ask God to forgive me. If he does not, I will never know.

I set out to die a warrior either way.

Over the next few days, I linger in the distance, standing guard over the two as Avery runs back and forth from the waterway to where Zhara lays tucked between large fallen trees and overgrown shrubbery. She is strong in her will, but sometimes that is just not enough to pull through.

Breaking out in chills and cold sweats in the daytime, her body shakes uncontrollably as the night comes. Avery holds her closely for warmth as his body shakes along with hers. There is nothing I can do for either of them at this point. Either she will live, or she will die along with that baby inside of her.

Therefore, it is up to God to look over us all, and up to me to look over them for now.

Morning brings new life with birds singing, water rushing down the stream, hitting rocks as it passes. My stretch allows the sun's rays to warm me and give me strength for the day ahead, as I have been sitting awake all night.

Walking toward Avery, he is body to body with Zhara, giving her his heat. Looking at me with a tear in his eyes, his teeth chattering from the cold, he tells me, "She is dead."

I explain to him this is what happens when we play God. When we put life into the hands of men, we lose.

Placing her head against the ground and covering her arms onto her chest, we begin our journey to catch up with the others at the next point.

Hearing a sudden cough, I turn, ready for battle, knife in hand.

"She is alive!" Avery shouts. Running to her, she has fallen into a deep sleep to help cure herself of impure blood, of that child that grew inside of her. Bleeding deep red blood from her woman's area, it pours from within and puddles around her on top of the ground and all that surrounds it.

Helping her to stand, we encourage her to gather all the strength she can muster and push. Rubbing her belly from top to bottom as Zhara stands, pushing in excruciating pain, we coax the remaining parts of the child out toward the ground.

"The animals will take care of the rest for us," I tell the two, now sulking in one another's presence. "They will carry off what is unwanted, so you can now be free of your past."

Resting for the night, Zhara is constantly brought fresh water to clean herself, and she rests to gather her strength for the journey ahead. We must not stay here much longer, or we will soon be found.

When morning comes, we will head out.

Over the years of bedding many women, never having children of my own, I have always wondered what joy others received from them. Maybe there is a bit of selfishness inside of me, or maybe I was never meant to have children of my own. Maybe if I was to have a child, I would have never run, I would have stayed to fight, to protect them. To die for them.

Maybe I was not meant to have children because I was building for this moment, to fight for their life by sacrificing my own.

I now see Avery is truly one of us. He cares what happens, he stands by our side and does not flee in fear.

.

It is a joyous occasion to finally reunite with the group after many days of traveling with Avery, while taking turns carrying Zhara through the thickness of the brush, bleeding a trail for animals to follow. Many nights we have stayed up chasing predators away from mauling us while we rest, gaining strength to push forward.

She is still weak, and with a fever, but she will live and grow stronger as the days pass.

There, waiting for us at the entrance to the new camp, is Richard. Anxious for our safe arrival, he embraces me with a tight brotherly hug, holding my head like a father holds his child. "It is good to see you, my friend. I grew worried in your absence," he shares with me.

Returning his kind gesture of words, we walk toward the rest of the group of men and talk. I inform him that Zhara is now without the child, weak and with fever. She will need a few days rest to grow stronger.

He explains, "We are in a safe place, a far distance from any land or any man looking to track us down. The brush here is thick with leaves and torturous with thorns to penetrate even the toughest of skin. We will hear anyone approaching from miles away. Our men are set deep into every corner of the woods, high in the trees to keep lookout so we may rest and plan for what is to come. We will need Avery and Zhara to carry out our plan against the Breeders, so here we will stay until they are both ready. Come, my friend, share your stories with us, and give us all something to let our minds have rest away from our surroundings."

Having traveled many days under great stress without the group, I find myself exhausted, yet I am always willing to share a good story.

We have spoken briefly of the plan to attack the Breeders' camp, and the use of Avery and Zhara going in alone. If they can penetrate the camp's walls, we will find their weaknesses, taking them over without much resistance.

We settled around the campfire, the men clasping my hand, glad for my return, and rightfully so. They would not succeed in this madness without my skills.

I paus looking around at each of them in turn before launching into my story.

"Hey, Richard, did I ever tell you about that time I stole that horse and road over to the next town and stole a family full of shoes right off they back porch? Boy, I hid in them woods for a full day, waiting for that family to come out that house looking for them damn shoes. They looked and looked and looked for them shoes. I guess they got tired and went on back

167

in the house to find some more to wear. I figure a family with this big ole house way out in the woods would have lots of shoes, but they all came back outside barefoot and started walking into town without no shoes on they feet.

"I road all the way around to the other side of the road before they were able to cross the path and dropped all them shoes right where they could see them. Hiding in the bushes, I sat back and watched them walk up on they own shoes as if they saw a ghost. They are only shoes! You think they need you to be in them before they just get up and walk away! Hell nah. They walk on they own!

"I ain't never owned a pair of shoes, but if I did, I could only imagine that my feet wouldn't look as good hiding in them shoes rather than being open and free to the air. I like to look at my toes while wiggling them and watching the dirt fall off.

"Man, when they found them shoes, the looks on they face was of pure horror. I laughed so hard and loud I sounded like the grim reaper coming for all of them.

"I rode that horse all the way back to where I stole it from, and before I could get to the farm, I ran smack dead into a posse of fifty men. They snatched me off the top of that horse so quick, grabbed a hundred-foot rope, and strung me up in the biggest tree they could find. I lay up in that tree wiggling, and kicking my feet like a jackass, choking, and dying. The men turned they back on me and started walking up the path. They did they job; they killed another ornery nigga for stealing a horse. I didn't steal it, I just borrowed it for a while.

"I wish I could have seen the face on them jackasses when they turned around and my black ass wasn't still hanging in that damn tree. They can't do to me what I haven't already done to myself. I know they hang niggas, so why am I not going to practice hanging myself? Every chance I got, I would practice making a noose and hanging myself in the barn. I would hang there for hours, even taking a nap or two until I got bored of hanging around and wiggled my way out.

"There is a keen way of getting your neck out of a tight noose, I almost killed myself a few times. They want to whip a nigga; well, I whip myself good. I got welts on my back not from getting whipped by them whites but from whipping my own black ass. I would bare my skin down to the muscles till I couldn't move, then I would lay on the ground, rubbing my back in the dirt to stop the wounds from bleeding, then head to the water hole to clean them out. Ain't nobody going to do to me, what I haven't already done to myself. I will wiggle my toes in your face, and if you chop them off, I will grow them back, because I have already chopped them off to eat them just to see how good I taste and grew them back on my own.

"One day, I am going to chop my whole arm off, tie it to my back, so that way I know how it feels to whoop another man's ass with one hand behind my back. I ain't playing! Can't no white do to me what I ain't willing to do to myself.

"Avery, are you willing to die for what you believe in, boy? You going to have to become everything you hate, everything you despise, you going to have to become white. Boy, you so white, that when other white folk stand next to you, they call themselves niggas.

"You going to have to take that girl Zhara there and act like she your slave and try to sell her off to them whites at the camp. Ain't that just funny, a slave owning a slave. I ain't never seen such a hoopla.

"If y'all make it out safely, then they all die. If not, well, then guess you don't have to worry about being a nigga slave anymore, so, good luck!

Avery

That man Cheeks doesn't like me much, but he is a good man. I see it in his eyes.

He could have left us behind, but he didn't.

Even though we struggled together bringing along Zhara, he still looks at me as a useless boy, a purebred white. I can understand his resistance to accept me among the men, but no matter what his thoughts are of me, I will stay strong and focused on getting at these Breeders.

When will this all end? Maybe after all the Breeders and their controllers are all dead, we can move toward the North, where I hear there are free men and women. Free to roam and own land, raise cattle and a family. I have never met a free black, or anyone from the North, but I imagine the rumors are true if they are told from generation through generation. I would only hope these rumors hold truth, if not, then running for my life will go on for the rest of my life, until I decide enough is enough.

Zhara is weakened from pouring out her child. Her fever does not go away quick enough and causes her to sleep all day and night. She seems to grow stronger by the day, but the men are anxious to leave this camp behind. Afraid of sitting still too long for fear of detection.

The group continues to plot our plan to invade the camp. Growing more and more afraid by the minute, I know that my part is important to our success, and if I am to fail, we will all fail and die. Having to keep in mind I must cut off my hair and clean myself to only become what I hate; my skin is what will get us into the camp.

I am sure I will find it almost impossible to smile and stand around with those whites who were responsible for taking advantage of my people on the farm that Christmas day. I must hold my anger to learn how we can dismantle them without much resistance. The best time to attack is when these powerful men are most vulnerable. When the controllers are at their worst, when no one can sound an alarm to our presence.

Our plan depends on Zhara being well enough to walk. If she does not make it through, strong enough to stand without collapsing, I do not know where our plan will take us. Remaining close by her side over the next few days, I sit and watch her grow stronger with each sunrise.

The same day all the men decide to abandon the campsite, leaving Zhara behind and making a new plan, she sits up.

Barely able to sit up straight for too long, the men gather around both me and Zhara and gave her the full rundown of the plan. She will play my nigga slave girl that I want to sell to settle a debt, but I will still be looking for work for the season from the camp controllers. Anything they have for me on their land, I am willing to do. Some of the men have gone into town

171

and stolen some clothes to provide me with, they have cut the mangled hair from my head.

Zhara, having had close favor with her master and his wife, helped to show me how I can best act like a white.

This is hard, I never knew I could be something I am not. Cheeks takes every chance he gets to make fun of me even more now than he did before. His white jokes toward me get more and more irritating, but Richard tells me if he makes fun of me, it's because he cares. I tried making a snap back at him, but apparently, I am just not very funny. All the men went silent, then busted out in hysterical laughter at my sad attempt at poking back at Cheeks. I will leave that up to him and keep myself learning about pretending to play something I am not cut out for.

Zhara has cleaned herself from her bloody child experience, only to get draped in tattered and torn cloth fit for a slave girl. She claims to have mustered enough within her to move forward with our plan, I can tell she only puts on a good face for the other men. She cannot appear weak or frail in front of the men. They are all expecting so much from her, a matter of life and death for either them or us.

Tomorrow will bring a day of reckoning for Zhara and myself. We make our final preparations to play our characters well enough to get into the camp of the Breeders. If she shows that she is weak, then she will not fetch any coinage for trade, and all will be lost.

Surrounded by the men, and Zhara, we must pray we have success. We all grab one another's hand in a circle around the campfire as I begin our prayer,

"Seeing the crowds, he went up on the mountain, and when he sat down, his disciples came to him. And he opened his mouth and taught them, saying: 'Blessed are the poor in spirit, for theirs is the kingdom of heaven. Blessed are those who mourn, for they shall be comforted. Blessed are the meek, for they shall inherit the earth.'

"For he is God's servant for your good. But if you do wrong, be afraid, for he does not bear the sword in vain. For he is the servant of God, an avenger who carries out God's wrath on the wrongdoer.

"Eye for eye, tooth for tooth, hand for hand, foot for foot, burn for burn, wound for wound, stripe for stripe.

"Amen…"

Putting on clothes the men have taken for me to wear, I am supposed to feel like a new person, but I only feel like a fake, a fraud, a masked man hiding behind falseness.

There is a feeling of betrayal that overwhelms me to the core. A man puts on clothes to change his identify, but black is not an identity easily shed with clothes, it is a hard life unwritten in history for us to obey.

The men have found some thin rope for me to bind Zhara's hands together to give the appearance of control of my slave.

I do not like this feeling that overtakes me, I am no longer comfortable with what is about to happen, but I know it is a necessary evil for us to portray what we hate the most. I guess we must become what we hate if we are to conquer those who destroy us, becoming thinkers of their same thoughts, their same actions, their movements before they move.

Walking closer to the door of the Breeders' camp's house, my knees begin to weaken, my palms and head sweat uncontrollably. Zhara seems pale and weakened, but I cannot help her or else someone might see and know we are false.

Straightening up, realizing there is no turning back, I take an extremely deep breath, stand erect and proud, and continue my path.

I am no longer a nigga slave, I am a white, and this is my slave girl.

Looking over at Zhara walking on unsteady legs, she sways from one side of the path to the other. In the distance, I see a man coming our way on his horse, I rear back my right arm, and give a big push to the back side of Zhara, causing her to fall helplessly to the ground. Laying there in pain, I hover over her shouting profanities at her, as she is useless and pitiful for a nigga girl.

The man rides past us, as I take a quick break from my ways to give him a quick head nod, then return to my yelling. Once the man has long passed gone down the roadway, unable to have us within his immediate sight, I apologize to Zhara for causing her so much pain and help her to her feet.

This weakness in my heart will get us both killed if I do not act according to the white law toward niggas.

Grabbing her by the rope binding her hands, I lead her toward the house. It may appear to others as if I am controlling her movements, but we both know now that I am helping her stay on her feet, helping her to not collapse again. I am giving her time to recover before entering the den of animals.

Arriving at the door, we stand for a second, fearful of what is behind it. Wondering if we will be invited in. I knock softly, timid, not really wanting anyone to answer. Zhara picks her head up, stands strong in her weakened state, and encourages me in a low tone to knock harder. Taking in another deep breath, then exhaling, I rub my hands together for better circulation of my blood and knock hard, as if to bang down the door.

Immediately, a large man swings open the large door, startling me, causing me to take a full step backward. Staring back at the large white man, I inform him of my want to sell my nigga slave girl. I am no longer in need of her and desire coinage and a job in return. Saying nothing in return, the man slams the door in my face. Wondering if he will return, I stand confused, looking at Zhara as she looks back at the ground. should I turn and walk away?

Instead, my fear is fueled by hatred to get inside, behind those walls. I knock again, even harder than I did before, and the man re-opens the door. Grabbing me by my shirt and shoulders, he slams me to the side of the house, yelling that they do not wish to purchase any ragged slave girl from some ragged white man, who looks like he stole the slave from her real master. Shoved against the ground, unable move the man's heavy grasp from my clothing, I wittingly spit a story of falling on hard times, gambling too much, and losing my family, and am in need of work and coinage.

He stares deep into my eyes. I can see his eyeballs shaking inside his head, his nose breaths smoke from him like a bull in a cold pasture. Grabbing me from the ground to my feet, the man releases me and allows me to straighten my clothes before looking over at Zhara.

Walking over to her, I am afraid he will harm her where she stands. Grabbing her face with one of his hands, he forcefully opens her mouth to inspect the inside. She squints her eyes, as he makes her open them to see how they look, are they clear, are they yellow, are they healthy.

The man fluffs at her body as if he is looking for soft portions of a woman. I can see that Zhara is in pain, but she does not allow the man to catch a glimpse of it, but I know, I can't tell she holds fast, trying not to collapse or scream in agony, she is strong.

With his inspection complete, he seems satisfied of the property I carry for sell. I am invited into the house, while Zhara is commanded to wait there. She is not allowed in the house until summoned. She must remain in her painful state just a little bit longer, hopefully.

Escorted through darkened pathways throughout the large house, I am pushed down to sit in a hard chair with no one around. Have they found out who I am already, that I am a complete fraud? My legs cannot stop shaking, and the man hovering over me notices.

As he's starting to pull out his carving knife from his waist, the door on the other side of the room opens, and in walks a very short, very large man with a hat on. The peacock feather that stands on his hat taller than he is makes me crack a small smile, but I quickly realize where I am, and it would not be appropriate to laugh at the man.

Carrying a large cigar in one hand and a libation in the other like my master used to do, the man greets me with lots of cheer, welcoming me to his home and apologizing for the way his man has treated me. Offering me a sip of whiskey, I inform the man of my position to sell a healthy and strong slave girl. Good for cooking and taking care of children, making good clothes. Ignoring what I have informed him of, he laughs a strong laugh, and asks my name. "Aver..." I pause for a moment and realize I cannot tell him my real name or else I take the chance of being discovered, I continue, "My name is

Adam. Yes, Adam Pickley, sir." Wow, if that doesn't sound like a white name if I ever heard one, then I don't know what is.

"Pickley, huh? Hmm… Never heard of a Pickley around these parts, son. Sure you are who you say you are?"

Knowing I must stay strong or else death will come my way, I firmly thrash out, "I am who I say I am!"

He chuckles. "Well, calm down, young man, we can't be too careful around here, ya know. We must make sure you are who you are, or else you take the chance of now walking out of here with your own legs carrying you. And where is this nigga slave girl you speak about so grandly? Bring her in here." He points his stubby fat fingers toward the man who stands guard over me to go fetch Zhara outside.

Turning his attention back to me, he croons, "By the way, how rude of me… I am Charles Heyward, everyone calls me Charlie, but you can call me Mr. Heyward, Adam."

Hearing his name brings a bad vibe to me. I have heard that last name someplace before but am unsure of where, as my memory escapes me for now.

While Zhara is finally brought in the room and pranced around to check her stature for weaknesses, I recall that Heyward was the last name of the mayor I killed who tried to hurt Lipi. His family is the heir to his fortune, and they are the controllers of the Breeders.

Pushing Zhara to stand in a corner furthest away from Mr. Heyward quickly brings me back to the place where we stand. "She is a frail one," the man shouts. "But she will do for what I need her for… I will give you one hundred dollars for your troubles, and that is being generous!"

Remembering what the men in the group told me, if I accept his first offer, which will not even be close to what she is worth, turn it down and walk out.

"Sir, do not offend me with your games. I may look like a boy, but I know the value of my slave. She can fetch three times that amount!" I counter, pausing to judge his reaction.

Mr. Heyward sits back in his chair, inhales his cigar, and lets out a huge puff of smoke that fills the air like fog. "I hear you are seeking work, boy? And I seem to be in a generous mood today, so... I will give you two hundred dollars for your nigga girl and set you to work for me, where you can make a bit more. If you keep your nose clean around here and mind your own, you might have a future here amongst us. We are like family around here. My uncle has created a fine business here, passed down to me after his untimely death. I am a visionary man, a modern-day Picasso, in the middle of creating my masterpiece."

Having taken the chance to negotiate a price for Zhara, I now worry what will happen to her. I know that she is strong, but in her current physical state, she might not survive much longer without rest and food.

I interrupt our moment of final negotiation, insisting, "My nigga girl must rest. If you want her to be able to show all her talents, she must rest and receive a day's food to regather herself from the extremely long journey we have taken to get here."

"Don't you mean... *my* slave girl?" he snidely responds.

Agreeing to my request, Zhara is taken off toward a room in the house, where Mr. Heyward has promised to take good care of his new house lady. "My house niggas are well taken care of. Can't have guests coming over seeing them weak and unkept, now, can we?"

Pulling out his billfold from the drawer in his desk, he starts laying out money on top. I am unsure of what two hundred dollars look like, as I have only seen coinage in the hands of Momma Ruby at the marketplace. Finishing counting the money, he covers the small stack with his hand and pushes it toward the other side of the desk where I sit for me to count. I am unable to count, and he knows that. He is a sneaky man, and I know his kind, I have seen his kind. They are all sneaky and conniving and cannot be trusted. I jump up in anger and tell him to pay me the money I am deserved and stop playing games with me.

Mr. Heyward sits back and laughs again. As he starts counting more money from his billfold, he smugly responds, "Just checking, boy, just checking," as he pulls more money out and sets it on top of the rest of the stack.

Informing him that I am no fool, he agrees to give me work tending to his property. His prized property of animals that he carries around for work. He offers me a room to stay in on the property out back and tells his man to get me some blankets before I catch a cold and wither away.

Stuffing my money into my newfound pockets, I begin to follow the man out of the room. I am immediately stopped in my tracks by the sound of Mr. Heyward's voice, "Hey, boy… Did you forget something?"

Unsure of what he speaks of, I turn to him and stare. Beneath his hand is a piece of paper. He has sat his drink down and traded it for a writing pen. "To make this here sale of this nigga slave, I need a Bill of Sale, a receipt for this nigga, or else someone might try to hang me by my neck for stealing

179

their property. And... well… we can't have that, now, can we? Sign here, Mr. Adam Pickley." Not hesitating even for a moment, I briskly walk over to the desk, pick up the pen, scribble a circle on the paper, slam the pen down, and walk away. "Show me my room please, sir, thank you!" I spit at Mr. Heyward's helper, and we exit the room.

I have never been so scared before in my whole entire life.

Putting together my things and getting ready to rest for the night, I can't help but have Zhara in my thoughts. When all has fallen quiet, and all I hear is snoring from every corner of the camp, I sneak my way over to the window of where Zhara was taken. Sneaking a peek inside, I am relieved to find she is resting, with a plate of empty food next to her. She has been fed well and given rest, just as he said he would. Even though he is a man of his word, he is still my enemy, but I thank him for making Zhara well again soon.

Morning comes and the same man from the night before comes to escort me towards where I am to work. We walk what seems like forever, as this is a large piece of land Mr. Heyward controls. It is almost a little town inside of a little town, so many different buildings to choose from. I wonder which one holds the Breeders. There are many slaves around, doing their work, children running at play as if they have no care of trouble. Before coming here, I imagine this to be horrid with caged animals, slaves chained hard at work, people being beaten and left for dead, but his is not what I had in mind. Everyone looks happy as the wave at me when we pass by and go back to what they are doing. There are some salve women in the distance tending to their own gardens, while kids are playing with domestic dogs. Continuing to walk up and around the pathways, we come directly to a large building surrounded by fields of vegetables and flowers. Nervous for my first day's work, we walk towards a small shed just on the side of the building. Opening the door, the man points to a stack of pales and directs me to fill them all up, and line them together. Walking away, I am compelled to ask him what the water is for, but I do not. Grabbing a few pales in hand, looking around the vast property, I am not sure where to retrieve the water from to fill the pales. Catching the eyes of one of the slave girls playing with her pet dog, she simply points. Looking at her looking at me, I smile and nod my thank you to her. Beginning to head in the direction she has pointed me, I only take a few steps before the door to the building opens, and laughter is heard coming from it. Looking into the blank opening of the door, there stands no one, only voices. Laughing and joking men start to pile out of the house. Very large, perfectly built, healthy and carefree men. It is the Breeders. Shocked at coming face to face with my enemy, the large group of men come directly towards me, until they are right on top of me. They pass right by me as if they hardly noticed me standing there. I am ready to pounce on each one of them. Feeling like beating them down, I desperately want to remind them of the torture they brought upon my farm, the gifts they wrongfully took from our women, the Christmas we will never forget, but I cannot. I stare at each one of them as they pass by me, I have hatred in my blood flowing through me, encouraging me to kill them all. I tell myself, in time Avery, in time. Richard has set a plan in motion, and we must all stick to the plan. With my heart pounding, and my arms trembling, I head off to fill the pales with water. Having lined them all up in front of the building, the man returns and tells me to take them inside. I do not want to go inside that place, where they stay, where they eat, where they sleep. Evil lives there, and it might take me over, smothering me from life. Grabbing a pale by its handle with both hands, creaking the door open with my foot, the grandness of this place causes me to gasp. Covered from wall to wall, the floor is filled with places to sit, pillows to rest on, and the furs of animals far and near for comfort. Piled in every corner of the place is the carcass of animals eaten to their bones, discarded. This is not the castle of kings, but a filthy place that holds men not worthy to be called men. They are the same as the filth they lay with. Entering the room, stepping over leftover bones and skin, I wonder where to sat down the water, what is the water for. sitting down the two pales that I have carried in, I turn to retrieve more, standing in the doorway is the man who brought me here. He asks me, why do I put the water down on the floor, when I should be using it to clean. That is why I am here, to clean the filth of the men who soiled my land? Knowing I must care for these beastly animals, knowing that Mr. Heyward calls him his prized property, and he takes them from town to town, I am sickened by the thought my task. I must do as I am told to keep anyone from suspecting I am here under false pretenses. I plan on killing these men, where they lay.

Knowing I have found where the Breeders lay at night, I must find a way to excuse myself from my duties, making my way back to the group to let them know what I have found. When night comes, and all are asleep, I work my way towards the end of the property headed to the hills. Suddenly, I am stopped at the sight of the same man blocking my direction. Questioning where I am sneaking off to in the middle of the night, and petrified he will harm me, I plead with him to let me go to see my sick and dying mother. He grabs me by my neck and lifts me from my feet. Dangling at the tips of his hands, my feet kick wildly, my hands hold his trying to loosen his grip, unsuccessfully. With death staring at me again, thoughts of failure come to mind. I have let everyone down who depended on me. Not careful enough in my ways, I did not see the dangers ahead, blinded by anger. What will happen to Zhara as he lay in the hands of Mr. Heyward, it is my fault I put her there. I walked her directly into the den of the Controllers and handed her over. Suddenly, as I am blacking out, I am released to plow against the ground, my limp body crashing down. My vision blurred from lack of air, my head pounding from lack of blood, Zhara stands over me with a knife in hand. She has penetrated the heart of the man through his spine, dropping him right there. It is good to see my friend up and healthy again. She looks good, even in the shadows of night, I can tell from her voice she is back to normal. Embracing one another, we realize this body must disappear, out of sight for no one to find. We work throughout the night dragging the body as far away from the Breeders camp as possible. When we stumble upon a cliff side with a creak below, grabbing both ends we toss him over the side. Satisfied of what we have done to hide our mistake for being caught, we decide to part ways. Zhara must return to the Breeders camp, and I must keep moving to find the others, sharing my information with them to further plot our attack. Walking for hours, I am surprised by someone wrestling me down to the grown. Immediately the man notices it is me, and I notice it is Cheeks. He is looking at me the same way he did when he first attacked me with a knife to my throat where the dog's fights happened. Scared he will finally have his wishes of killing me, he smiles in my face and kisses my forehead. Lifting me off the ground, he thanks the Lord for my return, as he hoped I was dead. He is not that funny to me, hoping I was dead. Informing the rest of the group of the Breeders location, and giving them the layout of the land, Richard and Cheeks plan to attack at dawn the next day. The Breeders will be tired and resting from too many libations, and food. Over-filled from eating way too much, they will be lethargic, and slow in their reaction. They are not warriors prepared for battle, they are lazy men groomed for battle with women, not men. Having completed my task, my eyes will not close to get rest, tomorrow will come quickly and I must be prepared.

Expecting an early raid of the Breeders, I wait in anticipation, Zhara knows she must take to the hills when it all starts happening. Even though she is better, she is not strong enough for the fight. Morning comes and goes with no sign of the men. Have they abandoned us without any sign? Have they coward at the sight of these perfectly formed men? Many thoughts run through my head, but whatever it is, I must now find a way out for me and Zhara. They will not look for me, but they will surely send trackers out after Zhara for missing. For now, I must go about my day as if nothing is wrong. Fetching and filling the pales of water to go clean the Breeders quarters, one of them stop me and demands I bring them fresh water for drinking. Filled with anger at the request, I take my time walking the stream picking various berries on the way. sitting at the water's edge, I suddenly start violently vomiting all the berries I have eaten. My stomach is cramping, my eyes are heavy, sweat pours from my skin soaking my clothing to the insides of my shoes. Laying in pain for hours, making my way back to my feet, I gather as many berries as I can and fill the pales. Running back to get more pales, I fill the others with water from the stream. I have left the water and all the berries at the doorstep of the Breeders and knock. They are surprised I have come bearing gifts for them and quickly start devouring what I have brought. The berries may not kill them, but at least it will give me some satisfaction they will feel like death is upon them for the night. Tired and drained from another full day's work, I lay down to figure how to get Zhara out. There is chatter amongst Mr. Heyward and the men as to where the big man has run off to. Where could he be, but no one asks me or even tells me that he is missing. It will be just a matter of time before worry sets in, and they go looking for him. If his body has not yet floated down stream, they will know he has met with foul play, with murder. With eyes no longer able to keep me awake, I allow myself to rest for the night.

Awakened at the sound of screaming, and immediately rising to my feet in fear. I listen for what is going on. The screams are at a far distance, it is coming from the Breeders. Quickly putting on my shoes and running on the backside of the land towards where the Breeders sleep, there is fire burning the quarters of the Breeders. Flames from torches surround the house, as the men throw them inside of every opening to the house. Finding a large tree, taking cover as to not be seen, my face glows from the lit building. One by one as the Breeders burst out, running from being burned alive, the men pounce, cutting each one down as flames cover them refusing to go out. Skins of the men roll off, exposing the meat below. They are weak, exhausted, ill from the berries they have eaten earlier, unable to defend themselves from our onslaught. They are easily overtaken and killed. Death comes to them quickly and without mercy, and I am happy to sit and watch it all happen. This is for Trita, and Hoof, and all the women they have ever taken from. God may have mercy on the souls of these men, as we do not.

Amongst the commotion of death, Zhara comes to mind. The others will soon come to the end of the land to see what has happened. The flames will guide them here quickly, as they will worry about the well-being of their precious prized property. That will give us time to sneak out the other direction and head for the hills to meet with the group. Running back towards where Zhara lay in the house, I run directly into Mr. Heyward, "What is happening boy?". "The men set their house on fire and is burning. Run sir, run! The flames will overtake us all if we don't!" Believing that is the truth, he runs towards the end of the property to see for himself. Grabbing Zhara from her sleep, we make our way through the night, disappearing towards the hills.

Returning to our previous camp, the men are all exhausted from their fight with the Breeders. Richard speaks of how he came across the head Controller, snuck up behind him and cut his throat. Leaving him for dead, Cheeks took his head off and sat it, staring at the burning building for him to see what he has created, and we have destroyed at the will of God. We have corrected what was wronged by mans greed. His will to create and destroy. We are bunching together our supplies to hurry on our way when we are ambushed without warning. Men in trees, hidden within the surface of the ground behind thickened brush attack from all sides. Their weapons penetrate the flesh of men running for cover behind fallen trees. There is no escape. They have lured us back into our hiding place and allowed us to feel safe before violently attacking. Crawling in the brush, bullets whisk passed my head, the ground is cold and wet with blood spilled by others. My head cannot stay up long enough to locate Richard or Zhara. Getting up from my hiding place I decide to run for it. Standing up to run, I am tackled back to the ground, it is Zhara laying her body on top of mine to keep me from moving, Richard by her side. If we are going to die, at least we are all going to die together. We have killed off the Breeders, and their men have come back to take revenge. Hunkered down just off the side of the hill, the deadly militia draws closer to our hiding place. Charging towards us is a familiar face, bloody and battered, he has been wounded by a shot to the shoulder and ear. It is Cheeks, the warrior, the beast, the teller of many tales. "We must flee! We must go our own ways or else we will all die here today!". We must not separate, we are a family, and must stick together. It is better to be in a group to help one another than it is to go it alone. We must stay together at all costs. Believing we are going to be over-run and killed, Richard agrees with Cheeks. Our best chance for survival is to separate, creating distance between us, so it will force their troops to thin out over the land. "We will go in pairs! Me and Avery, Zhara and Cheeks. If we are to survive, we will meet at the old canyon to the north that we spoke about." Even though I have grown to love Richard as a father to me, my heart hurts for Zhara to leave, she must be allowed to come with us. She must not leave my side, she needs me, and I need her. Grabbing her hand, I tell her to come with us, she refuses. I beg her again to come with us, she refuses again.

Tugging at her arm for her not to leave me, Cheeks quickly pulls her from me, heading down the hill towards a cliffs edge. Disappearing into the distance, Richard grabs a hold of me and forces me to run with him in the opposite direction. Looking back over my shoulder as we make distance between us and the militia firing their weapons all around, we slide uncontrollably down the side of the mountain, crashing into every bush and tree we tried to go past. Slamming with unmeasurable force to the ground below, we are both knocked unconscious. Barely breathing and unable to move, we lay stuck in the dense brush, hidden from others, unable to be seen from any direction. Thankful we are still alive, but unable to carry on any further, I rest awaiting death to sneak up on me and take me.

Richard

After coming to and finding Avery lying next to me in the bush still alive, I realized we are on our own. I worry about my friend Cheeks out there in the world, trudging through the land without me. He is a resourceful man, able to take care of his own, to watch his own hide. We have been through many battles together, many laughs, many of his stories. I hope to see my friend again someday. We lay here in this thick brush for two full nights, listening to men walking all around us, surrounding us at times, standing right on top of us at others. We dare not breath at moments, or else they will notice our position. Nights are filled with small critters crawling about our body and face. We take turns capturing bugs that crawl on us and eating them to keep from starving. Normally I would not like to sit in one place for too long, but we are safe sitting right here until the men that constantly, and unknowingly surround us move out and move on. When I am able to catch a few moments of sleep these last few nights, my dreams are filled with the images of that man. The main Controller who's throat I slit from end to end, Mr. Heyward. I knew of him from when I was breeding, he is the nephew of Mayor Heyward. Now he was running the show, inheriting all the Breeders and Controllers to keep it going. Well, no longer will he thrive off the backs of our people, using us to destroy our own. My stomach still becomes sick of the thought of what we have done to those women on the farms, throughout the towns we visited. Hopefully God will forgive me for the wrong I have done. If I am to die today, without moving forward one more inch, I will accept going home to lay in peace.

It is hard out here without Cheeks and the others. We were a family. Once the men who were always on our trail finally tracked us down, and ambushed us, I knew we had to get as far away as we possibly can. We have been traveling mostly at night and taking turns resting and taking watch in the day. Going from farm to farm taking food from the fields, traveling along the shallow edges of the stream to grab fish struggling close to its surface. Working daily to trap small animals in deep holes, dug with the edges of rocks, and limbs of trees laying on the forest floor. We throw whatever scraps we have saved on for from other animals to lure them to our traps. Trying hard to maintain our bodies strength, and our minds sharpness, always on the lookout for attacks, I can't help but think, where we are going. We walk as if I am sure, as if I am in command, but I have never traveled these parts or most parts of this land, as I am sure neither has Avery. He has grown into a fine young man, with many strengths. His ability to remember is more than I have ever seen in any man or woman. His hair has grown back into a matted mess, his clothes are torn from trekking through treacherous land, taking off his shoes and leaving them behind he tramples the land barefoot again. He complains they are uncomfortable, and do not allow his feet to cling freely to the earth. They slow him down. We constantly walk north, following the north star as my former master had always taught me if I was lost. Either way his small advice has given us a direction to travel, a way to roam. Eventually we will arrive at a place where maybe we can rest or be safe for at least a few days to get proper rest for us to move on.

We have not seen much of anything for the past few days. There are no streams or animals coming our direction. Exhausted, hungry, and thirsty, we work our way to the top of a high ridge so we can look about and see what is around us. It does not feel as if anyone is following us or trying to track us down. Maybe they think we are dead like all the others. Or maybe they have lost our scent in all the madness, either way my head does not feel the pressure of someone on our heels. Overlooking the greatness of this place we are now, there is nothing in sight. Nothing for miles and miles around us, except more and more large trees to shelter us from view, to shade us from the days sun, to keep us tired and weary. Spending so much time alone with Avery, I want to tell him that I am sorry for all his losses. I am sorry for what the Breeders have done to his family, his farm, to his home, but my tongue feels it is not time yet. I can't help but to wonder though. Why does he not get up and walk to freedom? He continues to run as if they are chasing him, but he does not realize, they are not chasing him. They have never been chasing him. They are chasing us niggas, us runaways, they chase our skin not his. He has made our fight his fight, struggling right along with us, but his fight is not the same as ours. I sit and look at him, and know he fights his own war deep within himself. How did he come into being a slave? A purebred white slave? I have seen many who have mixed with the whites at the hands of their master's lust. They carry both the whites and the black's blood in them. Their features are of both, black and white, but this Avery is not of one and the other, he is of only one. I do not know who has given this boy life, but whoever raised him raised a good man. One day he will figure it out for himself, but until then he remains with me.

We continue following the stars, leading us into what seems to go on forever without arriving in a place that appears safe. Hiding in the shadows of the trees we have spent many days and nights observing farmhouses and towns, sharing information between us about who seems to be who. Where people go, and what they do most of the day. Trying to find other blacks who can help us or lead us in a better direction, we have not found any, it appears the further north we get the less nigga slaves there are for us to lean on for help, for food, for water. Happening to come across a small farmhouse in the middle of nowhere, we need to seek shelter from this night's sudden freeze. We fill the chill in the air, and there is no other option or else we will freeze do death out here. Crawling underneath a short wooden fence along the tree line, hiding ourselves within the tall blades of the grass, we make our way on the backside of the farm. The small home on this land appears deep in a sleep, as there is only one small, dimmed light coming from a small window at the peak of the home. It flickers side to side as if a shadow dances in its wake. Sparking the attention of horses, and goats as we crawl pass them, they shuffle their hooves and scamper about, stirring one another up. Continuing towards the backside of the barn, coming to a large area piled to the roof with hay, we hunker deep inside. Covering ourselves with as much hay and debris as possible, shoulder to shoulder to keep safe and warm, we settle in for the night. We must not oversleep, or else we run the risk of a long rifle in our face, and a noose around our necks.

Morning brings a new day; we have slept a bit longer than expected. Our bodies must have taken more of a beating lately than normal, as we have moved quickly from place to place searching for food, and more water. Not wanting to make any sudden movements as to startle the livestock around us, there is a familiar double click. Frozen, not wanting to make any sudden movements, the end of a rifle clears the brush from my face to reveal me staring out. Still sleeping next to me, Avery goes unaware of the danger we are in, as he too turns to rise and stretch. His movement stuns the little girl standing above us in the barn, pointing a long rifle which appears larger than she is. She is a young girl, with a pretty dress on and dirty boots, she appears to mean business. Calling out to her Ma and Pa, we dare not make a move or self we might find ourselves deader than dead at the end of a rifle held by a little girl. If she wanted us dead, she would have already pulled the trigger with her tiny fingers that rest on it so eagerly. Banging at the side door still latched by a long wood slide, she keeps her eyes focused on us as she walks backwards to dislodge the door with one hand. Rushing in to see what is going on, her Pa with his handgun in hand, Ma with a crafty field tool, they insist she moves back away from us, "Get back! Get back now ya hear! These probably be those dangerous heathens we heard about. Them escaped boys!" He holds his gun steady at me, walking sideways but getting closer as he speaks. "Look here. This one caught him a little white boy. Holding him hostage for some ransom or something huh. Wait till the Sheriff get a hold of you boy. You going to hang for sure!". Daring not to say much for fear of my head going missing from my body, I can't help to speak out, "We ain't escape from nowhere sir. This here ain't no hostage for no ransom. This here is my master. We lost our way when some men tried to ambush us for our cargo, leaving us for dead a long way from home sir. We didn't mean any harm sir. We will get on our way, right away, if you just go ahead and put them guns away from our heads." He does not look convinced, but more confused than ever that I spoke before my master. Unknowingly, nudging Avery to speak out, he asserts himself with the farmer, "look here good man. I am a good Christian man in a bad place. Is this how one treats their neighbor in need? I am cold and hungry, and my nigga here needs tending to for our long journey. Let him care for your animals this morning, in return, maybe you can provide us with something to eat, and some water to carry with us home?" While speaking to the family, Avery has worked his way to his feet, brushed himself off from the bed of hay to reach out and shake the man's hand, thanking him for saving us. Reluctantly welcoming him into the house, the family turns to walk away, Avery walking right along with them. The man pauses, turning towards me, "When you done picking up after them animals, you come on to the house and get something to eat, hear?", with hesitation, and somewhat surprised at his sudden invitation, "Yes.....Yes sir, will do.", as I nod and shuffle to my feet to work.

Walking towards the house after finishing taking care of the few animals they have on the farm, I dare not walk in the open fields, but take a route closer to the backside of each building just in case we are watched from the trees. Reaching the porch, the family and Avery sit, eating and talking. Seeing that I am standing there, Avery stops what he is doing and stands up. Understanding the relationship between slave and master I quickly put my head to the ground to not look him directly in the eye. He is confused at my actions. He is expecting me to greet him as a friend, yet if I do this family will discover we are not who we say we are. A silence comes over the porch, earie as haunted land filled with silent prayers, until the farmer speaks, "Glad you finally made it, I started to wonder if you crawled up into one of them damn animals and died off! He lays out an unsure chuckle towards me, and his family. "Come on up here and fill your stomach with some of this good food the misses made. It ain't that good but she still does it with lots of love.". Lifting my head, I realize this family does not care that I am a black, that I am a slave. They welcome me to their table and feed me as if I am one of them. I have not sat at a table with a white, since my master and I would share meals and a laugh at night after he had cheated someone out of their money gambling. It feels good to rest and have a meal with a family who doesn't see the color of my skin, but another person sitting across from them enjoying the same meal as them. "I'm Tim... This is my wife Cookie, my oldest child here is my boy Champ, and my baby girl, princess Christy-Marie. We don't have much, but what we have we are willing to share with you all. We can give you a place to rest in the barn back there where you were, except instead of you all sleeping with the hay, we can provide some blankets to keep you from catching cold. Then you can get on your way to wherever it is you all are heading.". He is a kind looking man, I can look into his eyes and see his good nature, but he knows we are not who we say we are. I can tell he knows something more than he is putting on. Staying a few more days, we help around the farm feeding and cleaning the animals, gathering, and chopping wood, setting it aside the house, and fixing things that need fixing. The boy and girl run around having a good ole time, chasing each other here and there, laughing and rolling around the fields. Their Ma and Pa always getting on them about doing their chores and getting to work, but they keep running about, freely ignoring the demands. It's a nice place here, always work to do, from sunup till sundown, followed by not so good meals. She doesn't cook very well, mostly burnt food that taste like bricks, but at least Cookie cooks us food, so we eat it. Avery seems to adapt well to the family, and they adapt well to him. I can tell they like him, and probably want

195

him to stick around for a while, but he keeps telling them that we must be on our way soon. Having hinted at the fact we must leave; Mrs. Cookie starts to prepare us food and water pouches to carry with us on our journey. Mr. Tim will carry us as far north as he can before letting us go on to find our way. Having our final day and night come near, our next journey the next day, Mr. Tim decides to send us off by roasting one of his small pigs, instead of hurting our stomachs on the road with Mrs. Cookies bad cooking. Sitting on the porch, we all begin digging in at the meat and vegetable piled on the table, when a voice comes over us.

"Finally, all of you, be like-minded, be sympathetic, love one another, be compassionate and humble.

No one should seek their own good, but the good of others.

Therefore encourage one another and build each other up, just as in fact you are doing.

Keep on loving one another as brothers and sisters. Do not forget to show hospitality to strangers, for by so doing some people have shown hospitality to angels without knowing it.

For the entire law is fulfilled in keeping this one command: "Love your neighbor as yourself."

Amen…"

Avery stands for a moment, eyes closed, head towards the sky. He has moved us all; it feels like time stands still if even for a second. We all stand here, ready to eat and share. Not as whites and blacks but as equals. In the morning, we will go on our way and continue north.

With wagon all loaded up to carry us away, we thank the good family for their warming hospitality, and food for our journey. Accompanied by his young son Champ, Tim takes the reins, slaps at them with a quick snap of his wrist, and off we head down the road. Sitting in the rear with Avery looking back at the farm family in the distance as we draw further and further away, I can tell he misses his own family. He wants a family of his own. Rocking back and forth, the wagon bumping against every rock in the road, I reach my hand out and put it on Avery's shoulder, my other hand on his arm. Sharing a small moment to internally reflect at the possibilities of more peace to come, we both know, they will be far and few.

Mr. Tim

Heading down this road for a few hours now, none of us has spoken more than a word. They have not even asked me where I was taking them. My son Champ cannot stop his chattering about every tree, bird, lizard, animal that he thinks he sees, but no one else can see when he points it out to us. Occasionally, when he calls out an animal, I just keep my head forward, "Oh, yeah... That's nice boy!" and keep our wagon moving. Before long he begins to nod off. I lay a blanket down from the back

197

of my wagon on my lap and lay his head atop the blanket to rest easy. Maybe my mind can rest too now that his mouth no longer blabbers at everything and anything. He is a good boy, just a bit rambunctious, at times a bit high strung. He is a good boy non-the less, my boy. Riding along I can't help but to inquire to where they were coming from and where they were headed to when they were ambushed for their goods. They do not seem like thieves, and they did not come to harm my family in any way, but I have seen a master and his slave, and they are no master and slave. What is it they are hiding, or rather who are they hiding from? "I have seen many parts of this country. In love with this country as much as I am in love with my wife and children. They mean the world to me, and I don't know what I would do with myself if I was to ever have to give them up. Every day I wake up and go out to them fields, feed them animals, plow the land, and work from sunup to sundown, I do it all with them in mind. I understand, family don't have to carry the same blood, or even the same skin, because they share the same beating heart. You two want to tell me what in God's green earth are Y'all really doing out here? You all running, hiding, scheming? ". They just sit there rocking back and forth, looking at me then looking back at one another, seemingly confused at my story, followed by my questions. "Don't worry. I am not here to judge you or turn you in. I have done many things in my life that I am not proud of, that I should have been condemned for, but slavery was not one of them. This slavery business is not one I wish to embark on, nor have anything to do with. But it is here, and it is now, and I need to know what is going on so that I don't put my family in any further danger.". Pausing for a moment to catch my breath from all the talking and trying to keep my voice to a minimum not to awaken my boy still resting on my lap, I hold fast. "Mr. Tim, this here man you see riding with us. He is a warrior, a big man with a big heart and an even bigger dream. He dreams of freedom, of roaming this land without chains, without men chasing at his heels. That man is a nigga slave. He is my friend; he is my brother. We do not share the same blood, but like you said, the same heart. His beats for mine, and mine for his. Unusual circumstances have brought us together and to your home, with your family. It is not that we are running from something, it is that we are running to something. I was born a nigga slave. Everyone I have loved has been murdered at the hands of the whites. Butchered and gutted, beaten, and raped, as I have witnessed it all with my own eyes. You ask what do we run from? With all due respect Mr. Tim, I don't want to remember what we run from anymore...... I much rather think about hope, and what we are running to". Sitting for a few, pondering what I have just heard, I can't help to feel the passion in which Avery speaks, the pain, the hope. He speaks the truth from deep within. "Le garçon ment. Je ne veux pas oublier d'où je viens. Je ne veux pas le laisser derrière moi pour vivre dans un fantasme. je veux me souvenir de tout ce que j'ai laissé pour ne jamais oublier ceux qui sont morts pour que je puisse vivre. ", Richard pauses, "The boy lies. I do not want to forget where I come from. I do not want to leave it behind for me to live in a fantasy. All that I have left behind I want to remember, so that, I never forget those who died so that I may live.....This young man here, this man with only one name, Avery. I did not save his life as he thinks, he saved mine. Many nights, laying in complete darkness, I have doubted my existence, my purpose. Knowing this life will end, but not knowing when or how, was already killing me inside. Just like

199

the animals we hunt for food; they hunt for sport to hang on walls. I do not want to be hunted down like an animal for sport. His words from that book kept me alive. The words he spoke and continues to speak gives not only me hope, but all those who followed, all who heard them, believed in them. No, I did not save his life, he saved mine. And now we both search for a new land, with new life, together.". There remains a long period of silence, as I am taking in all that is being said. The wheels in my head turn from the heartfelt stories they tell of their lives. I too have stories, dreams for my family, fantasies of how this land should be. Without wanting anyone to feel any more uncomfortable, "A white slave, and a black Frenchman, well that's just proof. When you think you seen it all, you ain't!". Chuckling, and with another quick snap of the wrist and reins, I make sure my horses stay steady on our course as close to the state line going north as possible.

Traveling the country for a few days and nights, we set up camp again and again once night fall came over us. Finding out more about these two men and their stories, and how they came to arrive at my farmhouse, I can't help but to think about how this country has disappointed us all. How we are all slaves of some kind to those with money and power. We try so hard to carve out a little bit of heaven in this land, raise our family, be good Christians, but it never seems to be good enough. We pay taxes on everything we buy, even everything we own. It seems we work harder and harder, and still gain more and more of nothing, at least nothing we can truly call our own. Not even our thoughts are our own. They tell us what to think, and how to think it. They tell us who we are supposed to be and how we are supposed to act. Their stories make me wonder, where and when will the change come? What will this land hold for my children, and my children's children? All I have to leave them is that small piece of land, and a rundown house with a bunch of ailing animals barely able to produce much of nothing. This white slave and this black Frenchman are the change. Me, I will drop them at the norths line, so they may carry on and move forward, while I go back to my home, my family, my life.

Early, before the sun has a chance to rise over the mountains, we packed up our belongings back into the wagon, and head off. Hungry for a good bit of breakfast, my stomach talks to me, singing its own tune while the wagon stumbles down the road. Coming around a bend just close to the state line, in the distance I notice a posse full of men on horseback, others standing on the ground. We quickly take notice as they have now noticed us moving in their direction. There are way too many of them for us to try an outrun. We have no choice but to keep moving forward, and hope for the best. Encouraging the two to let me do all the talking, and for my boy to keep quiet, we draw closer and more nervous. Within range of the small posse of men, I notice they are soldiers in uniform. What are they doing here? There is now war going on here, so there is no reason for them to be here, to hold us. Reaching the front line of the soldiers, I slow command my horses to slow down and stop. "Whoa," I command my horses, followed by a click click of my tongue. "Good day gentlemen. What's all the hoopla about?" As I sit back up in my seat, looking over all the troops standing around. "There a way you can make way for us to keep moving on down the road here?". Giving a little chuckle and a smile at the soldier standing there atop his horse, a few troops next to him now taking positions surrounding my wagon, I grow nervous. Looking around my wagon to observe what they were doing, I take my hat off and wipe my forehead, complaining about the morning heat. "Good day!" in a commanding voice, "I am Captain Jerimiah Littleberry of the Union Army, Infantry. Do you have a pass to travel these roads?". Sitting confused as to why I would need a pass to travel a road I have traveled many times before; I sit still looking around at the other troops surrounding my wagon. "If you have not heard already, there is a war happening. The North and the South are at odds. The south has separated from us and wish to rely on their own resources, mainly nigga slaves as their main labor force. We in the Union, don't much like the idea of freeing them, but don't much like the idea of them being held as slaves either. Now, we are seeking good men to fight a good fight, strengthen our numbers. Both blacks and whites to join the Union. Any man or boy old enough to carry and shoot a weapon, we need. Any man who loves his country, we need. Any black who wants to set himself free, we need.". Not wanting to interrupt, I sit fidgeting uncomfortably in my wagon seat, looking about for an answer within my now crowded mind. Just having had the conversation with Avery and Richard about change, and making changes, but not having the chance. Well, now the chance is here, and in my head, I just want to run away, back to my family and my land. Back to my everyday life where on a day-to-day basis, things are simply normal, ordinary. I couldn't leave my family right now, what would my wife and daughter think if I ran off to war and abandoned them to take care of the farm? What would my son do if he didn't have me around to show him how to become a man, how to shoot, hunt, fish, roll the dice, and play cards? No,

I can't volunteer for a war that has nothing to do with me. Looking over at my Champ, these thoughts running over me, he stands on top of his seat, "I will fight!", he must be out of his mind to even think of such words coming from his mouth, "I will fight if no one else will! Me and my Pa, we ain't scared of no body! Ain't that right Pa!". Stunned at his sudden blurt of unrealistic enthusiasm, I quickly grab his harm and sat him in his seat, "Hush down boy. You too young to be fighting in any man's war. Hush down and keep quiet.". Staring him down, almost daring him to attempt another move like the stunt he just pulled, he sits pouting like the boy he is, for not getting his way. Returning my focus back to the captain, attempting to further our uncomfortability to his line of questioning to draft us into their war, when without even one breath being spilled, "I'll fight that war.", my head whips around to see who said that. "I will fight that war, if you going to let me free.", Richard peeks everyone's attention at his sudden plea to join for his freedom. Putting his head back down after his claims, as to not offend the white captain,

Avery abruptly stands and jumps off the back of the wagon and begins walking towards the front side where the captain is, "You know what? War sounds good right about now. War sounds good. Do we get to eat, and sleep in a warm bed?". Avery continues inquiring, but the captain simply nods and gestures in agreement with all he asks. Hopping off the wagon, Richard joins at Avery's side just below where I sit, between myself and the now smiling Captain Littleberry. Pleased to have two more ignoramuses join their war, I am now left looking like a fool in front of my young son. It is time for him to become a man, fight his own war, be his own man. I have taught him all that he needs to know for now to take care of himself. Turning to look at his precious young face, barely able to grow any hair on it, still soft as a baby's bottom, I place my hand on his upper back, "Son, there is a time in every man's life where he makes a choice to live or to die for his family. It's time for you to be a man now, and go fight your own war, find your own way, and become your own man. No more chasing after me asking me what I would do. I already taught you all I can teach you, and you already know what to do." Hesitating to catch my breath, making sure this is the right decision for him and me, "You take these fine horses, and this wagon and you carry yourself home to your mother and sister. You take good care of them, look out for them, be the man." Having to hush him a few more times from him wanting to plead for me to go with him, I had to save his honor in front of the other men standing watch. Leaving all the supplies he would need to carry him through the few days travel back to the farm, I grab a sharp hold of the lead horse, turn him around back in the direction which we came, and give him a hard slap on the rear to get him going. As Champ rolls past me, I can't even look at him in his eyes, knowing he will shed tears, bringing my heart too much pain. I have just sent my boy off into the land, with only food and blankets to keep him long enough to get home. He knows the way as he has traveled these roads with me since he was a tiny one. Always pointing out everything and anything. He knows these roads better than I do; I am sure. Every tree, every stream, every mountain, and valley around every turn. He will be fine, until I return.

Watching my boy disappear down the road to become a man, my heels stay stuck for a moment, embracing the time I still must watch him rolling away. Will I ever see my boy again? When I return will he have already grown into a young man with his own family, my daughter married, my wife still mine? These are no longer my worries to carry, my burdens, my cross to burn. Turning back towards the men, I find they are all frozen in time, staring at the back side of my wagon rolling away. It would appear, they have all gone through the same moment when leaving their families behind. They too know the feeling of abandoning their loved ones for a purpose much bigger than us. A dream for change, a better future for our children, and if not our children, then our children's children. Their war is now my war, my fight, my change.

Captain Jerimiah Littleberry

Traveling the better part of this country searching high and low for any man who would join our fight, we have yet to see any battle. My battalion has been put in charge of roaming and gathering supplies from every farmhouse we come across for a hundred miles. I don't feel good about myself, leaving my own family behind to join this war, but it is my duty to protect the faith of this great nation in which our fathers have bled for. The soles of my boots have worn down to only threads, barely held together with just a few left-over strings. Our troops are unable to receive food and supplies quick enough to keep them strong for the fight. The waiting for our supplies, feels worse than the damage presented by the war itself. More and more of us die each day of dehydration, and starvation, that killed at the hands of the enemy. This land we fight for has become more of an enemy than those who attack from the front. Today we came across two white men and a slave to join our fight. One man had a young boy, not old enough to fight, but not young enough to be a child anymore. He wanted to fight, but his father sent him on his way, back home to look over the farm. Sent him home to take care of his Ma and sis. Having left my family behind for many years now, I felt his hurt, his pain of leaving all you love behind, for all you believe in. Watching this man boy vanish in the distance was like watching my life come to its end. I have yet to understand why this battalion, this group of men that I command, has yet to see any parts of the battle. Why do they hold us in the rear, supplying others who fight with supplies? We are not a supply unit, we are a fighting unit, a unit of two full battalions. On one side we have our Union infantry fighting men, on the other we have our Union blacks trained and ready to fight at a moment's notice. We march up and down these mountains, set up camps and break camps down, only to keep marching. Passing other battalions, we all see the way they look at us, as if we are nothing, as if we are not worthy of saluting, or praise for our efforts. On a nightly, thoughts of my command being foiled by orders to supply troops are constantly interrupted with skirmishes breaking out amongst the white troops and the private we call Avery, one of the men found back on the road to the north. He doesn't appear to fit in with most of the others in the battalion. The white troops and the black troops normally keep to themselves. Each has their own areas they retire to build their camps at night, and they respect that space. This Avery boy tends to cross the lines every chance he gets to go and hang out with his slave Richard, falling asleep next to the fire as if he is one of them. The other blacks in the troop used to complain about him eating with them and hanging with them after sundown, but he seems to feel more at home amongst his slave and the blacks. Tension grows every night he breaks the rules. Although we fight this war of equality, there are still do's and don'ts to this war, and the handling of our troops. I am stuck in the middle here. How do we tell a group of white and blacks to fight together, to fight for one another, to fight for the freedom of all people, and the abolishment of slavery, and yet still separate them at the core? It is up to me as the Commander in charge of these men, to bring them together, to fight as one unit, to see the front lines of war and achieve our goal. I am not without compassion for the black troops, as I have been set in charge to appropriately over-see much of their training, getting them ready for battle. Even though we have been ready for battle at a moment's notice, we continuously fail to receive any orders to proceed. Hearing we are having trouble stopping the flow of supplies to our enemies to the south, I have taken it upon myself to put together a small group of men to move in silence, gathering intelligence about the south. They are responsible for destroying any pipeline of supplies to the Confederate Army, any field they encounter growing food, tobacco, corn, sugar, or anything of use to the souths Army. We will choke off their supplies causing the head to fall off and the body to wilt.

Avery

The captain has forced me to fight with the whites. I am told it is for the best, for the moral of the other troops, but I don't understand how we fight for freedom but don't have the freedom to fight. They have made me and Mr. Tim part of a small platoon of men responsible for roaming the back country deep within enemy lines, behind the fighting to destroy the flow of food and supplies to the Confederate south. We are just a handful of men, not many of us much older than the next, but entrusted to look after one another, keep one another alive. Not agreeing with most their tactics, or beliefs towards the south, I keep to myself majority of the time. Expressing my concerns to Mr. Tim as we spend time marching along, he has become a friend in these times of need. Days are spent marching through clouds of mosquitoes, biting bugs, and snakes squirming about us. Our nights are cold, we don't dare light much of a fire for fear of detection by the south's troops. Most of us are chosen because we are either originally from the south, or volunteered to walk many miles, be on our own. It would appear we are vagrants and thieves, no better than the south, as we do not carry enough supplies to last us through this journey. We are forced to pilferage and plunder farm fields, taking shelter in homes on the way, from the cold nights. Our troop eats, what is sometimes the last bit of scraps from those we take shelter with, denying their family of its own much needed nourishment during these hard times. Although we fight for freedom, this does not feel free. Telling me we must see the bigger picture, that we have no choice but to take so that we may later give, it all seems wrong to me, but every day we repeat the cycle and march on.

We have marched many days and night, over high mountains, and through thick brush tearing at us from every reaching branch that touches our filthy uniforms. Mr. Tim is having a tremendously exhausting time dealing with having left his family behind. He constantly complains as to why we are here, deep in the woods, fighting nothing or no one except for our own lives against starvation and persistent bugs. Assuring him we will eventually see a fight, and to not wish something that will surely come as the days themselves, he can't help but to fall into wallowing for his loved ones at home. If he does not pull out of it while the enemy is all around us, he will succumb to being part of the soil at the end of our enemy's shovel. These men we travel with are no more my friends than they are my enemy, but I am unable to bond with them, as they laugh and make jokes about the nigga slaves they fight for, the ones they fight to free. None of them have never even seen a real slave, let alone be friend one, or encounter one. They do not realize that I too am a slave, I too am the one they have been sent to fight for, to free, and yet I stand right next to them unknowingly, and still not free. Their laughter cringes my skin, brings fear, anger and pain to the surface all at once. Do they not know the true meaning of what they fight for? How can I ask that question when I do not really know myself.

Putting our differences aside, as I do not dare share my discomfort with any of the other men besides Mr. Tim, one of the men returns from patrol to inform the rest of us, that we have come upon a large plantation with plenty of growing fields in bloom ready for picking. My heart starts to race, my blood comes to the surface. Our orders are to set fire to all blooming fields we encounter, under darkness, moving away quickly without being seen, gaining as much distance in as short period of time as possible, on to the next, wherever we may find it. My thoughts are, they have sent us out here to die, blind in our mission, suffering in our starvation. Huddled together, a plan to burn the fields from all angles is set for nightfall. These men who I travel with, do not know, by burning these fields of food ready to harvest, they not only destroy food for the troops, but the only food supply for the blacks in the south. The only food available to keep them alive. They are starving the already starved. The large house is set in the very middle, surrounded by crops, the slave quarters in the distance along the side of the property. Setting fire to the crops will engulf both houses, causing death to all who remain inside of them unable to escape in any direction. I cannot with good conscious allow them to burn the crops without warning the slaves of their coming demise. We cannot kill what we have been sent to set free. Taking up rest before night, as others take watch over us, I take a moment to look around, making sure all are fast asleep. Sprawled onto the floor of the forest, I crawl from the center of the troops, and off into the bushes, headed towards the tall crops of corn. Making my way to the other side of the farm's land, I come face to face with the overseer of the land. His horse rears high in the sky, his rifle discharging a great flash of light into the airs sky. Rushing backwards I retreat into the cover of tall crops, trying to make my way full circle back in the direction of where the slave's quarters would be, the overseer trampling close behind, torch in one hand, rifle in the other. Making my way back towards the other side of the land, my lungs start to quickly fill with smoke, they have set the fires, trapping me inside along with the others. Having set out to save others, I am now in a desperate fight for my own life, struggling to breath or see through the thickening clouds of smoke, filling every creasing branch of corn stock. Unable to mask my desperate cough for air, I know it is a matter of time before I am overrun by smoke and flames, burning to my end. The smoke is thick, I cannot see my own body laying here. My eyes want to leap from my skull, face feeling tremendous heat coming closer and closer as I lay here helpless. Shoulders feeling a tug, gunshots ring overhead, I am drug by my feet and arms, my body still scrapping a path on the ground. Rushing to the fires edge, clear from its direction, the blacks have taken the overseer, bringing him down from his horse, and to his death. They have heard we were coming, and kept look out for us, and our sign. I do not know how they knew, but I am glad they did. Retreating into the forest, I am assisted to my weakened legs by others, carrying me further into the belly of the forest to safety. Unorganized from our first assault on a supply farm, we, along with the other troop members erratically scatter throughout the woods, moving away from the farm fire as quickly as possible. Clearing my head, bringing my eyes to focus, surprised to see Mr. Tim sitting next to me, "I knew you would try something like this boy, I could see the wheels turning in your eyes.". Having a sense of relief, I realized I am not in this fight alone. Mr. Tim followed me, witnessing me running into the overseer he continued awakening the slaves, warning them of the fire to come. He is a good man, this Mr. Tim, he is a good man.

With the fire behind us growing greater and greater, we are forced deeper into the forest. Moving further away from the smoke and flamed filled trees burning in all directions, we are unaware of the consequences our actions have caused. Shuffling along, unorganized from scattering we now face the alarming reality, there are more mouths to feed, more people to hide, and more lives to protect from the south. With this fire burning fiercely, it is sure to be seen four towns over, bringing others to investigate. Now we run from fire chasing us, and the militia filled Confederate Army of the south burning to kill all who rebel against them.

We are surrounded with nowhere to run, no place to hide. All that is in front of us is set ablaze, tearing at our emotions, sickening us with anxiety. If Captain Littleberry only thought further ahead, we would have all seen that coming deep into the other side of the enemy's line, starting a fire, would start a burn of the entire south, maybe he would have realized we were sent on a death mission. We would not have been expected to return but given orders to set the south ablaze at all costs, including our own lives.

Our troop platoon has now become saviors to those men, women, and children in desperate need of fleeing from burning to death, the souths troops not far behind us. We are unsure of where we are at in all the confusion, but we must keep moving in a direction or else succumb to the blistering fire crackling at our heels. More alive and fierce with each tree it burns, each bush it devours. The land around us has once again becomes our enemy, it holds our footsteps hostage, tracking us at every turn, whispering songs of death in our ears. Its breaths fire out of its mouth like the ancestor's stories of the devil's serpents chasing souls from heaven back to hell. We are left with only one choice of escape. Taking a path given to us by one of the other slave girls, we are led at a water's edge, down past a fall, and across to a rocky, watery sand pit filled with left over harvest. Pushing past to the other side, in the distance, we can make out a few dozen men hurryingly coming our direction. Quickly alerting others of the oncoming danger, we gather everyone together, hushing them up to hurry down the stream, to stay in the water as we travel. We are not deep enough in the brush to have proper cover from our enemy. If it is not for the thick smoke covering our every limb, we would all perish in the open. The smoke lingering enemy has become a gift, given to us by our own hands, our own idiotic mistake grown to camouflage us from our foe. We cannot cover ourselves enough to protect us from the air tainted with charred debris, as our lungs fill quickly keeping us from much needed deep breaths. The children cough the most. Their lungs are young and tender, fragile, and too weak for this type of exposure. If the others cannot find us through the smoke, their coughs will blindly guide them directly to us.

Unable to go any further down the path of the stream, we find ourselves hunkered down, troops right on top of us. It is too late, they know where our position is, where we hide along the stream. We begin randomly firing into the smoke-filled sky. Even the shadows of trees from our rifles flash, move like our enemy. Swift and exact, they are indeed better trained than we are. Moving flawlessly through the woods, it appears they

213

know our every move before we do it, our every plan before we even think it, as they are there before we are there. They fight as if they have the strength of ten men, moving methodically from position to position. Continuing our onslaught of rapid fire, a silence comes over us all. We realize, we are the only one's firing. No one is firing back at us, but why? "Avery! Avery... Tim...... it's us." I hear an eerily familiar voice in the far distance. There is no way. It cannot be. "It's me... Richard...". Confused and petrified at the same time, thinking someone is calling out to confuse us into showing ourselves to be killed, I yell, "Who is your best friend?" Waiting for a moment, all is quiet, "Not you!" the voice bellows, as Richard stays concealed behind trees of smoke. A chuckle comes deep inside of me, thoughts of Cheeks come to mind, and I know my friend has come to join us, join our fight.

Following downstream, up to our waist and necks in rushing water, our weapons held high above our heads, we are deep into the mouth of the dangerous south and its fire clouding our judgment. Reunited with Richard, informing us they have followed our tracks for two days after our departure from the battalion, there is no wonder they were there to rescue us from ourselves. Orders came to the captain for our battalion to join the fight elsewhere, we are headed to war, to the front lines and must return immediately or else be considered deserters. How will we return to a place where we don't even know where we are anymore? We have traveled many weeks and have lost our way in all the confusion. There is no course to our madness now, we simply move in a direction, furthest away from the blaze. Trapped between fire, and hidden southern enemies, our mission is now to save ourselves and the others we have released from bondage, escaping from behind enemy lines. Unable to move in silence or cover much meaningful ground, coming to the end of the smoke screening our position I can hear the women muttering to the children to keep quiet. If we are to get out of here, there can be no loss of life, no one left behind, or else we have failed. This halfhearted mistaken death mission, the men coming to rescue us, the start of the blaze burning down the south, will all be for nothing, will be forgotten.

Reaching a point, far enough away in the hills, we are all tired and exhausted. Many have fallen far behind; it would seem our minds have unconsciously split unknowingly leaving some behind. With our troop resting under the dense cover of thick trees, we can see the fire burning throughout the land, clouds dancing atop drowning the treetops below. Richard kindly gives me a canister of water to sip from, and some dried meat he has been saving. There is no sign of Mr. Tim, as he was far in the rear responsible for taking care of anyone of had fallen behind. Hours pass while we huddle together trying to plot our next path after all has gathered as one again. We can feel the chill in the air, but the fire burning the woods below takes some of the nip off the air, its bearable for now. Rubbing my hands together to stay warm, woman and children curl up next to one another, the men pacing, standing look out over the hills prepared to warn us of anyone approaching. We can't wait here too much longer for Mr. Tim and the others, but we cannot leave them behind either. Deciding we need not scatter ourselves thin, as we may need all the help, we can get to fight off any troops, we hunker down for the night, close to the opening of a deep cave. With a small fire lit to the very back of the cave to keep us warm from the freezing cold cave dwelling, some of the men and I gather large fallen trees, bushes, and boulders to cover the entrance, leaving only a small opening. As the night falls more and more, retreating further into the cave, I can't help to feel this place can easily become our tomb, our final resting place. If the enemy decides to take us over, there is no place to run and hide, we will trap ourselves with no way out. Fearing the worse, I sit outside the cave along with Richard, we don't say much of anything, simply look out on the night sky, watching the fires burn in the distance. Ambers swaying and dancing in the midnight sky, as I have seen my family dancing around the fire during Christmas. Cold and hungry, I am missing Momma Ruby, and her good cooking. She makes the best bread, and beans so good it made us all pass gas like a competition. The sounds that would come out of Hoof was like a musical instrument. I never knew how he could make so many sounds, coming from his little body. I wish I could tell Trita, that we killed those bad men who took her innocence. I want to thank her for saving my life, taking my place for killing the mayor for trying to hurt Lipi. The silence of this place reminds me of the clearing, where I loved to spend time alone, listening to the winds pushing past me, watching the morning dew trickle down off leaves, creating puddles on the ground below for animals to drink from. I have carried my bible, my gift from Lipi, with me everywhere I go. It has stayed wrapped around my waste, tethered with twine, but has become extremely brittle from being battered by the elements. Even though I am unable to read, holding it close to me brings me great comfort, knowing it holds those I love close to me no matter where I travel, no matter who tries to harm me, they are with me.

Richard has become somewhat of a father figure to me. Never having someone like him look out for me before, I look to him for direction, for experience. As strange as it sounds, he worries me when he walks off speaking French to himself, as if he is fighting within himself. Never telling me what he says to himself, I can only wonder if he speaks to Cheeks, if he worries where his friend is, if he is ok. I am sure this worries his mind, makes it uneasy for him to focus, but he is a large man always demanding respect. Beginning to hum a tune Momma Ruby used to hum while working around the farm, Richard quickly me from behind, covering my mouth with his hand. My eyes grow large, his finger silently points in a direction nearing a completely blacked out area where the trees come together. Knowing we can be surrounded and killed at any moment, we are both tense of the rustling of trees and bushes breaking as something pushes its way through. Kneeling, Richard moves his hand away from my opened mouth. Unable to warn the others of oncoming danger, with only the whites of our eyes peeking from the cover of trees and boulders, we nervously wait for the enemy to show his face. Readying our weapons in the direction of cracking debris, we steady ourselves for a fight. This is it, the moment we did not want to come is here, they are here. Richard leaning away from my position onto a rock, steading himself, he reaches over and places his hand on the top of my weapon, lowering it. Mr. Tim and the others have returned, stumbling through the bush, making their way closer to us. Knowing we have dodged death once again, we quietly reveal ourselves, inviting them to hurry along into the warmth

217

of the cave, with the others. Embracing Mr. Tim as my brother, he has a relief of worry on his face, imaging he would never see us or his family again, if left alone to traverse enemy land. For now, we are together, fighting for our lives.

Awaken at the sound of Mr. Tim's voice, telling us all the hurry, they are coming, we scurry to wake all others huddled in the caves shelter. Leading everyone away from the hill, we can see silhouettes of troops climbing towards us, the blaze of trees following close behind. The fire has shifted with the winds and is now headed right in our direction. Unable to know if they are running from being swallowed up or charging us, we scramble from our position high on the hill, racing downhill away from them. Crying uncontrollably from the sudden awakening, the younger children alert the southern troops of our presence. They have started firing at us, they know we are here. Now having a mission, and target, they relentlessly pursue us, heavily firing their weapons in our direction. I don't know if anyone is hit, or who is behind us following together, but our lives continue to have no meaning for others. A huge blast lights up the night, balls of fire burn the ground beneath us, legs leaving the safety of the earth's surface as our troop and others fly through the air. We have been hit, but what has struck us from such a distance is unknown. Looking around, many lay wounded and crying, screaming in pain, but I am unable to reach them. Disoriented by blast after blast coming our direction, Richard blindly grabs a tight hold of my seared uniform, encouraging me to get to my feet and hurry along, "We have to move Avery, get up boy!", my legs weak, my head clouded, my weapon gone, we stumble through the night away from our attackers. "Wait! Where is

Mr. Tim and the others?", my concern grows with more distance, with noticing only a few others of our group still bunched together moving side my side. Limping from one leg hurting from the blast, Richard carries me to lean against a tree, helping those behind us to catch up. Grasping my breath, piercing into the center of where the blast landed, Mr. Tim's body lay in half, separated at the waist from his upper body, still caressing the small hand of one of the children he was once helping along. It is an unbearable sight to see. We have joined this war to make a difference, to fight for freedom, but we are mistakenly killing those we have set out to make free. My heart cannot help but to suffer for the many deaths I have witnessed, for lives lost at the deadly hands of the south. We must hurry along towards the norths line, if we have any chance of surviving, any chance of saving ourselves.

Richard

We have traveled many days and nights without much food or water to keep us going. Fallen ash from burning forest trees in the far distance blankets everything around us, making it easier to see our tracks. Walking in circles at times to cover our tracks from the enemy, it takes us twice as long to progress forward. My eye lashes shake pieces of ash from my face with every irritating blink. We are weak and tired, suffering within ourselves at times to keep going. Losing so many of our group in such a short period of time to an explosive attack, having to leave Mr. Tim's mangled body behind, these images burn into my thoughts. Normally these memories lay deep in the back of my mind, never to think of again, because they are the deaths of my enemies. But these deaths are of the innocent, victims of war, a man with a family who only joined under the convincing eye of his anxious young son. They will never see their families again, see their children grow to marry and have children of their own, live to know how it truly feels to be free, taste freedoms sweet juices. Myself and Avery, plus a handful of others are left struggling to find our way back towards the norths line, back to our battalion, back to safety. Out from underneath the blanketed fog of the fires cloud, the night sky becomes clearer, with only small sprinkles of ashes falling like snowflakes from the sky, making it easier in finding the bright star that leads us north in the right direction. Following it back is our only hope of saving the remainder of our fallen group. With only a few healthy, able bodies, the rest are starving women and crying children, some wounded, others slow and unmotivated from losing their loved ones. Avery's health and mind seem to be ailing from exhaustion, his fire in his eyes seem to dim with every passing night we aimlessly wonder in these woods. Assuring him we are headed in the right direction, he pops in and out of focus, one moment egging on the group to keep pushing forward towards the norths line, the next limping off into a dark space someplace to set alone, talking to himself. I think he has lost his faith, as he has not said a word from his book, his bible. If he does not pull out of it, he will perish like the others, having no choice to leave him behind succumbing to the same fate as the rest. Leaving the group behind to rest, I move forward to scout a better path for us all to pass through. There must be food around, water to drink, as we need to give strength to those who have very little. Working a path through sticky brush, thorny branches, and walls of trees, I make my way up to the top of a ridge, where I can see far into the distance. We seem to have gone far enough that the south soldiers no longer care to track us, but not far enough to safety. This land from here has a familiarity to it, as if we have been here before, me and Avery. We have stood atop this hill, or close by on our first journey trying to get north. Another days walk from here I believe is Mr. Tim's farmland, where we can find food and shelter for a night or two, maybe encourage the use of the wagon to carry us further faster. Informing the others of my thoughts, letting it be known that I am not completely sure of what is out there, but clearly out of options, we are set to start moving again once the sun disappears behind the mountains.

Continuing to backtrack our own tracks, we have traveled additional days, much more than originally anticipated, and we have yet to find any sign of the farmhouse. Maybe my sense of direction has failed me, I am unfocused with worrying of the group failing to stay close together, others continuing to all behind as we wait for them to catch up. Avery worries me, I have seen him at his strongest, and now at his weakest, he is fading quickly and there is nothing I can do to help him snap out of it. Finding a stream deep into the valley, the bugs flying around us are relentless as they pursue us, mosquitos bite at every inch of skin we have uncovered, the water freezes our feet as we move in and out of the water, warming ourselves just long enough to keep going, but we must travel at its edge to keep from being seen. The trees are thick on both sides, completely shielding us from seeing what is around us or being seen from anyone not within fifty feet. We continue to struggle to find food for everyone to eat, besides dew covered leaves, and small berries left on vines. Some of us have gotten a bit sick from the berries, others are showing signs of cramping. Unsure if it is from dehydration or the berries we have cautiously consumed, but we must keep marching forward. Coming to the end of the infested stream, deep into the side of the mountain, the farm sits in shade. The land is more grown than I recall, it is unkept, and worn from time and lack of attention. I can see a small light on the side of the house, twinkling in the distance like the star we follow. I can't help to for my mind to wonder if we will be welcomed with opened arms or a closed fist arriving without Mr. Tim with us. I do not want to have to tell that family we have come back without him, his body left in the mud of the woods, separated in two. Anxious from the possibilities of food and shelter for the night, we cautiously make our way towards the house, clinging to the run-down fence lining the property. leaving the others at the rear of the property, bunched together hidden behind the outbuilding, Avery accompanies me to the back door of the home, hoping not to get shot at by Mrs. Cookie. Deciding not to approach the door for fear of death before we can get help, we take cover behind an old broken-down wagon not far from the back door, hauling small rocks at the back door, until we see a shadow inside. Calmly approaching the back door where we lay far enough away out of harm's way, the door slowly cracks open, rifle barrels peeking out. "Mrs. Cookie…... Mrs. Cookie… It's me… Richard, and Avery…", pausing and awaiting an answer or the blast of a rifle, we hear, "What the hell… What are ya'll doing back there. Get on in here now, it's freezing out there.". Coming from out behind the protection of the wagon, knowing it is safe, I can see the confusion on her face, as there is only two of us, knowing there is supposed to be three. She notices we are without Mr. Tim. As she hurries us in the house, she peers past both of us looking into the night air, hoping her fallen husband is close on our heels, coming to embrace her to receive his welcome home. Only standing for a brief moment waiting for his return behind us, her face tells us she knows he is not coming home.

Pulling the rest of our small group into the comforting warmth of the small, crowded farmhouse, most huddle quietly about every corner of the homes wooden floor. The smell of fresh bread, and earthy soup fills the air making our stomachs sound as if they are arguing back and forth of who's getting the first bowl. Water pails are past around trying to quench the thirst of all who gather, exhausted and barely able to move another muscle. Sitting at the family's small dinner table, Mr. Tim's daughter, Christie-Marie, and son Champ quietly stand close by the hot stove, looking directly into my eyes with worry. Staring back at them, but unable to keep eye contact for too long, feeling shame for not bringing their father back, I stand. Wiping my face of ash with a dampened rag given to me by Mrs. Cookie, I squeeze the rag in my hands knowing I must share their father's death with them. I know they know, but there is nothing like knowing the truth. Their father was a courageous man, fighting for his family's future, for our future. Gaining the courage to look the family in the eye, and tell them their father is not coming, I am interrupted before sounding a word,

"Greater love has no one than this, that someone lay down his life for his friends.

He who walks righteously and speaks uprightly, who despises the gain of oppressions, who shakes his hands, lest they hold a bribe, who stops his ears from hearing of bloodshed and shuts his eyes from looking on evil, he will dwell on the heights; his place of defense will be the fortresses of rocks; his bread will be given him; his water will be sure."

"Amen..."

Breaking his silence in a crackling voice of sorrow, feeling accomplished at having given us good words from the book, Avery takes his bible from his waist, looks to the children's faces for comfort he only finds blank sadness, he turns to walk out of the room into the next. Left to finish, I do not believe there is much left to tell them, the thick air of silence tells no lie.

Avery

Standing in the cool air of the night, its sky so clear, stars twinkling, shaking their brightness showing they are very much alive. My shivering pale hands together in prayer. We have come to this farm for shelter, for food, rest, and water, but what have we brought with us? News of death without flowers, stories of war without hope, slave women, men and children begging for freedom but there is none. Our hope is to get to the norths line back to our battalion before we are called deserters of the war. What do we get out of what we have done? Maybe a slap on the shoulder to say welcome back, maybe hung by our necks for unwillingly deserting at the ambitious orders of our commander's mistake. I refuse to die at the hands of the unrighteous, the unforgiving, the heartless, yet as a slave I am at the mercy of those who desire to play God with mine and everyone else's lives. They kill at will what they do not understand, what they do not control but wish to control. Maybe I do not desire freedom, as I have been enslaved all my life, and know nothing else. Maybe I simply desire a name of my own, an identity to say I am a person, I am more than the animal they make us out to be. I am human. This air of fake freedom, being able to stand here plays tricks on my mind. It gives me false hope, standing here without shackles, but I am still not free, they trap me still. This quiet night being still seems to bring all critters out to play in the tall weeds. Hearing them rustle around, crickets sounding off one overlapping another like fiddles playing a tune, I can't help but feel this too will end as all else does.

Early morning brings roosters crowing, with cows moving closer to the barn's trough for their morning feed of grain and corn. Unable to sleep, I find myself walking the outer area of the land, deep at its edge searching for peace. Sitting under a ledge of a cliff, underneath a large overhanging, overgrown bush by a small creek, I watch fish come to the shallow waters surface and back down again disappearing into the cracks and caves below. Bedding down into my surroundings, with pops and crackling of branches from critters all around me, I do not notice I am completely surrounded by southern soldiers, stalking past me towards the farmhouse.

225

Running will do no good at this point. I am trapped where I sit with no escape. If I bolt at this time, I will be shot down like a rabbit running from its hole. All I can do is watch them stalk past me and hope to go unnoticed. Man, after man, I see ease towards the farmhouse, where all stay resting, completely unaware of the approaching danger. Peeking up and out I keep checking to see if all the men have passed me by or are there more to come. How many are there? I cannot tell if they are many or just a few, or if they are closing in from all sides, what weapons they may have. Why would they attack a small farm in the middle of nowhere? Having looked to see if anymore are coming, noticing there are no more, I caringly move the brush from my hiding place, making my way around to the other side of the farm to warn the others. Racing through thorny brush, and sticky branches, I cannot catch my breath, my heartbeats rapidly for fear of not getting there soon enough. Ducking under the belly of cows in a sea of manure, I see Richard and one of the men next to the entrance of the barn. Looking over and seeing my face laying there crawling towards them, I wave and point to warn them of men approaching. They just look at me, smirk and laugh at me laying in piles of manure, then turn to continue their business. Continuing to feverishly crawls towards them, they take a second look at me. Noticing the seriousness on my face, waving my hands again, and pointing they realize we are in danger. Immediately taking shelter back into the house to alert the rest of the group of southern troops, jumping to my feet I head towards the house for protection. Growing closer to the entrance, I hear a deafening boom, followed by a steady tone whistling in the air, as if some horn blows with one large, long breath. A flash of light passes through me, my eyes blinded by debris charging my way, the

226

tiny farmhouse maliciously exploding into unrecognizable pieces bursting into flames, scattering throughout the now destroyed farms land. Feeling in my body goes away, clouds of smoke quickly overtake me, unable to breath from the thickness of blackening smoke my lungs fill with choking ash. I cannot see anything, I am unable to move, while my eyelids grow heavier by the second, it is time to rest here.

It seems that I have been laying here for hours. Waking, extreme pain pounds my head, it is unbearable. Unable to get to my feet, I lay flat on my back trying to look around. Eyes clearing from passing out consumed by the blast, starting to focus on what is around me, I can only see from one of my eyes, there are smoldering bodies all around. All of them are dead, they have killed us all. We have failed tremendously at getting to safety, from the tyranny of the south's deadly oppression. Pain pierces my entire body, as I feel most of my pain in my arms and back. Not being able to move, barely seeing from one of my eyes, I find myself staring at my mangled leg, twisted to the side at my knee. Realizing I am at the mercy of the soldiers, my eyes close to sleep, and await my fate. We are too far from the norths line, and no one knows we are here. There is no one to help us now. I am again, completely on my own.

Coming to and passing out again and again throughout the night, my eyes focus on a figure hovering over me, dragging my body by my one leg, my damaged leg cupping the ground forced to follow. Unaware of who is left alive to drag me, I am left to imagine the worst. It is the southern soldiers clearing the area of death, carrying me to willfully dump my remains in a massive grave along with the others. Passing out from excruciating pain and coming to again, I find myself awakening, lying motionless on the hard-cold floor of the wagon. More bodies lying next to me, wounded, bleeding, crying in pain, but still alive. A man not in uniform heavily shuffling in the distance carries another atop his shoulders towards the wagon. Coming closer, I try my hardest to focus my one eye on the man to see who it is that piles us together, who takes us off to our graves. With a straggly body on top moaning in pain, the two come closer and closer. Carried, almost lifeless, body limping from all sides on the shoulders of the man is Richard, severely wounded, the man carrying him, our long lost but never forgotten friend, Cheeks. He has come back from the wild, deceptively hiding out to save us, and those who survived the souths lethal blasts. Relieved to see a friendly face during such deadly turmoil, my eyes can no longer stay open, they weigh heavy on my swollen face, shredded with debris.

Chattering whispers all around me, sounds of clinking pots fill my head with emotions not yet allowed to penetrate my senses while at rest. Hearing all that's going on around me, struggling to open my eyes causes me to feel anxiety, restless to move. The fog slowly clears from my head, eyes heavier than they had been before, slowly I awaken to find myself in a strange place filled with people running around tending to others next to me. Forcing myself to sit up right to see what is going on, I find my surroundings completely unfamiliar. This is a place I have never been before, a strange shelter filled with others sick and dying, wounded from war. Tending to my wounds, is a nurse standing watch, moving from bed to bed, next to me then across the room and back again. She moves like an angel saving dying souls ready for their date with heaven or is this heaven and I am already dead. I do not know, as I have never seen heaven before. This is not how I imagined heaven would be, seeing the dead and dying, the wounded and the living all in one place. Holding myself up to look around, my arms shake from lack of strength, shoulders not might enough to bare much weight on them for too long, I collapse back into my bed. Stretched out from head to feet, I cannot feel my lower half, neither one of my legs are working. My clothes still bloodied, and ripped, bandages wrap clear around my head and eye, I am unsure if I even have an eye left. Pulling covers back that barely drape my lower legs, I want to see my feet, I want to know if they are still there or did, I lose them. Convincing my own mind, I am fully prepared to find myself without any legs. Pulling the covers back far enough reveals they are still there, still attached to me. Swollen beyond recognition, discolored to the core, the black and purple bruises that dress them covers like a badge of honor. She comes closer to me again, realizing I have awakened, she stops directly in front of me and gives me a soft smile, it is my Lipi. I have dreamed of this day since I last saw her face. She has grown into such a beautiful young woman, graceful in how she walks, a light to brighten this dimly shaded room filled with sickness. Grabbing a hold of my hand, she gently rubs it, comforting me with every kind stroke. The scent of wildflowers, and jasmine leaves fill my nose with thoughts of us holding hands, walking in the clearing by my old farmland. I told myself, if I was to ever see her again, I would never let her go, never let her out of my sight for a second. Always wanting to stay by her side, we will walk this land proud to love one another till the end of our days. Focused on her, nothing else in the room seems to matter, except a whisper in the back of my head that keeps calling my name, "Avery... Avery.... Pshhh... Psst.... Avery..", the sound seems to get louder and more irritating with every whisper, "Hey, Avery... Psh.... You awake?", jolting myself awake, startled at someone standing over me, I am now wishing I was dead. Suddenly realizing I was only dreaming about my Lipi being here with me, my reality spoils my desire to be alive. Laying in my bed look directly up is a face that I never thought would be the first face I encounter, waking up, "Cheeks? Is Lipi here?". Completely unaware, maintaining a puzzled look on his face, "What the hell is a Lipi?", as he rubs the back of his neck, brushing flies away from his head. "Boy, I thought we lost ya... it was a bit touch and go there for a while. Always knew your head was harder than a bull trying to mate with a miniature goat on a Sunday.". Not feeling much like smiling or laughing at Cheeks silliness, I interrupt his madness by asking him to help sit me up right. Grabbing a firm grip of my upper body, he helps me put a pillow behind my back, so I can take a look around, "Where exactly are we? I ain't never seen a place like this before.", looking around he takes a deep breath, "We at the get-well place. They bring you here to take care of you and make you well again. Either that or they bring you here to die. I wasn't exactly sure which one it would be until I seen you over here moving your eyelids like you was anxious to talk to me. So, I came right over. Hello!". Getting a hold of my bearings, I need to know what happen, where are all the others, where is Richard? Looking around for a place to sit, Cheeks give me a little push at my hips to move over and make room for him at the edge of my bed, "Boy, you been sleeping for a long while now. Days turned to night and nights turned to day.

230

I can't count, but I know it was too many. Wondering the backwoods, I come across smoke filling the air just behind one them big hills. I came to check it out and see if I can find some food, but instead I find a bunch of bodies lying around, blown up. That's when I noticed one them bodies still breathing, still alive. It was a young white boy all beat up and barely breathing. I started to walk away, but he called out to me to help him. I ain't one to help white folk, but he was just a boy, and I couldn't walk away, my feet wouldn't let me. I seen the wagon and carried him over to it, then noticed another and another. Some dead, some still breathing. I turned one them whites over, and it was you Avery. I thought it was all white folk burnt up, but it was blacks laying there. You ain't doing too well Avery. Doctors here are not sure if you will ever have the use of that eye again, and your leg is a mangled mess, look like a dog been chewing on it for weeks. And... well... Richard... they put him someplace else, but they are not sure if he is going to make it either. He still sleeping, not sure if he is going to wake or stay sleep forever. I sit by his side day and night, rubbing his lips with water from my fingertips, hoping one day he realize it's me rubbing his lips. Maybe he will jump up and give me a punch in the face. At least I know he is going to be ok if he does. Everybody is gone Avery, everybody, every last one of them people at the farm ended up dying, except you. You are the only one left... ". Barely able to absorb all that he is telling me, all I want to do is fall back asleep to a place where all this is not real, not true, a place where I can continue to dream about Lipi, and how beautiful she is now. Grabbing a firm grip to my hand, Cheeks begins to walk away, "Thank you", I spat out, "Thank you, for saving my life... I know it must have been hard for you.", not holding my breath for a welcome in return, he turns to look straight again, away from me, "We are brothers", he says proudly, "We are brothers.", walking away like a man finally coming to grips with his own reality.

It has been a few days since I have last seen Cheeks or had anymore dreams of Lipi. With only time on my hands laying here, it gives me time to reflect on how I ended up here. The circumstances surrounding me running away from Master Reginald and running into Richard. No one can tell me anything about where he is or if he is ok. No one even knows Cheeks, as I try to explain to them, he is the one who brought me here. He is the one who brought us all here, who saved our flesh from being devoured by the elements or wild animals scavenging for a meal. Barely able to wiggle a few toes on one foot, a few fingers on either hand, and with only the sight of one eye, I am left to the care of those who have volunteered to support the war and care for the wounded. Keeping me pumped with drugs when they can, when there is not a shortage, which there always seems to be a shortage around here, I drift in and out of consciousness, other times I lay here dying in pain, suffering within myself from the loss of everyone I have ever known. I am awake for now, in this coffin of a bed. They say I must lay here, still as possible for my body to heal, but I feel as if I am seemingly wasting away day by day. With no one around me to that I would care to speak with, I talk to myself, telling myself stories of great victories, of men, women, and children escaping the clutches of slavery, becoming equals, even taking over this land as their own. I know it is just a dream, it is simply my imagination accompanied by the lack of oxygen to my brain, and pain killers, but it is all I have to keep myself from going completely insane. A tall white man walks the aisle, those who are alert and can, salute him as he passes. Barely able to salute myself, my arm starts to draw up to my forehead long before he gets close enough for me to salute. "At ease soldier.", as he salutes, then greets me, stopping at the foot of my bed. "Well now, don't you just look like a ray of sunshine.", Captain Jerimiah Littleberry has come to claim me as a deserter. The same man whose motivated ignorance sent us off to die, on a death mission never to return, stands in front of me with a shifty smile perched on his smug face, pretending we have won the battle. "Between you and me Avery, I have come to visit you with orders from higher than me. They have come a long way to deliver them to me, and I thought I would deliver the news to you personally, since it was my idea to send you off to interrupt the food supplying the southern troops. They have heard of your bravery, of how you set fire to the fields of food, how set the blaze in motion burning down the south, but that is not what they are commending you for. They are giving you the Medal of Honor, signed by President Lincoln himself, for saving all those people on the farm after the south had attacked, and blown the property to pieces. They say while wounded, your leg shredded, and barely able to see you carried every person on that farm to a wagon, and road off for two days till you reached the safety of a northern battalion of soldiers making camp. This is truly a great day for the north, as there has never been such a higher honor bestowed upon anyone in any other war, except this one son.", not believing the story he is telling me, my stomach begins turning, the temperature in my head drastically rises, causing me to vomit all over my chin, and chest. Covered in my own vomit, my words cannot come quick enough in shame, "This is truly....

Truly… a disgrace, and I will have nothing to do with it, this medal of dishonor, of dishonesty. You say we fight this war for equality, but you fight for yourself, and no one else. I did nothing of the sort. You sent us off to die, and we burned down one field, we bumbled our way through the woods almost dying at the hands of our own idiocy, killing most of the people that we saved on the way. I am no hero, I am nothing! I sat under a tree, hiding, watching the southern troops pass by me, scared like a beaten dog. I sat cowering, as soldiers approached that farmhouse filled with innocent men, women, and children taking refuge. I… too... was in pieces. I too was blown up and unable to move, unable to breathe, left to die. You did not come to save us; you left us to die. If anyone deserves a Medal of Honor for bravery it is a man without a uniform, a proud man who fights for love, for honor, for his people, it is Cheeks who deserves to stand and accept the Presidents orders, not me…. He is a slave as I am a slave. I am Avery… a black man, I was born a slave, the skin color of yours, but I wear the scars of my people. He tried saving all those people at the farm... Not me.", closing my eyes, I pain turning sideways away from his pitiful face, the sight of him brings utter disgust to me, and I don't wish to throw up any further. "Leave me alone Sir…. Please, just leave me here, alone.". Before, I am fully able to absorb what is happening to me, a familiar voice penetrates me to the core, "Is this him?", I am frozen. I remember that voice calling out for my death at the farm when they came for the mayor's killer. Creaking my neck back towards the direction of the voice, the scarred face stranger who stood next to the Sheriff in our town, now stands next to the captain. Covered from head to toe in heavy clothing, scarf draping his head and shoulders, keeping is mutated face staring right at mine, confusion tramples my thoughts. What is he here for? Did he track me down to take me back to Master Reginald after all this time? Does he know that I killed the mayor for attacking Lipi? He simply looks me up and down without saying a word. Reaching out, he touches the bandages surrounding my head and eye, as if to pity my wounds. Slightly moving away, not wanting the touch of this stranger, he slowly pulls his hand away from my face, and back into the warmth of his coat pocket. With his voice raspy, and unclear, he is slow in his speech, "News travels very fast in these parts. I have heard of this white slave they call Avery. Brave as any ten men, a soldier without a home. A man without a tribe of his own, a man without a last name. I knew of a boy like this once, he was left to die at the hands of his mother. Clarah was her name. "Interrupting him at the shock of him knowing who my mother was, I have to know more". In a shocked low toned voice, "You... You knew my mother?". Overlapping our thoughts, the man continues, "Yes... you are her son...... As, you are mine." No words can explain the pain, sorrow, excitement that tears at me deep within. Hardly able to contain my emotions from erupting, I ask to know more. Agreeing to tell me the of my family, the strange man who now claims to be my father, insists on my silence without interruption. Wanting to know all he knows, I concede to his terms, allowing him to speak freely. "Your mother Clarah. She was a beautiful woman, a smile to brighten anyone's mood, filled with life and a love for anyone down on their luck. She would take in any hurt of lost animal she could find, bringing them home and caring for them until they were well enough to go off on their own again, free. Losing her... well losing her was like losing myself. She was all I had left in this world, and nothing else mattered more to me than keeping a smile on her face. Her smiled mirrored that of her mothers, God rest both of their souls.", chocking up for just a moment, the man gathers himself to begin again, "I am sorry for having a lapse. I have put this story far back into my mind, hoping it would go away, but it torments me every second of every day. I was angry. Oh, so angry for losing everything in the fire. My house, my life, my Clarah… and then, there was you. I found you lying in waste, covered from head to toe in mud. Crying out, I couldn't help but to hurry to find you before the animals carry you away. My anger consumed me, more than the fire that burned my entire body, and I became lost. Covering you with my coat, I carried you back to the house, still burning, everything collapsed into one big pile of smoldering nothingness, with my Clarah smothering underneath it all. I had not money to eat, no place to live, no way to survive or to take care of you. Men came because they saw the smoke from the fire. These were great men of wealth, passing through on their way to a traveling convention of scientists. Finding me hunched down, covering you with my body, they offered me a way out. They offered me money for you, to take you off my hands and put to better use. They promised me they would look after you, that you would become useful to mankind, a type of scientific experiment to better understand humanity. I needed to eat, and rebuild my home, so... I handed you over to them, when you were just a day old, no bigger than the palm of my hand. I knew letting you go was letting go of the little bit I had left to remember Clarah by, but I knew it was for our best. Years later when I was down south in the town I grew up in, at that farmhouse, the farm of Mr. Reginald, I knew it was you. I saw you at that farm that day, looking for the murderer of the mayor. I knew it was you, a white slave boy joined with the other nigga slaves. That is the moment, I realized those scientist's men who bought you, left you as the experiment. They knew if someone found you, especially a slave farmer, they would think you were not of pure blood, that you would be of mixed blood left at the hands of a master and his black mistress. You were left to grow up as a slave, without a real name, without anyone to properly love you. For this I am sorry. For this I have suffered every waking moment of every day I have lived sense. God has punished me for all my wrongdoing, giving me these scars burned deep into my skin, deforming me to walk this land for the rest of my life. He spared me death, only to torment me until I made right what I have made wrong. You know who you are Avery. You have a ma and a pa…. please son… please forgive me in the name of God…" His tears tell of his pain, of his truth, but I do not want to hear his truth, as his truth is now my lies. Painfully turning away to ignore the stranger's plea for forgiveness, my eyes cry for the thought of my mother Clarah. Hearing his footsteps disappearing in the distance until I no longer hear a sound, my mind racing does not allow sleep to give me solace until the next morning. Exhausted at even the thought of more filth tainting my soul, my body sleeps for days. Not eating or taking a sip of water for many days, those around me, entrusted to helping keep us alive and recovering from our injuries grow increasingly concerned with my now failing health.

Having nothing left, not believing in my own life, my existence has become meaningless. I too am a lie within a lie. Crawling out of my bed, going unseen I make my way out of the makeshift tent for the sick, and under the sheet guarding us from outside. Rain pours down, heavier than I have ever seen in my life. This is a sign from God himself. Crawling on my belly, one arm dragging me gripping deep into the mud, my only leg pushing me further along inch by muddy inch. Exhausted from my slow accomplishment, soaked in rainy mud, I flop flat to my back and stare into the rain pelting my face.

"While he himself went a day's journey into the wilderness. He came to a broom bush, sat down under it and prayed that he might die. "I have had enough, LORD," he said. "Take my life; I am no better than my ancestors."

"Amen…"

Made in the USA
Columbia, SC
05 February 2024

31471758R00134